Praise for Tu-Shonda

The Ex Factor

Essence Bestseller

"An arousing story of three sisters hitting the curveballs that love throws their way." —VIBE VIXEN

"Chock-full of raw dialogue, ghetto slang, and enough scintillating sex scenes and bedroom romps to make even a grown man squirm, *The Ex Factor* grabs its readers' full attention almost immediately." —*Amsterdam News* (New York)

"Tu-Shonda once again proves why she is one of my favorite authors!" —K'WAN, national bestselling author of *Street Dreams*

"Tu-Shonda L. Whitaker's novel, *The Ex Factor* evokes feelings that you never thought you possessed. You will find yourself laughing out loud at times and crying on the inside at others. Whitaker deals with passionate sex, to-die-for love, traitorous adultery, bitter jealousy, and the inability to love one's self. *The Ex Factor* is a guaranteed classic." —KEISHA ERVIN, author of *Mina's Joint*

"*The Ex Factor* reads like a movie and will keep you entertained from the first page to the last!" —DANITA CARTER, co-author of *Success Is the Best Revenge*

"*The Ex Factor* is a scandalous story of self-discovery and growth, and Tu-Shonda L. Whitaker has a unique talent for combining humor, vivid characters, and a compelling story line." —CRYSTAL LACEY WINSLOW, author of *The Criss Cross*

"Whitaker has an amazing ability to mix raw emotion with comedic flare. *The Ex Factor* is another hit waiting to explode!"
—BRENDA L. THOMAS,
Essence bestselling author of *Velvet Rope*

Game Over

"Tu-Shonda Whitaker stands and delivers again! Whitaker writes characters that jump off the page and pull you into the story. *Game Over* is realistic and filled with gut-wrenching emotions, drama, and authentic conflict."
—DANIELLE SANTIAGO, bestselling author of *Little Ghetto Girl*

Flip Side of the Game

"Tu-Shonda L. Whitaker's strong imagery of characters from the ghetto is stunning and authentic. There will be more great tales from this gifted writer who has a strong edge on the urban world."
—RAWSISTAZ

"Street lit with a romantic twist . . . raw and uncensored."
—SHELIA M. GOSS, author of *Roses Are Thorns, Violets Are True*

"From the very first page the author screams a raw, gritty, and moving tale. The voice of her character leaves an eerie echo in your head. You won't be able to put this book down because it calls you with an alluring ghetto whisper. By far one of the best street tales yet." —JOYLYNN JOSSEL, bestselling author of *Dollar Bill*

Millionaire
Wives Club

Millionaire
Wives Club

A Novel

Tu-Shonda L. Whitaker

ONE WORLD TRADE PAPERBACKS ● BALLANTINE BOOKS NEW YORK

A One World Books Trade Paperback Original

Copyright © 2009 by Tu-Shonda Whitaker

Published in the United States by One World Books, an imprint of The Random House Publishing Group, a division of Random House, Inc., New York.

ONE WORLD is a registered trademark and the One World colophon is a trademark of Random House, Inc.

Library of Congress Cataloging-in-Publication Data

Whitaker, Tu-Shonda L.
Millionaire wives club : a novel / Tu-Shonda L. Whitaker.
p. cm.
ISBN 978-0-345-48667-7 (pbk.)
1. African American women—Fiction. 2. Reality television programs—Fiction. 3. Rich people—Fiction. 4. Man-woman relationships—Fiction. 5. African American families—Fiction. 6. Domestic fiction. I. Title.
PS3623.H563M55 2009
813'.54—dc22   2009035731

Printed in the United States of America

www.oneworldbooks.net

1 2 3 4 5 6 7 8 9

Book design by Christopher M. Zucker

To you, the reader, for always being there.

What's love got to do with it?

—*Tina Turner*

Season One

The Club

illions of dollars in premier fashions and champagne diamonds were on display at Manhattan's 40/40 Club as four ultrarich and ubersuccessful women—America's newest addition to reality TV—strolled the red carpet and smiled at the flashing lights of the paparazzi. The clicking of their designer stilettos was like exquisite steel-pan beats as they crossed the club's threshold, and the sultry sounds of Maxwell's live performance filled the air. Despite their individual insecurities and doubts, at this moment as they sauntered into the sunrise of superstardom, what mattered most was that they'd gotten their own piece of the latest in rich bitch candy.

"Ladies, ladies," a reporter from *E! News* said, motioning for the four of them to come together and meet him across the room. "Can you all tell us a little about yourselves?" He looked at the woman to his left. "May we start with you?"

"I'm Milan Starks, wife of the great Yusef 'Da Truef' Starks, number twenty-three on the New York Knicks." A lovely mix of her cinnamon brown Dominican father and golden-skinned African American mother, Milan had an effortless beauty that didn't require makeup or facials to be perfect. She had a Marilyn Monroe mole on the corner of her top lip, hazel eyes, and her Beyoncé-like hips were a size ten, twelve at most, and she had a true apple bottom.

"Wasn't he suspended?" Evan Malik said and then quickly covered her mouth. "Oh, my apologies, I didn't mean to say that."

"He was suspended," the reporter said, following up on Evan's comment. "Do you want to tell us how you feel about that?" he asked Milan.

"My husband is a great man." Milan smiled. "Sure, he hit a rough patch, but he's on his way back and will be better than ever."

"Thank you, Mrs. Starks, now on to you, Mrs. Malik," he said to Evan. "Is it true that you were the first to be cast for the show?"

Milan shifted her weight from one Christian Louboutin python pump to the other, praying the nausea she felt as she sized up Evan would go away. Evan stood five eleven, fabulously slender, a figure eight shape, and skin the color of butterscotch. Her hair was cut in a short and spiky Halle Berry–inspired 'do with touches of honey blond that glimmered in the spotlights.

Milan hated that she and Evan had ended up in the same circle, because every time she saw Evan, heard Evan's voice, and was in her presence, Milan was forced to deal with the fact that Evan had won. Evan had ended up with the only man who made Milan feel true love was obtainable: Kendu. But since image was everything in this business, Milan planned to do her damnedest and pretend that they were all friends, even if the knife she had for Evan's back weighed down her Chloé clutch.

"Why of course, sweetie," Evan said. "Who wouldn't want to start with me?" She winked.

"It's been five minutes," Chaunci Morgan, Milan's neighbor and one of the four costars, whispered to Milan while maintaining a smile, "and already I'm sick of this bitch. Did she forget that she was a video ho?"

"Seems so," Milan whispered back.

"Excuse you." Jaise Williams, Evan's friend and their costar, turned toward Milan and then eyed Chaunci. "What did you just say?" she snapped.

"I said that she looks fabulous." Milan smiled at Evan. "She gives retired video hos, I mean vixens, a good name."

"Umm-hmm," Chaunci added, snapping her fingers in a Z motion. "A true fashionista. You better work it, girl."

"So, Mrs. Malik," the reporter said, "tell the world who you are and what it means to be on the show."

Evan paused. The microphone pointed toward her and the spotlights shining in her face caused her to draw a blank. There was no way she could say, "*Millionaire Wives Club* is a last-ditch effort to save my life, something to keep me busy and silence the self-destructive thoughts running through my mind." And she definitely couldn't say, "I may be married to Kendu Malik, linebacker for the New York Giants, but it's an unending struggle holding on to the motherfucker."

"Mrs. Malik," the reporter interrupted her thoughts, "is everything okay? Do you want to fill us in?"

Evan blinked and shot him a Barbie-doll smile. "I am a beautiful wife"—she arched her eyebrows—"an outstanding mother, and I have the talent and the foresight to seize the moment. And being on the show will allow all women to see what it takes to be me."

"And what exactly does that mean?" the reporter probed.

"What she means," Chaunci mumbled to Milan, "is that she thinks us peons are pissed that we didn't hit the same groupies party that she did."

Milan tried not to laugh, but then couldn't hold it in any longer, and when she looked at Chaunci they both cracked up, neither one of them stopping until they noticed everyone standing around them was silent.

"Oh," the producer, Bridget, said to them, batting her eyes, "don't stop on the boom mic's accord. For ratings' sake, carry on."

Milan was embarrassed; the last thing she wanted was for her and Chaunci to be seen as the troublemaking pair. "I'ma ummm"—Milan pointed to the bar—"go and have a drink."

"I'll join you," Chaunci said, as Bridget motioned for the camera guy, Carl, to follow them.

Once they were at the bar and had ordered their drinks, Carl tapped Chaunci on the shoulder. Both she and Milan turned around. "When I cut the camera on, tell us what happened over there. Why'd you say those things?"

He turned the camera on and pointed it at them. "Evan works my nerves," Chaunci said, popping her lips. "I've known her for three days, since we met at the studio, and already she's been in my life too long." She shot Milan a high five. "And believe me, as editor in chief of *Nubian Diva* magazine everyone knows that I'm too classy to lose my cool, but trust me, I will not hesitate to tap dat ass." She pointed toward Evan.

"But since this is a nice place," Milan interrupted as she sipped her drink, "we're not gon' tear it up."

"So we're just going to sit here." Chaunci crossed her legs.

"And enjoy our evening," Milan added.

"Thanks, ladies." Carl smiled and turned away.

Jaise stared at the *E! News* reporter, wondering how she should introduce herself to the world. Should she tell people the made-for-TV parts of her life story or should she lower the boom, let 'em know the truth, and maybe, just maybe, some sanity-teetering superwoman somewhere would understand that this single-mother-doing-her-thing bullshit was overrated?

She stood next to Evan and her eyes shifted from the people mingling across the room to the reporter standing before them. Her open-toed pencil heels were aching her feet, and she wondered why she had committed to doing reality TV, especially when her postdivorce resolution was no drama. Yet here she was drowning in it. All because she and Evan had sworn that cable's *Millionaire Wives Club* was the new bling they needed to rock.

It was public knowledge that Jaise had married and divorced ex–heavyweight champion Lawrence Williams, but she wondered if anyone knew how much she had suffered in silence during their marriage. She'd been slapped, punched, kicked, and humiliated, almost daily, by her ex. And if people didn't know it, would revealing it make hers a story of empowerment or weakness?

Then again, maybe she would look like a shero if she revealed how she had walked out on Lawrence by placing a sedative in his nightly shot of Hennessey, waited for him to drift to sleep, grabbed her son, and then escaped to a battered woman's shelter.

But she had been married to him for seven years and never once publicly complained. There was no way she could now admit before the world that a man with money had clouded her judgment. And since some shit was better left unsaid, Jaise stood there, waited for Evan to finish, and when the reporter turned to her she had her intro down pat.

"Mrs. Williams," the reporter said, "can you tell us a little about yourself? We hear that you're superwoman. A single mom, the owner of the online Shabby Chic antique business—you seem to be doing it all."

"Superwoman," Jaise responded, laughing, "is a myth." She flung her emerald-and-rhodium-draped wrist. "But I am handling money and power quite well." She chuckled a bit. "I'm just so excited to be in the company of some remarkable women."

Once Jaise was done the reporter shook the ladies' hands and said, "Good interview, ladies. Now I need to go and speak to your costars."

As he turned away Jaise let out a sigh of relief. She sat down at one of the tables and lit a cigarette, and Evan sat across from her. As Jaise eased her feet from her four-inch heels, she said, "I hope

I can survive this shit." She looked at Evan and took a pull. "I keep thinking and rethinking what to say and what not to say." She let out the smoke. "I swear somebody is going to think I'm crazy."

"Girl," Evan said, as she watched Milan and Chaunci laugh and converse at the bar, "just be yourself."

"Be myself?" Jaise smirked. "Yeah, right."

"No seriously, I mean, hell, I have no problems being me. I meant what I said to the reporter."

"Well, I'm not that put together. I'm stressed and sometimes I feel beat down. And you know that's too real for TV."

"It's *reality TV*," Evan insisted. "Speak to the camera as if you were talking to me."

Jaise laughed. "Okay, I'ma relax this bill collector's voice, put on my Brooklyn-mami twang, and say, 'I'm so goddamn tired of faking the funk. The truth is my sixteen-year-old son needs a man to call daddy and, hell, I do too.' "

Evan laughed, but her eyes were on Milan. She couldn't help but wonder what Milan had that she didn't. Why had Kendu chosen Milan for his best friend and why was Milan able to touch places and parts of Kendu that he wouldn't dare let Evan into? Kendu's rejection of her had steadily become Evan's obsession.

"What are you thinking about?" Jaise asked Evan once she realized she'd lost her attention. Jaise followed Evan's gaze to Chaunci and Milan. "Fuck them."

"That's it!" Bridget unexpectedly walked over to their table and said, "That's the spirit. Fuck them, and just so you know, they just finished calling you two a buncha rats' asses."

"What?" Jaise said, slipping her shoes back on. "They don't even know me."

"And from the sound of it," Bridget said, "they don't want to."

"Let's go and straighten this out." Jaise looked at Evan as she rose from her chair.

"Sit down," Evan warned Jaise. "I wouldn't give those low-budget bitches the satisfaction."

"Low-budget"—Bridget grabbed a napkin and a pen and scribbled down what Evan had just said—"bitch-es."

"I thought most producers didn't get involved with the cast," Evan snapped.

Bridget, who resembled a redheaded Heidi Klum, smiled and tossed her red hair over her shoulders. "Meet the new and improved way to produce."

"Anyway," Evan said, looking back at Jaise, "we have more going for us than to argue with a pair of half-dollar hos."

"So what makes you different from all the other women?" the *E! News* reporter asked Chaunci.

Chaunci did her best to hold a steady smile and act sober considering she and Milan had had one too many shots of Patrón and glasses of white wine. Milan smiled sweetly, knowing that if her friend said even one word it was sure to be slurred.

"Well," Chaunci attempted to speak in a steady tone, although her being tipsy was evident, "what makes me different is that I have my own, and all the rest of these women are uppity skeezers on the stroll." She turned to Milan: "No offense." Turning back toward the reporter she continued, "I'm not upset with them, though, not one bit. What woman wouldn't want to marry well?"

"But then they'd have to worry about groupies," Milan managed to add without slurring.

"Any advice about that?" the reporter asked.

Chaunci laughed. "Certainly, I have some advice. As soon as some groupie comes shakin' it around your man, bust a cap in her ass and then put one in him. Shit, I can't say he won't cheat, but make sure he's a handicap motherfucker doin' it. Alright." She and Milan exchanged high fives again.

"So what do you think people will learn from the show?" the reporter asked Chaunci.

"That when these Jones come down"—she sipped her drink

with one hand and pointed her index finger with the other—"it's gon' be a motherfucker."

"And there you have it." The *E! News* reporter turned to face the camera. "I present to you the ladies of *Millionaire Wives Club.* Stay tuned!"

One Truism in Life

Evan

Evan's French-manicured nails tapped nervously on the lava vanity in her guests' bathroom as she looked in the mirror and wondered if all the luxuries she had were worth the burning feeling lining her stomach.

Never had Evan begged a man—any man—let alone her husband, to make love to her—at least not until last night. Kendu had told her that they needed to talk. But she couldn't bear to listen. She didn't want to face what his actions had already said. He didn't love her, didn't want her, and she wasn't good enough to change his mind. So instead of listening she had kneeled before him, slid down his chest, and filled her mouth.

To fight off the anxiety heightened by the mixed emotions she felt, Evan took a bottle of Vicodin from her purse and popped two in her mouth.

The Vicodin always calmed her, but the fact that she needed a pill to do that made her feel as if she was less than perfect and more like a beautiful freak. Three years ago after a failed suicide attempt, where Evan slit her wrist and was prescribed Vicodin for the physical pain and lithium, which she took, off and on, for the mental, she quickly became addicted to the cocktail high.

Evan continued to stare in the mirror. Her heart raced, and instead of seeing her own reflection she saw her mother's face. Instantly her mother's voice filled her head: "I hate you! You and your young pussy wanna take my husband away from me!"

"He makes me do it," Evan responded to her mother's voice, while pressing her fingers deeply into her temples.

"You're lying!" her mother's voice responded. "You wanted it, because you think you're better than me! But you ain't shit! And you'll never be more than a whore!"

"Stop it!" Evan shook her head feverishly and wiped the sweat from her face with the back of her hand. She looked around the bathroom, and made sure the voice was only in her head, especially since her mother had long been dead.

Evan pushed herself away from the sink and lit a cigarette. She tried to clear her mind, but as soon as the flashback of her mother left, the disarray with Kendu took over her thoughts. She eased smoke from the corner of her mouth and watched it do an evaporating dance. *I have to swallow the fucked-up feeling and handle my business,* she thought. *Besides, I have this . . . it doesn't have me. And if that fails, then fuck it. I'll lay down the law and let him know*—she anxiously took a toke—*that at the end of the day I don't need a man . . .* She released the smoke. *All I need is to stay black and die . . . Shit*—she gave a slight chuckle as she sucked the butt of her cigarette—*I already told him I'm tired of feeling like the only one loving me is me. And if he wants to leave, then I'll gladly open the door and watch his ass disappear into the elements.*

Evan took one last pull off her cigarette before walking over to the toilet, dropping the burning butt into the water, and listening to the hiss of the dying flame before flushing it away.

She popped a stick of gum into her mouth, cracked the door open, and caught the smell of the burning food she had left on the stovetop half an hour ago.

Once in the kitchen she looked at Kendu, who sat on the sectional in the den area of the kitchen, sipping a cup of java and reading the morning paper. "What's your problem? You can't smell and shit?" she snapped. "If you would stop being so cheap and giving the chef every other weekend off, I wouldn't have to deal with this cooking shit."

Instead of responding, Kendu rattled the paper and flipped a page.

"I know you're not ignoring me." Evan shook her head. This was not what she had planned. Already her emotions had her going against her "be calm" constitution.

Kendu didn't budge; instead he continued what he was doing.

Evan hated to be ignored; it enraged her and she felt she was slowly unraveling out of control. Her head was spinning and her mind kept telling her to relax. She walked over to the refrigerator, removed the orange juice, and set it on the counter.

"Evan," Kendu said, looking toward her, "we need to go someplace and talk."

Evan slammed a glass on the island. "Oh, I know damn well you're not speaking to me now?" She pointed to her chest. "I thought you were reading the paper? Well, read the motherfucker then." She knew she was starting to spaz a little too much.

"Evan . . . ," Kendu called.

She swallowed. The tone of Kendu's voice rang in her head like raging drums.

"Evan—"

"What?!" she screamed.

Kendu sighed. "I'm asking you nicely to please let's go to lunch, dinner, or something—"

"I'm so sick of motherfuckers," she said more to herself than to him.

"Evan, it's not my intention to hurt you. I just think we need to live in two different places."

"For how long?"

"How am I supposed to answer that?"

"It was your bitch-ass idea. I mean really, since we're being so fuckin' adult"—she threw her hands in the air—"let me ask you this: Are you gon' still fuck me, or you bouncin' wit' the dick too?"

"I'm not doing this with you," he said.

"Oh really, I thought we were keepin' it real. Tell me, Kendu, we gon' still fuck or does your leaving come attached with the line of 'we can still be friends'? Or are you"—she made air quotes—" 'honest' enough to admit that you're looking for some groupie-ass bitch?!"

Kendu narrowed his eyes. "That's enough."

"I thought we were talking, Mr. I-Need-Some-Space." Evan spun on her heels. "You know I'm not stupid, don't you?! I know you've been out there on the road after one of your games, fucking some bitch! I know it; I should've known I was too good for your ass!"

"Too good? Have you lost your goddamn—" Kendu paused and started pacing the room, the cuffs of his black Versace pants swayed over his matching Prada loafers. The arguing and cussing, especially like this, was taking him out of his element. He was used to being cool, calm, and collected, with the ability to say how he felt and bring peace to the situation, all while never having to raise his voice. It was how he'd remained one of the New York Giants' star players and had avoided scandal.

It wasn't that he didn't know what he'd said to Evan was hurtful; he did, but, shit, it was hurting him even more to look in her face. "Like I said: This is done," he said. He grabbed his keys and walked toward the front door.

"You must be cheating on me!" Evan blocked his path and shoved him. "I'ma kill that bitch! I promise you I'ma kill her! Who is she?!" Evan yelled so loud that specks of spit flew into his face. "Just admit that it's Milan!" Evan attempted to shake Kendu, but he was too big, too strong, and his six-foot-three muscular frame was too burly for her to move him.

Evan could tell he was getting angrier by the second because of how his jaw tightened and his pecs thumped twice. She knew she was pushing her luck, but there was no way she could stop now. "How could you do this to me?!" She slapped him.

Kendu lifted his hand and, midway into his instantaneous reflex to slap her ass back, he stopped. "Didn't I tell you before to keep your hands to yourself?" he warned. "Stop fuckin' putting your hands on me. Because if I bring it, I will knock your ass down and you will not get up." He turned away from her and toward the door.

Evan ran around him and blocked his path once more. "Oh, you wanna hit me!" she screamed. "You wanna beat me now?! Do it! Just do it. I know you want to." She shoved him again.

Kendu looked at Evan in disgust. He was tired of the dramatics, of her mental instability, and her constant nagging and begging. He didn't hate her, but he was starting to, and if she continued to put her hands on him when they were arguing, he knew it would be only a matter of time before he blew his fuse and gave her what she'd been asking for.

Even though he was the athlete, Evan was the one who'd had the affair, citing Kendu's long playing hours and constant time on the road as the cause. And yeah, maybe he was away a bit much. And yeah, maybe instead of nursing his injury and entertaining plans of going back to the team, he needed to consider retiring so he could spend some time with his family, yet still, he had never expected that his wife would throw a tantrum by fucking another man, and then act as if he'd asked for it.

Didn't she understand that although he was famous and had enough money to last him several lifetimes, he was a man and that he hurt too? That he didn't deserve to be making love to his wife and smelling another man's scent? He didn't deserve having to find out from their daughter that Mommy had a new friend who was some played-out one-hit wonder named Cash. And then when he asked Evan if she knew Cash, she lied and forced Kendu to find out the truth by secretly following her to a hotel. After he caused a scene, Kendu left her and promised he'd be gone forever.

But then there was Evan's suicide attempt and Aiyanna suddenly became ill, which made him feel guilty, as if he needed to work things out with his family. Which ultimately he did . . . but things were never the same. He fucked Evan, yeah, laughed with her, yeah, but there was always something in the pit of his stomach, something that ached his backbone and aggravated his pride that never allowed him to get over Evan having an affair.

And it wasn't the friendship Evan may have had with the other man, or the emotional attachment to the attention that Cash may have paid her. What bugged Kendu was his imagination and the dreams of his wife sucking another man's dick, riding it, and cumin' all over it. The nagging-ass question of if she called this man's name, if he was hittin' it from the back, and making her say who the best was and who her pussy belonged to.

That was the shit he couldn't deal with, and no matter how many times he tried to rid the thoughts from his head, it never worked. Instead, six months later after he'd come back home, he found himself pissed that he was still married to this chick.

"For the *last time*," Kendu said, "this conversation is finished."

"Don't try and put this on me! You were the one working all the time." She pointed her finger at his face. "I needed you, our child needed you, and instead you were out tossing some fuckin' ball around. You never listened to me when I reminded you that you had a family!" She pushed him on his shoulder.

"Go ahead," he said, more as a warning than a statement. "Enough." He waved his hand under his chin.

"You had a wife . . . ," Evan continued, as she shoved him again.

"Ai'ight now!" He grabbed her hand but she slipped from his grip and pounded into him.

"You practically forced me to be with someone else. You didn't give a damn about me! Do you know what you had?!" She pushed him. "Why are you doing this to me?!"

He grabbed her wrists. "What you want me to say, Evan? Huh? I told you I wanted to leave. But you don't seem to hear that! So tell me what you need to hear to get the goddamn hint? Do you want me to tell you that I can't stand looking at you? That I hate to even see your fuckin' face? That I'm not attracted to you, and that the only reason my dick gets hard is because you suck it so goddamn well? Is that what you want? I'm tryna be a man and tell you that I'm done as peacefully as I know how, but that's not enough for you. I *don't* like you anymore, Evan. I *don't* want you anymore. Even the perfume you wear stinks to me. I'm sick of fuckin' lookin' at you. Do you get it now? Do you understand that I want you out of my life?!"

"We are a family!"

"You are *not* my fuckin' family!"

Evan was stunned. Her mind told her to kick his ass, but judging from the way the veins on the side of his neck were jumping she thought better of it. Instead, she wanted to be taken out of herself . . . because this here, this shit that Kendu was doing, was some bullshit, and last she checked there was no rehab for it. Here she'd been injected with raw, throbbing, and excruciating heart-break and this niggah had the nerve to feel himself . . . all because she had made one mistake, and now suddenly he was above loving her and she should get over anything she felt for him? Forget about the time when he said she'd given him the most precious gift of all: a beautiful baby girl?

Did he understand all the lonely nights she had spent, or had he forgotten? And now suddenly his ass wanna buck? He wasn't getting off that easy. Fuck that. Evan turned to Kendu. "You want space?! No problem, you only have to tell me once. Your wish is my fuckin' command." She charged down the hall. "You don't have to leave, we'll leave! Aiyanna!" Evan screamed. "Aiyanna!

We're not a family?" she said, quickly turning around and squinting her eyes at Kendu. "You would say some shit like that to me?"

"What are you doing, Evan?" Kendu followed her as she
stormed into their eight-year-old daughter's room, pushing the
double French doors open on Aiyanna, who was sitting with her
legs crossed Indian-style in the middle of her canopy bed amid
Bratz dolls and her dog, and watching *High School Musical* on TV.
Evan yanked the girl off the bed by the elbow. Aiyanna instantly
started crying and the dog barked in a frenzy.

"We're leaving! Your daddy said we aren't a family!" Evan said
frantically. "He doesn't love us anymore, and he wants us gone! So
hurry, we don't have much time! Get your dog and get your shit!"

Immediately Aiyanna started screaming like never before.
Kendu didn't know if she was hurting from the pain of her
mother's hold on her elbow or the gut punch of her words. "Let
her go, Evan," Kendu said calmly, attempting to get her to let go
of Aiyanna.

"No!" Evan snatched Aiyanna around. "Didn't you just say that
you wanted us out?! So we're leaving!"

"Evan . . . I'm warning you." He turned Aiyanna toward him.
"Daddy loves you—"

"Your father's a fuckin' liar." She snatched her daughter back.
"You know he left you before, and he just told me he's going to
do it again. So all your friends will know! Your teacher will know!
Everyone!"

"It's not like that." Kendu turned Aiyanna toward him.

Evan twisted her back. "You listen to me, he wants another
family."

"Aiyanna."

"He ain't shit. He said we weren't his family! We're not good
enough. Don't worry, I'll work on getting you a new daddy—"

As soon as Evan said that Kendu drew back his hand and
smacked her so hard that her entire body froze before she fell to
the floor, screaming, "You put your fuckin' hands on me?! I been

waiting for this day, motherfucker! Call the cops! Give me the phone, Aiyanna!"

"No! Mommy!" Aiyanna yelled. "Don't call the cops on my daddy! Please, not my daddy!"

"I'ma have him locked up!"

Aiyanna screamed as if she were going crazy, and though Kendu heard her crying he couldn't stop himself from lifting Evan off the floor by her neck, and pressing his left thumb and index finger deeply into her jugular vein. "You keep testing me because you don't believe that I will kill you. Well, you better believe it, because I will take you outta here, Evan, I swear to God I will!"

"Daddy!" Aiyanna pulled on his leg. "Daddy, stop!"

"You gon' tell my daughter some shit like that?!" Kendu yelled.

"Daddy, I know you love me! Daddy, please." Aiyanna started to hyperventilate and wheeze profusely.

Evan started to gag, and Aiyanna continued to pull on Kendu's legs. "Daddy, please stop! You gon' kill Mommy, Daddy! Please, don't kill my mommy!"

Instantly Kendu removed his hand from Evan's throat and she slithered to the floor like a dying snake.

"Daddy!" Aiyanna coughed and wheezed, still holding on to his leg. Kendu could feel the tears pushing against the back of his eyes. He hated to see his daughter crying like this, and he especially hated that he had put his hands on her mother.

He picked his daughter up and held her in his arms.

"Shh, calm down, you need your asthma pump." He picked it up off her nightstand and Aiyanna took two whiffs.

"Don't leave me, Daddy."

"I'm not." Unexpected tears rolled down his face. "Daddy loves you. Daddy would never leave you."

Aiyanna wiped his eyes with the back of her hand. "Daddy, do you want me and my mommy to leave? Say no, Daddy," she cried.

"No, not you. I don't want you to leave." He was now wiping her tears away.

"You love me, right, Daddy? Say yes."

"Yes, I'ma always love you."

"You love my mommy?"

Kendu stared at Evan, who was still holding her throat. He wanted to say no. "Yes, baby."

"Then make up," Aiyanna cried. "Make up and say sorry, Daddy. You said boys not s'pose to hit girls."

He placed Aiyanna on the floor and looked at Evan. "You'll never know how sorry I am." Kendu walked over to Evan and helped her up off the floor.

As Evan was steady on her feet Bridget and the camera crew walked into the room.

"Oh, Bridget." Evan faked a laugh. "I didn't expect you so soon." She held on to Kendu as if she were giving him a hug. "How'd you get in?"

"The door was open."

"The bell works," Kendu said as he slyly pushed Evan away.

"I don't believe ringing it is in my contract." Bridget looked at Evan. "Why do you look so disheveled? And what was all the commotion we just heard?"

"Kendu was just teaching us some football techniques. You know he loves contact sports."

"Yo," Kendu said, disgusted and disturbed by what had just occurred, "I gotta go."

"Honey, wait." Evan kissed him on the cheek and he whispered to her, "Get the fuck away from me."

Kendu looked back at Aiyanna. "Daddy needs a minute."

"Wait, Daddy!" Aiyanna cried.

"Why is she crying?" Bridget pointed toward Aiyanna.

Evan ignored her, and as Kendu continued out the door she turned to Aiyanna. "Get dressed," she said with precise diction. "I am going to get my purse. Today is the day they film us shopping."

Milan

"Close your eyes and count backward," the nurse said as Milan lay on the gurney.

Only a week had passed since the show had begun taping, and already Milan was avoiding the cameras. Today was supposed to be one of her shooting days, but there was no way she could allow this to be taped.

As Milan was anesthetized into sleep her mind felt like it weighed a thousand pounds and her thoughts even more. She knew that one day she'd pay for this, but that was a chance she'd have to take. She was definitely pro-life, but right now the life she was pro was her own . . . and at this moment her desire not to wallow in defeat gave her little room to think of any other options.

Besides, the day that she sat at the kitchen table with morning sickness, bills overflowing like water, and Yusef sitting at the other end of the table, complaining that he wasn't about to get a job and be reduced to a minimum-wage piece of shit, was the day when she knew this had to end.

There was no way she could worsen her situation by having

this baby. It didn't matter how much she wanted Yusef to change. What mattered was that instead of gold he'd turned out to be the pot of shit at the end of a pissy-ass rainbow, and she could make no more excuses for it.

There was no way to explain away how in the last year her life had gone to hell. How they had gone from living in the lap of luxury to being the king and queen of late payments. From being carefree to being stressed out all the time. From having a staff to keep the apartment clean to her being solely responsible for the maintenance. No one in their right mind would understand this nonsense.

Therefore she had to do what she had to do. She had enough liabilities. And she needed time to think and regroup, because right now she was drowning in fear. Fear of having to leave all of her plans behind and start anew.

"Ms. Andrews," the nurse whispered and patted the side of the bed. "Ms. Andrews, can you hear me?"

Milan lay still for a moment before she realized that the nurse was calling her by the false name she'd checked into the clinic under. Milan peeled one eye open at a time and scanned the room. She was no longer in the operating room; she was lying in the recovery room, separated from the other women by a white curtain.

"Try and sit up," the nurse said. "As soon as you get yourself together, you can go home. Would you like for me to call you a cab?"

Milan nodded as she grabbed her clothes. After a few minutes of collecting herself and fighting off the drowsy side effects of the anesthesia, Milan began to dress.

A little while later the nurse peeped back into her section. "Your cab is waiting." She smiled.

Milan nodded and made her way out of the clinic.

Rain poured from the sky and beat against the cab's hood as she slid in. Once she gave the cabby her address she heard a knock on the window. Milan looked up and a protestor had plastered a picture of a dead fetus against the wet glass with a bleeding hand-written note: STOP SLEEPING WITH THE DEVIL.

The protestor ran off, and until the cabby removed it, the picture stuck to the window.

As they took off down the highway tears ran down Milan's cheeks.

As she approached her apartment she could hear a throwback of Boogie Down Production's "Bridge Is Over" screaming from the CD player. She turned the knob, and the smell of fried chicken and weed filled her nose.

"Happy Birthday!" Yusef smiled, holding his right arm out and puffing on a blunt with the left. He walked over, held Milan in his embrace, and kissed her on the lips.

Milan looked surprised; she glanced up at the calendar: October 5. She looked at the small card table and saw a birthday cake. She turned thirty today. She couldn't believe it; she'd actually forgotten one of the biggest days of her life. The day by which she had promised herself she'd have a white picket fence, two point five kids, and a dog.

"I was hoping to surprise you." Yusef smiled. "Where've you been?"

Milan didn't respond; she couldn't, especially knowing how much he wanted a child. Instead of answering she walked over to the small, round table, held her hair back, blew out the candles, and then lay down on the suede sectional.

"What the?" Yusef mashed the blunt in the ashtray and said in disbelief, "You sick or some shit?"

Milan turned over on her back and looked at the ceiling. "Yeah." She nodded. "Yeah—I am."

"Oh, I was 'bout to say, black man can't do nothin' for yo' ass." He laughed.

Milan arched her eyebrows and turned back on her side. She wasn't in the mood to discuss his version of race relations.

"Yo, dig," Yusef said, walking over to her, "I been thinking . . ."

Milan could tell by the way he was breathing that this was the intro to an argument. "Yusef . . . I'm not in the mood."

"So what is you sayin', Milan, fuck Da Truef?"

Milan rolled her eyes. "Look, I never said that."

"So what is you saying?"

She carefully took a deep breath. "I'm not saying anything."

"Ain't no sweat, Milan. If you too high and mighty to hear what Da Truef got to say, it's cool."

"Know what? Just tell me."

Yusef sighed. "Ai'ight." He sighed again. "But first, just let me talk. Don't interrupt, 'cause I don't wanna hear no bullshit and no opinions. Just hear me out."

"What is it?"

"I made a career change, baby."

"A career change?"

"Look, I ain't gon' tell you if you gon' be sighing and shit."

"Would you say it?"

"I'm tryin' to."

"Oh God."

"Why you always gotta start an argument?"

"Would you say it!" she screamed.

"Ai'ight, I invested some money in this dude from Wyoming to train me."

"Wy-who? What?" She sat up. "What did you just say to me?" She looked at him, confused, hoping she had heard wrong.

"Check it, I'ma 'bout to be in the WWE. You heard of Superman, well I'ma be Da Truef Man!" He jumped up in glee. "Yo, I'ma be knockin' suckers out!" He rocked from side to side. "I'm 'bout to the best fuckin' wrestler they've ever seen. The Rock ain't gon' have shit on me."

Milan blinked. Maybe the anesthesia had made her delusional. "What just happened here? You about to be a who?"

"A wrestler."

"Oh . . . my . . . God . . . are you that desperate for the lime-light?"

"You tryna play Da Truef? What's the problem? Wrestlers got groupie wives too. You'll be right at home."

She ignored his groupie comment and went straight to her biggest concern. "And how much money did you invest into this business?"

"A million dollars."

Milan's eyes welled with tears. "Are you crazy?" She couldn't believe this; they had only two million left. Half a million was for her to buy new furniture and designer digs for TV, which she saw as an investment. The network would pay her fifty thousand an episode, but she wouldn't receive any of it until the end of the season's filming.

But if he'd just spent a million, they had only one million left, and judging by the letter she had just got from the IRS, half of that was about to be tied up in taxes. Milan felt herself about to pass out, but she fought with everything she had to stay conscious. "Why didn't you come and talk to me about this first?"

" 'Cause I didn't think I owed you an explanation seeing as how I was by myself when I was up and down the basketball court, and truth be told you the reason we don't have any money. So I didn't really see what I needed to discuss with you."

"Excuse you, Yusef?" Milan blinked. "I wasn't the one who snorted up a multimillion-dollar contract."

"No, 'cause yo' ass was too busy shoppin'!"

"What did you just say to me, Yusef?" Milan snapped.

"You heard me: You the reason we don't have any money."

"Yo' ass was gettin' high, motherfucker! Don't try and act like you were Michael Jordan, Pooky."

"Don't be tryna shine. You know that shit was weed."

"Tell it to the damn drug exam that came back positive for co-caine!"

"You know that came from that medication I was taking."

Milan felt herself getting dizzy. "Look . . . leave me alone."

"I get it." Yusef snorted. " 'Cause you graduated college and I didn't you the best ma'fucker round here. What, you hot shit all of a sudden?"

"What are you talking about?!" Milan screamed. "I graduated from college because I wanted more. I didn't wait around for somebody to give it to me!"

"You ain't say all of that when I gave you that fuckin' ring and married your ass." He pointed to her left index finger. "You was all on my dick then." Yusef shook his head. "Yo it's whatever," he snapped. "I been thinking that maybe you need to step off anyway. My mother been telling me for years that you a problem and I shoulda never married your ass. So you know what? Do you. If you here when I come back then cool, if not then that's cool too."

Milan couldn't believe it. Now she knew for sure the abortion had been the right decision. "I can't do this anymore," she said. Milan placed her hand over her mouth and looked around the room. "This is crazy. Absolutely crazy."

"What-the-hell-ever, Milan. If you can't love a black man when he's down on his luck, then do what you got to do." He flicked his hand as if he were performing a magic trick.

"So what are you saying?"

Yusef took a step back. "I'm saying you ain't shit, like the fuck I been saying. If you can't accept Da Truef like he is, then ain't no need for you to stick around and wait for Da Truef to get back on his feet. Man, please. Your Puerto Rican ass—"

"I'm not Puerto Rican."

"Whatever, I betchu you understand 'Adios motherfucker.' You gotta lotta dreams that ain't gon' amount to shit, 'cause you ain't shit. You're talentless, and you're fat as hell. When I met you, you were cute, exotic and shit."

"Please, you were just hung up on me being black and Dominican."

"Well, now I'm hung up on you being a spic-ass trick. Since we don't have any money, why don't you go down to the corner and hop on the back of a truck with the rest of the goddamn Mexicans. 'Cause I don't need you in my face."

"You ain't shit," Milan snapped. "All the other athletes' wives are living lavishly, and here I am stuck with the fuckin' towel boy!"

"Oh, so that's what this has come to? You wanna put me down? Well, if yo' big ass think you can come up with something better than Da Truef, number twenty-three, then who is Da Truef to hold you back? Da Truef shall set you free." He opened the front door and walked out into the hall. "I ain't gotta take this." He slammed the door behind him.

"And neither do I!" Milan screamed, as the automatic locks clicked in place.

After sitting still for a few moments she walked over to the wall of windows and looked down at the busy Manhattan street. "How do I get outta hell?" Milan said to herself as she turned around and leaned her back against the glass. Suddenly she felt the room was closing in on her, and if she didn't leave now she knew her fear would never let her out.

"Happy Birthday," she said, sliding her wedding band off and dropping it on top of the cake. She lay back on the couch and rubbed her empty belly.

Jaise

Jaise was tired of carrying the weight of a strong black woman on her shoulders. She didn't want the responsibility of being seen as Mother Earth, Nubian Queen, or an I-don't-need-no-man-all-I-need-is-me being.

She wanted to be vulnerable without being taken advantage of. To be able to cry without being charged as emotional. The permission to stand up, place her hands on her voluptuous hips, shake her fly-ass hair, and say, "Yes, I need a man for more than dick," without any judgment.

Jaise wanted to be submissive without anyone thinking she lacked substance. And she might be rich due to her substantial alimony checks, but she was tired of paying her own bills. She wanted a man—her man—the infamous "him" to do it . . . and not complain about it.

And she wanted to cook for "him" . . . hell, she liked to cook. She wanted to hold "his" hand while he took charge.

And no, Jaise wanted to shout, *no matter how you slice it, how many goddamn support groups, testimonies, and self-help books there are, I can-*

not be my sixteen-year-old son's mother and father. She was failing miserably at it.

But since she couldn't voice her true feelings, and because what everyone else thought of her mattered more than what was in her heart, she swallowed her emotions and glided into her bedroom where her on-again, off-again boyfriend, Trenton, was lying in her Civil War–era antique four-poster bed waiting for her.

Jaise moved from side to side, her see-through nightie showing every erotic gift she had. She placed her hand on the retractable pole in her bedroom and started a sensual dance, moving her size-sixteen hips in a seductive rhythm. She could see Trenton's dick hardening and seeming to grow by the moment. Jaise spun around the pole and grooved like a Vegas stripper. Trenton gripped his dick and squeezed the tip, as the pre-cum glistened and eased out the sides. "Shit, Jaise," he said, "I want you over here."

Jaise smiled and hoped that him wanting her had a double meaning. "You want this?" she took her index finger, slipped it into her sweetness, and licked the wetness. "Are you sure you want this?"

"You know I do." Trenton said, "And I'm selfish as hell too, so I want all of it."

The closer she got to Trenton, the more she prayed that he saw in her what she saw in him: security. She knew convincing him that they should be a family would be hard to do, especially since he and her son, Jabril, didn't interact other than a head nod or a sincere-looking wave. Jabril had already told Jaise that if Trenton wasn't gone by the time he was eighteen he would either bounce or snuff Trenton out, but either way one of them had to go. As far as Trenton was concerned, whenever he spent the night, which was more often than not, everything was all about him: He showered, Jaise fed him dinner, and they went to bed.

Yet despite the inner anguish Jaise felt about the situation, she was determined to make do with the man she had. There was no way at thirty-five, with a sixteen-year-old son and a ton of suppressed relationship baggage, that her selection of rich men was endless. Besides, Jaise knew plenty of women who kept their children and their man separate.

It wasn't as if Trenton mistreated Jabril; he just didn't do children. But she'd concluded that her son was her responsibility anyway. At least Trenton was a good role model. He had an MBA and his own company, invested his money, and was able to show Jabril what it was to be a successful black man, especially since Jabril's daddy never had. Lawrence was too busy making love to his white wife and floating like a butterfly and stinging like a bee for the boxing commission.

The music floated behind Jaise as she stood before the bed and dropped her black satin negligee to the floor, revealing her smooth and glistening brown skin.

"Damn," Trenton said, admiring what he saw. "I've been wanting that pussy all week."

"You should stop waiting so long to come home and get it." She smiled. "It's yours all the time, baby. And it's waiting for the day when we can share last names."

"Didn't I tell you to stop thinking about that? When the time is right, I'll let you know."

"Shh." Jaise climbed on the bed and placed her wet index finger between his lips. "Let's just enjoy this moment." Jaise slid down his scrumptious body, parting his legs, and expanding her cheeks. She licked the length of his hardness and as his toes curled against her sides, she started doing his favorite thing: tea-baggin' him.

"Fuck." His eyes rolled to the top of his head and as Jaise sucked every ounce of him, his phone started singing.

Jaise stopped for a moment, long enough to at least open her eyes and wonder why this ringtone was different from the others. Before she could come to any conclusions Trenton pushed her head back to his dick and she continued to deep throat him.

Jaise tried to get back into the erotic rhythm that her slurping mouth had mastered but she couldn't. She just wanted him to cum so she could be done. So as she sucked his dick she ran her middle finger along the slit of his ass and within a matter of moments it was over.

"That was the shit, baby," Trenton said, shaking his head, as if waves were floating through him. "Damn." He hollered in delight as Musiq and Mary J started singing from his phone again.

Trenton reached for his phone on the nightstand. Jaise looked at the clock: one a.m. "Trenton, why is your phone ringing this time of the night?"

"What I tell you about questioning me? In my business this could be anybody."

"At one in the morning?"

"I talk to people from all over the world. It could be three in the afternoon for them," he said, flipping his phone open. "Hello?"

Jaise heard a female voice on the other end of Trenton's phone, causing a lump to gather in Jaise's throat and make her gag on the residue of Trenton's stickiness. She attempted to kiss Trenton on the lips in an effort not to allow jealousy to prick her pride.

He looked at her as if she'd gone crazy, and instead of kissing her back he turned his face to the side, muted the phone, and whispered, "You know I don't do that. Go brush your teeth and come back."

"Excuse me." She blinked. "That's your dick."

"Why don't you ever do what I ask you to do the first time?" He gave her a warning eye. "I really don't like that."

Every part of Jaise's being told her not to get her ass out of bed, but in the pit of her stomach she knew if she pissed him off he wouldn't think twice about leaving for the night, and that was not what she wanted. So she went into her master bath, handled her business, and came back out.

Trenton was still on the phone, and she could clearly see that he was aggravated. She lay down next to him, and while she ran her hands through the curly hair on his chest she heard the woman on the other end crying.

"Listen," Trenton spoke sternly into the phone, "I'm being extremely rude right now and I have to go." He paused, and a second later said, "This could've waited for the morning's meeting. Your calling me this time of night is not acceptable."

Jaise's heart thundered in her chest. It was obvious that Trenton was attempting to pass off whomever this was as a business associate.

Trenton continued, "Look, I will deal with you later in the a.m." He clicked his phone off and tossed it back on the nightstand. He rolled over on top of Jaise. "Where were we?" He licked her now-soft nipples.

"Who was that?" she said, watching him suckle her breasts.

"An associate." He cuddled her nipple with his tongue.

Jaise stared at Trenton. She wanted desperately to ask him what type of associate, but she wasn't so sure what he would say. There was a possibility he would lie and a possibility that he wouldn't, and at this moment with her feelings resting on the tip of her clit, which he was now sucking better than he ever had before, she wasn't so sure if the truth or a lie would be worse.

Besides, she'd already surmised that most of Trenton's ambivalence came from his never having been involved with a woman like her. And since she was just getting into the groove of convincing him of what life and love with her would be like, Jaise made up her mind that she was willing to put in the time it would take to reshape Trenton into the man she longed for him to be.

So . . . what was a phone call with a crying bitch on the other end? After all, if he wanted the other chick, he wouldn't have been in Jaise's bed.

"Eat it up, baby," Jaise said, with melting sugar running between her legs. Trenton pulled her clit between his teeth, and as she grabbed the base of his neck her phone rang. Trenton stopped what he was doing and looked at the clock. "Who the hell is call- ing you this time of night?"

"Karma," she said, watching the phone vibrate as it rang on the nightstand.

"Oh, you're being smart?" he said, pissed, as her phone stopped ringing and quickly started again. "Answer the motherfucker, since it's karma. What you waitin' on?"

"Jealousy is so unattractive." She smiled as she answered the phone. "Hello?" There was a pregnant pause. "Hello?" she said again.

"Hi, uhh," an unfamiliar male voice said on the other end of the line. "What's your mother's name, son?" she heard the unfa- miliar voice say in the background, and then he was talking to her again. "Hi, is this Mrs. Jaise Williams, or is she available?"

"This is she," Jaise said nervously. "Who is this?"

"Ma'am, my apologies for bothering you so late, but I'm Offi- cer Asante and we have your son, Jabril, in custody. He was pulled over and the officers found alcohol in the car."

"What?! Alcohol! He's only sixteen, and he told me he was spending the night at a friend's house!"

"Spending the night at a friend's house?" She could hear that the officer was put off. "Isn't it a school night?"

"Your point?" she said defensively.

"I guess if you can ask that question I don't have much of a point."

Trenton looked at Jaise. "Are you okay?" he asked, sounding genuinely concerned.

She shook head her no.

"I know this is upsetting," Officer Asante said, "but your son has been playing games and not giving me or any of the other of- ficers your phone number, and it wasn't until I told him he was about to catch a free ride down to juvey that he gave me what I needed."

Jaise's stomach flipped. This was the second time Jabril had been arrested this month. "Please don't send him anywhere." She held tears back. "I'm on my way."

"You need to hurry, because the way he's acting, he's about to be on the next bus out of here."

The officer hung up and Jaise held the phone to her ear in shock. She'd never felt like such a failure. For the most part, although Jabril had his ways, he had always been a good kid. The problems started about a year ago, after she had practically moved Trenton in and Lawrence and his new wife had their own son. Jabril said that he felt like he was on the outside looking in. Jaise had tried to talk to Lawrence about it, but he accused her of jealousy, not liking his wife, and he took no account of his son's feelings, treating Jabril as if he were simply being ridiculous. Which left Jaise stuck with a kid who was suddenly all over the place.

She wiped the tears slipping from her eyes and onto her cheeks. "Look, ummm, Trenton, we need to go and get Jabril."

"We?" he said, surprised. "He doesn't even speak to me, and now I have to go and get him? Where is he, in jail again?"

Jaise hung her head. "He was arrested."

"You do realize," Trenton said matter-of-factly, "that this is the second time this month?"

"I can count, Trenton."

"Don't get nasty with me. Shit, since you can count you better start tallying up how much bail money you're about to spend on your l'il in-house gangstah."

"He's not a gangstah, he's a follower, and he's following these damn no-good niggahs around!"

"You better stop thinking that boy is perfect, 'cause he's not. Believe me, from what I can tell and based on the way he acts around here, he's the leader in his criminal activity."

"You can save your smart-ass comments," Jaise snapped. "Furthermore, I didn't ask you for analysis on my baby."

"Babies are not six feet tall and wear a size-twelve shoe. He's sixteen years old."

"Trenton." Jaise paused. "I don't think you wanna go there."

"Go where?"

"The way you're talking about my son."

"I'm not talking about your son!" Trenton raised his voice. "I'm just saying that you make excuses for everything he does. If you really want to teach him a lesson, let his ass stay there. This isn't the first time, and he's always in something or another. Now I have to get up early in the morning for a business meeting. I'm not going anywhere, and neither are you."

"So what am I supposed to do, leave my child there?"

"He needs to be taught a lesson." He pulled Jaise back to him, her firm breasts pressed against his chest. "Trust me on this."

Immediately there was a collision in Jaise's head, and everything in the room, including Trenton, started to spin. Why was she in this dead-end relationship with him? Why? Was it the dick, the addiction to being rich? Or was she a slave to being mistreated?

Jaise looked at Trenton and blinked in disbelief: As he rubbed his hard dick against her thigh, there was not one wrinkle of concern on his face to show that he gave a fuck about her son. She pushed him on his shoulder and sat up. "Are you crazy? Don't you ever in your damn life think your bustin' a nut in my pussy in any way comes before my son! When you have a kid, you dump that niggah in the trash, but let me inform you, Jabril Williams is not up for negotiation, so if you don't give a fuck, stay not giving a fuck, but don't ever give me no fucked-up advice about my son's life. Be clear, that is not your damn place!"

"Oh, but it's my place to take you on trips, spend my money on you, refurnish your house and shit, so you can ball on TV. But it's not my place to tell you what I think about your son. Listen, it's cool, after all he's not my kid."

"And thank God for that."

"Yeah really," Trenton snapped as he started to dress. "And when he grows up robbing and killing folks don't call me."

"Don't you worry about him!"

Trenton grabbed his car keys.

"Where are you going?" Jaise asked.

"Listen, go take care of the thief you're raising, and when he's sentenced to prison and is finally out of the house, call me."

"I can't believe you said some shit like that!"

"Believe it, because I said it. You're so busy complaining and all up in my ear about when are we going to be married. Well, from where I'm standing, outside of fucking you, there's no future with you. You nag too much, you have a life filled with drama, and any man that comes up in here and takes you seriously will have to fuck your son up because you won't. Here's some advice: If you want to raise a strong and productive black man then find a man to be his daddy, because Lawrence ran away and I don't have the tolerance for it." And he slammed the door behind him.

Jaise could hear Trenton's car tires screeching down the street as she sat naked in the middle of her bed. *If only my son would behave,* she thought, *I wouldn't have these problems.*

A few minutes later she was dressed and practically skating down the stairs and into her car. She placed her car in reverse and saw the camera crew's van revving its engine behind her. Jaise couldn't believe it; they had actually camped out across the street from where she lived. She knew it was reality TV, but damn.

As soon as Jaise pulled up in front of the precinct with the camera crew on her heels, she flew out of the car and into the station. She found Jabril handcuffed to a metal bench, surrounded by a room filled with busy officers and other handcuffed criminals. Jaise's heart dropped. Although Jabril towered over her at six feet, he still looked like a sweet and innocent baby to her . . . a toddler at the most, with big brown button eyes, deep dimples, and a sweet smile. She could tell by the way he was biting his bottom lip that he was nervous.

"Jabril," she said breathlessly as if she'd been running in a marathon, "what happened?" She ran her hand along the side of his face. "Did anybody hurt you? Are you okay? What the hell happened? Why are your eyes so red? Did somebody put their hands on you? And who are these so-called thugs?! And alcohol, Jabril? Why won't you listen to me?!"

"Man, don't start questioning me." Jabril sighed and sucked his teeth. His breath reeked of alcohol, and contact with the stench almost made Jaise high. She felt as if she were having an out-of-body experience, because there was no way the baby she'd nurtured in her bosom, carried on her hip, loved more than herself, protected like a grand prize, and had dreams and aspirations for was sitting handcuffed in a police station drunk . . . Maybe she was in space. Yeah, that was it, she was in the Twilight Zone.

Jabril pushed his mother's hands from his face. "What does it look like happened? And what took you so long?! And get that camera outta my face before my friends think I'ma cop."

The innocent vision of Jabril quickly faded. "Who the hell are you talking to?!" Jaise lost it. "I'm worried sick about you and this is how you speak to me? And on TV? You think I like coming to get you from jail? Is this what you want out of life—to be a crackhead?" She mushed Jabril in the center of his forehead.

"I don't do crack. It was Banana Red Cisco. And what you worried about it for?"

"I'm your mother!"

"I ain't the one who needs to recognize who the mother is."

"You better shut your fuckin' mouth, talkin' all high and crazy."

"Whatever."

"I can't believe you're sitting here drunk, Jabril! What is really going on with you?!"

"I like to drink, Mama." He cracked up laughing.

Jaise reared her hand back and slapped Jabril so hard that the sting from the slap resonated around the room. "I'll kick yo' ass before I let you be reduced to nothing!"

"Ma'am." One of the officers walked over to Jaise. "Don't put your hands on him again."

"Don't tell me what to do! I pushed his ass out, not you!"

"Ma'am, can you please calm down. The assigned officer will be out here to see you in a minute."

"You lucky I'm handcuffed!" Jabril spat.

"And what you gon' do, but get fucked up!" Jaise yelled. "The day you even look like you wanna hit me I'm shuttin' the world down!"

Before Jaise could go on, a voice drifted over her shoulder. "Hi, I'm Detective Asante, and you are?" He held out his hand.

Accepting his gesture, but never looking into his face, Jaise said, "I'm Jaise. This is my soon-to-be-bust-upside-his-head son, Jabril."

The detective looked at the cameras strangely. "And they are?"

"Her new boyfriends," Jabril interjected.

"Shut up." Jaise squinted. "No, Detective Asante, they are the camera crew . . . for a reality TV show I'm doing." Jaise rolled her eyes, hating that the cameras were recording this.

"Oh-kay," he said. "Well, maybe you need less reality TV and more reality with your son, who's quickly making a rise in under-age drinking."

"Excuse me?" Jaise said, offended. "I didn't come here for you to judge me."

"I haven't judged you. I'm just calling it as I see it. But as I was saying, it seems your son was picked up for underage drinking. There were open containers in the car. He was the only one caught. The others took off."

"First of all, my baby isn't drunk."

"Stevie Wonder can see that he's drunk."

Jaise looked at Jabril and he gave her a stupid one-sided smile. She quickly took her eyes from him because if she looked at him a moment longer she was sure to slap the shit out of him again. "Well, maybe he's a little tipsy, but he didn't buy the alcohol."

"How do you know that?" the detective asked.

"Because . . . we're better than this. Do you know who his father is?"

"His father doesn't concern me."

"Listen, I don't have to go back and forth with you. Like my son said, he didn't buy any alcohol."

"He didn't say that, you did," Detective Asante said.

Jaise looked at Jabril. "Tell him."

A sly smile ran across Jabril's face. "My dude," he belched, "I ain't buy no alcohol."

"Listen," the detective said, "we're not equals, and you're a kid, not my friend. So as far as you're concerned, my name is Detective Asante."

"Yeah, ai'ight, Detective Asante," Jabril said sarcastically.

"Now," the detective continued, "if you didn't buy the alcohol, who did?"

"You the cop, you tell me."

"As far as I'm concerned you did, and since you were the only one caught, guess who wears the charge?"

Jaise placed her hands on her wide hips. "I think it's unprofessional," she said to the detective, "the way you're going back and forth with a sixteen-year-old kid."

"This isn't about him being a kid. This is about him committing a crime."

"I'm not raising a criminal!"

"No, you're just raising a problem."

This was the second time tonight that everything for Jaise had come to a complete standstill. She couldn't believe this man had the nerve to stand his big and muscular, six-foot-three-inch fine ass, looking like Boris Kodjoe on his best day, with skin like butter-colored silk, perfectly white teeth, and a raspy voice that let her and everybody else standing around know that he didn't play much, and tell her any damn thing about her baby.

If she hadn't noticed how fine and how big he was, she would've risked her freedom and slapped him for talking to her crazy. "Listen, I don't have to argue with you," she said. "I'm sure there's a reasonable explanation for this."

"Like what?" The detective blinked.

"Like this new group of friends he suddenly wants to hang with!"

"Whatever," Jabril yarned. "Don't talk about my friends."

"Shut up, Jabril, right now!" Jaise snapped. "Stop acting like one of them niggahs in the street!"

"You better back up out my face. And I'm not playin'!" Jabril went to lift his hand and point his finger, but the handcuffs halted him. "Get me out of here! Stop talking to this dude and get me out of here now! You don't never listen to me. Get on my nerves!"

"Who are you talking to, son?" Detective Asante looked at Jabril strangely. "You aren't that drunk, so I know you couldn't be talking to your mother like that."

"Man, this between me and my moms, not you, so mind yours."

"Jabril, shut your mouth!" Jaise peered at him. "And you got one more time to get into some shit and you getting out my house!"

"I ain't got to live with your miserable ass. All you got to do is tell me when to bounce and I'm out!"

"Ungrateful ass! I swear I'm tired!" She turned to the cop. "I'm really trying—"

"Don't be discussing our business with this cat. And what I tell you about yelling at me like that! And get this stupid camera out of my face."

"You need to calm down, son," Detective Asante said.

"Get out my face."

"Jabril—" Jaise said, embarrassed.

"Shut up and go see if I can get bail or something. Just get me out of here."

"I will not stand here and have you talk to your mother like that," the detective said.

"Yo, uncuff me and lose yourself!"

"Jabril—" Jaise gasped.

"Whup . . . his . . . ass," a man who was being fingerprinted shouted. "Cut them cameras off and fuck him up. That's why I'm in here, for fucking my son up!"

Jaise turned to Detective Asante. "He didn't mean what he said. Listen, we've just been going through a hard time right now. His dad and I are divorced. He doesn't come around too much anymore. It's just me and—"

"You don't have to explain anything to him," Jabril snapped.

"Shut your mouth," Jaise said sternly.

"You need to shut your mouth!"

"Yo dig," Officer Asante spat at Jabril, with enough bass in his voice to beat a drum, "let me kick it to you in a language you understand. If you say one more ill-ass thing to your mother, I'ma lock yo' drunk azz up. Now I hate to see your mother's pretty face in distress, but you being real foul right now, so calm yo' li'l ass down. 'Cause true story, you ain't that bad, thugged out, and on the real you can't bring it to nobody, so you and all that punk-ass mouth you have can fall back, fa real. Now, if you got other thoughts and you think you that tough then buck." He paused. "I didn't think so, trust me, the streets ain't for you, 'cause you gettin' caught too soon. Now, you are a man and a man's job starts with loving and respecting his women, and if you can't even respect your mother, then you gon' have some problems. Now be clear, if I see your face on my streets again I'ma make sure you don't see the sunrise for a long time. Now apologize to your mother, right now."

"Acting like a damn niggah in the street," Jaise said, pissed.

"And you"—Detective Asante turned to Jaise and twisted his lips—"what is it with you calling him a niggah every five seconds? You raising a niggah or a man? 'Cause if you raising a man, then you better straighten this shit out. I get tired of seeing these young boys float in and out of here and nobody gives them anything to stand up to. Let him know you have expectations, and this isn't what you had in mind. You want him in jail or on a job? Because at the end of the day you're his mother, so it's your call. So my suggestion to you is to see what your son is really saying to you underneath all this nonsense and deal with it."

Jaise looked at Detective Asante in shock, and instead of responding Jabril sucked his teeth.

"You testin' me, bruh?" The detective looked at Jabril as if he could see through him.

"Nah," Jabril quickly spat out.

"I didn't think so. Now, didn't I tell you to apologize?"

"Sorry," Jabril mumbled.

"I can't hear you," Detective Asante said.

"I said sorry."

"Sorry who?"

"Ma."

"For what? And say it like you mean it."

"For being disrespectful."

"Now bounce." He uncuffed him.

Jaise didn't know whether to say thank you or to cuss the detective out for speaking to her and her son like that. After deciding that Jabril deserved the treatment he received, and maybe she did too, she signed the papers releasing him into her custody and they headed home.

Jabril was quiet the entire ride home. A zillion things raced through Jaise's mind. She knew she couldn't lose her son to the streets; the only problem was she didn't know how he'd gotten there. The last she remembered he was riding in her car in a booster seat with his feet barely touching the floor, and now suddenly and without warning he was sixteen, towering over her, with the body of a man.

"Jabril," Jaise said as they pulled into a parking space, "I can't condone your drinking alcohol."

Jabril looked at his mother, sucked his teeth, slammed the door behind him, and headed into the house.

"Do you wanna smack him again or something?" Bridget

asked, startling Jaise, who had forgotten that Bridget and the camera crew were there. "Let us know," Bridget carried on, "so Carl here can run in the house first and get a close-up."

Jaise started to read Bridget, but she quickly changed her mind and decided the drama wasn't worth it. Instead she opened her front door and slammed it, leaving Bridget and the camera crew outside.

Chaunci

Chaunci sat in the center of her king-size bed, her back resting against the seven-foot-long black leather headboard, with her six-thousand-thread-count sheets caressing the back of her thighs. The evening lights of the New York City skyline bathed her sage bedroom walls as she did her all to focus on the sketched designs for her wedding gown.

Yet no matter how hard she tried to focus or reason with herself that brokering a marriage based on financial security made more sense than marrying for love, she couldn't nix the loneliness that slowly crept into her chest and hung out there. She hated wondering what it would be like to love again, because it forced her to ponder a series of what-ifs, and she despised that, because in all of her thirty years what-if had turned out to be one great big hopeless motherfucker.

This was why she had accepted the marriage proposal of her silent business partner and lover, Edmon. She knew he loved her, but she also knew that her not being in love with him placed her in the position of control. She wasn't interested in their situation being upgraded to romance. She wanted to be a power couple, sharing the perks of money, influence, respect, and good sex.

Love was always easier for Chaunci when she could pretend it didn't exist, or better yet when she could act as if she didn't need it, didn't want it, and wasn't lying in her bed at night aching for it. She could do without the risk of bruised emotions and hurt feelings. Everything in her life was about business. Marriage, sex, work, play—even the reality show she considered to be a season-long infomercial for her magazine.

"Okay, Mommy, Anty Dextra said it's time for your party!" Chaunci's six-year-old daughter, Kobi, pushed Chaunci's bedroom door open, relaying the message from her au pair. Kobi hung on to the doorknob and swung into the room.

"What are you doing? And what are you wearing?" Chaunci looked at Kobi, who, decked out in a Cinderella gown with a towel wrapped around her neck, was spinning in a circle.

"This my freakum dress."

"Excuse you?" Chaunci snapped.

Kobi slapped her hand over her mouth. "I mean this is my ball gown." She curtsied. "Anty Dextra and I just had a tea party. Would you like a cup of tea, ma'dum?" she said in a playful British accent while picking up her mini porcelain teacup.

"No."

"Why?" Kobi placed the cup to her lips and pretended to sip. "You're going to be late to Ms. Evan's party?"

Chaunci rolled her eyes to the ceiling. She couldn't stand Evan, and the thought that she would have to pretend to like her for the rest of the night was unbearable. As far as Chaunci was concerned, Evan was the mistress of bitches, and the only reason Evan probably wanted Chaunci at the party was so that *Nubian Diva* would cover the event. Chaunci's magazine was one of the hottest on the stands. It was the only African American magazine that ranked at the top with *Vogue* and *Glamour,* so anybody who was anybody would of course invite her to their party, especially if they wanted it to be the event of the year.

She looked at the clock and realized she had only an hour to prepare for the evening. "No," she said, her spirits dragging, "I won't be late for the party."

"So what are you going to do at the party?" Kobi climbed into the middle of her mother's bed as Chaunci sorted through her closet.

"I'm not sure. What do you think I should do?"

Kobi pretended to sip again. "I think you should get us a new French-say."

"A what?"

"Mommy, the man you're marrying. French-say."

"It's 'fiancé.' "

"I thought his name was Edmon." Kobi looked confused. "But anyway, I heard Anty Dextra say on the phone that she doesn't think Edmon is right for you. I have to agree with her. We need another one."

Chaunci spun on her heels. "Who said that?"

"Anty Dextra said it. And she said that you needed a real man-ringo to handle you."

"Oh, wait a minute, I know she wasn't talking like that in front of you?!" Chaunci snapped. "Dextra"—she opened her bedroom door—"please come."

"Mommy," Kobi whispered, in excitement, "you're going to get me in trouble. Anty Dextra told me to leave the room when grown folks were talking, but I liked what she was saying, so I stood by the door and listened. Don't give my secret away, Mommy." She folded her hands. "Please."

"You are a little too grown," Chaunci said, pushing the door closed, as she reluctantly decided to keep her daughter's secret. "And whatever 'new' *French-say* I need or don't need is a little out of your six-year-old league."

"Huh?" Kobi said, confused. "What does that mean, Mommy? To mind my business?"

"Forget it, Kobi. Just let me get dressed."

"I wanna see what you're going to wear," Kobi insisted, pretending to sip her drink again.

While Kobi sat in the center of Chaunci's bed, Chaunci pulled on a supertight navy blue velvet corset, which made her D-cup breasts look like an overflowing river of flesh. Her curvaceous hips were complemented by a Dolce and Gabbana eighteenth-century-inspired formal navy chiffon skirt, which draped to the floor and covered her pencil-heel Manolos.

"Mommy."

"Yes," Chaunci said as she snapped on her sapphire bangle.

"How come everybody in my class knows their daddy but me?"

"I'm your mommy and your daddy."

"I told them that and they laughed at me. I had to tell Asia that I would kick her butt if she laughed one more time. And Mommy, I hate to break it to you, but you have to be a man in order to be a daddy. So do you think my daddy, the man-daddy, doesn't like me?"

Chaunci had always sworn that she would be the type of mother who was open and honest with her child. She promised that she would never speak an ill word about Kobi's father, but the older Kobi got the harder it was not to say that her father was an asshole. That when Chaunci had told him she was pregnant he had lost his mind and tossed three hundred dollars in the air for an abortion, not caring that Chaunci's pregnancy was too far along for that.

Chaunci looked at Kobi and thought about ignoring the question altogether, but seeing the intensity with which Kobi watched her she said, "Your daddy is a great man, he loves you, and we'll talk about him later."

"Well, Mommy, when is later? Because every time I ask, you always say 'later,' and later never comes. I keep waiting and waiting, looking at the clock, and later is taking its own sweet time."

"You're too grown," Chaunci admonished Kobi.

"Why does everyone keep saying that? Can I sleep in your room?"

"Only for tonight. Now go put on your pajamas."

"I want to sleep in this."

"Okay, well, I have to go. And you know the rules, no candy and nothing to drink."

"We have to pray, Mommy," Kobi said as Chaunci headed toward the door. Kobi kneeled on the floor. "Mommy, come on."

Chaunci knew she couldn't refuse, especially since this was their nightly ritual, but she hoped like hell she wouldn't pop the hooks and eyes on her corset. She started to tell Kobi that in the interest of her girdle, she needed to pray standing up, but since Kobi didn't know what a girdle was, Chaunci grinned and bore it, while slyly practicing breathing techniques. She kneeled. "Okay Kobi, it's your turn to lead the prayer."

"Mommy," Kobi whispered, "I always forget if I'm supposed to begin by saying Amen."

"No," Chaunci whispered back, "you save that for the end. Start with 'Now I lay me down to sleep.' "

"Okay." She began to pray, "Now I lay me down to sleep— Wait, I forgot to say, 'Hi, God, how are you? I hope you're fine, and I hope You and Jesus had a good day, too—' "

"Kobi, God always has a good day."

"But we don't know that, Mommy, and you said it's rude not to ask people how their day was . . . Oh, and Anty Dextra said it's rude to interrupt people when they prayin', too."

"Just pray." Chaunci laughed.

"Okay. Now I lay me down to sleep. I pray the Lord my soul to keep. If I should die—Wait, I don't like that part. I'ma skip it. Dear God, bless my grandma, my pop-pop, Anty Dextra . . . God, can you ask my mommy to get me a dog? Oh, and God bless my mommy so that we can get a new husband. No one likes Edmon—"

"Kobi!"

"Sorry."

"Now finish praying."

"You think God is asleep, Mommy?"

"No, Kobi."

"He doesn't have a bedtime?"

"Finish praying, Kobi."

"I'm done. Bye, God. Amen."

They rose from the floor and Kobi hopped into bed. "Good-night," Chaunci said. "Good-night and Mommy loves you."

"I love you too, and you look real fly."

"Don't I always?" Chaunci started to pose.

"Work it, Mommy!" Kobi screamed as Chaunci closed the door behind her and stepped into the living room, where Dextra was.

"Anty Dextra," Chaunci snapped, walking into the living room, where her au pair was directing the contestant on *Wheel of Fortune* to buy a vowel.

"Yes, chile," Dextra said in her thick Trinidadian accent, never once taking her eyes from the TV. "Aiye-yi-yi, but what de hell is dis? Just buy an *A*!" She looked up at Chaunci. "You look beautiful."

Chaunci sucked in a breath and a smile ran across her lips. "Good-night, Anty."

Dextra smiled. "Good-night." She looked back at the TV, and as Chaunci closed the door she heard Dextra solving the puzzle.

The Club

The glow of the full moon complemented the flashing lights of the paparazzi as the A-list guests—athletes, music moguls, Hollywood stars, and politicians among them—arrived at Evan and Kendu's sprawling Sag Harbor estate, all the while rocking their vintage masquerade finest.

Nothing said new money like shallow excessiveness. Diamonds, furs, Bentleys, stretch Hummers, Rolls-Royces, Excaliburs, and horse-drawn carriages created a foreground of bling against the waving ocean. This was just one of the many fundraiser play dates for the rich, many of whom had their own charitable foundations.

The live jazz band's rendition of Nina Simone's "I Put a Spell on You" drifted into the master suite, where the hosting couple dressed silently. Evan could tell by the look on Kendu's face that being here with her was difficult for him. She felt as if she desperately had to find a way to regain control over the relationship, to make him love her more than she loved him.

"Kendu?"

"Evan," he sighed wearily.

She swallowed. "I just want you to know—that—Aiyanna may need a spinal tap."

"What?" Kendu said, caught off guard. "Why?"

"So the doctors can find out what's wrong and begin treating her."

"But she had a spinal tap last year, and I've never seen her cry like that. I don't want her in that kind of pain again." He turned around and faced her.

This was the first time in a long while that he had looked at her with sympathy in his eyes. That bit of attention meant the world to her. "So what do you want? Her to die?" Evan asked.

"Are you for real asking me something like that?"

"I'm sorry," Evan quickly relented. "I'm stressed out and it's just so difficult." She shook her head. "All I want is for my daughter to be a normal eight-year-old." Tears filled her eyes.

Kendu swallowed. He knew Evan loved Aiyanna, and her illness had taken a toll on both of them. "Listen"—he grabbed Evan's hands and placed them between his—"this will work out. We have the best doctors, the best hospital. You said this new specialist she's seeing is much more knowledgeable than the others."

Evan wasn't sure but she thought she could hear the love he once had for her starting to reemerge. She knew if he was gently holding her hand that some of his coldness had to thaw. He loved her, and the softness of his touch said so.

Besides, he was way too beautiful for her to let him get away. His skin was the color of midnight. Smooth, radiant, and beautifully black. He wore a well-groomed goatee with premature sprinkles of gray, and his regal nose complemented his full African lips and charming chestnut eyes. Evan found herself craving his touch. "You're right." Evan tried to calm the tremble in her voice. "And I'm going to try and enjoy this night." She placed her arms around his waist.

"There you go." Kendra stroked Evan's cheek.

She smiled and straightened his tie. "And hopefully we will

raise a lot of money so that other families who are not as fortunate as we are can get the help they need for their sick children."

"Exactly." He wiped the tears from her eyes. "Besides, you look too beautiful to be crying." He kissed her on the forehead.

Evan closed her eyes. She'd found that feeling of heaven again. "You think so?" She stepped back to allow him to soak in the vision of her in an emerald green off-the-shoulder Vera Wang ball gown trimmed in Australian crystals.

"I know so." He brushed her cheek.

Evan wiped the remaining tears from her eyes. "Kendu, I know what happened between us the other day was crazy, and I just want you to know that we can work this out—"

"Work what out?" He took a step back.

"Us. Our marriage. I know that you love me."

"Evan—"

"No, Kendu, you don't have to explain." She could tell by the change in his tone that he was working on bursting her bubble. She thought for sure cutting him off mid-sentence would curb his rejection. At least for this moment.

"Listen to me, you know I will always love you," he said, then paused. "But I need you to know that I haven't changed my mind about no longer wanting to be with you."

"But you were just—"

"Evan, even if I laugh with you, smile with you, speak nicely to you, unless I *specifically* tell you that I want you, then I have not changed my mind."

"Kendu—" She could swear he heard her heart crack.

"Listen to me: I do love you, Evan," he said with confidence. "But I love you because of our child, because we have beautiful memories, but that's it."

"No." She shook her head while batting her extended eyelashes. "That's not true. You love me because we have a tomorrow. We have years left. Eternity."

"Our divorce will beat us to eternity."

Evan shook her head feverishly. "Why are you saying this? You always claim you're not good at expressing yourself, but you have certainly found a way to say all of this to me."

"You don't give me a choice."

"How fuckin' dare you, Kendu!" Evan pushed him.

Kendu took a step back. "I can't do this."

"Kendu, wait."

"No." He walked out of the bedroom and slammed the door behind him.

Evan stood, looking around the room, her eyes wandering from the balcony to the brushed nickel knob on the bedroom door. She could feel a manic episode coming on, and she knew she would never be able to function tonight without shots of vodka and a Vicodin. She opened her clutch and popped a pill in her mouth. She walked over to the small bar in their bedroom and poured a shot glass of Patrón to ease it down.

"Why are you drinking that?" Milan asked Yusef as they arrived at the estate.

"Because I'm grown," he snapped. The brown bag he held in his hand crumpled as he took the forty-ounce of Ole English to the head. He wiped the sides of his mouth with the tips of his fingers and said, "Why, you want some?"

"No," she said, tight-lipped.

He shoved the bottle to her lips. "Drink it."

"I don't want it." She slapped his hand.

"Yes, you do." He pressed the rim of the bottle so hard against her lips that she was forced to open her mouth.

As Milan shook her head, the liquor splashed against her mouth and dripped down her cleavage. "Didn't I say no?!" She slapped the bottle from his hand, spilling the drink on the floor.

"Shit!" he screamed, rearing his hand back.

"Please do it and we'll box up in this motherfucker tonight."

Before she could continue the driver opened the door and she stepped out, leaving a pissed-off Yusef behind in the car.

As soon as Milan stepped out of their onyx Phantom, which no one knew was rented but them, cameras flashed and photographers were everywhere. Instantly her counterfeit reality took over and she worked it to perfection.

Milan went from pose to pose as her hair flowed like a calm ebony river midway down her back, while her smooth Dominican brown skin glistened like shimmering lotion.

The Michael Knight royal blue gown she wore snaked like the number eight across her tight midsection, giving sneak peeks of her full and firm breasts, and the skirt rested perfectly on her hips.

Yusef walked up behind her, placed his arm around her waist, and posed for pictures. "You gon' fuck around and get your ass kicked," he whispered against her hair.

Milan hated how quickly she was failing at being the reality star she'd envisioned for herself. "You really don't care about the cameras, do you?" she asked Yusef, tight-lipped.

"Of course I care. Isn't this a reality show?"

"You know it is."

"Well, welcome to your reality," he said as they posed for another picture.

Jaise sat in the back of her silver Rolls as the driver cruised up the highway. She pressed her cell phone to her MAC-covered lips, wondering what exactly she should say to Lawrence about Jabril. She hated calling him for anything, unless it was about her alimony check or child support, because she knew outside of that he didn't care.

"Hell with it." She dialed Lawrence's number.

After several rings a soft female voice answered, "Hello?"

Jaise sucked her teeth. She was instantly pissed as she realized the drama that was sure to arise with Lawrence's jealous and overbearing wife picking up his line. "Robyn?" Jaise snapped with a little more edge than she intended.

"Who is this?" Robyn's soft voice quickly dropped an octave and picked up a tinge of attitude.

"It's Jaise"—she sucked her teeth—"how are you?"

"Look, my husband is busy."

Jaise chuckled. "You never cease to amaze me."

"What do you want?"

"I need to speak to Lawrence—"

"If you think you're calling here to start your around-the-way drama, you're dead-ass wrong. And if you have a problem with me telling your son that he is not to call our house after nine at night because the baby is sleeping, then tough. Like I explained to him, his little 'I've been to jail' story didn't impress me, especially since we don't deal with hoodlums. So I don't need you calling here to defend your son and argue with my husband about a sixteen-year-old gangster."

Jaise was in shock. Jabril never told her he had called his father. Now she knew what his most recent attitude must've been about. "What you tell my baby, bitch?!"

"How intelligent of you. I see why your son's a thug."

Jaise tapped the driver on the shoulder. "Cancel Sag Harbor and drive me over to Montclair, New Jersey. I got a bitch I need to drag."

"In case you missed the memo, I'm not scared of you, so you can approach me if you want to and see what happens. Oh, and I'm not going to be too many more bitches. Now, what do you want? My baby is crying."

"Are you crazy? Really? Are you? Have you lost your fuckin' mind? Fuck you and that goddamn baby. All I know is that Lawrence has a son with me, and I need to speak to him about him. Now, my suggestion to you is to put him on the phone, because if you don't, wherever you are and whenever I see you, I'ma kick yo' motherfuckin' ass!"

"Who the hell are you talkin' to?" Lawrence shouted into the phone, while Robyn screamed and cried in the background, "I'm tired of her. How could she say that about our son? I really don't believe this!"

"Oh, now you're on the phone, asshole?! Tell your wife to meet me someplace and see if I don't backhand the shit outta her!"

"You better cool your heels, Jaise, because I'm not going to have you calling here and speaking to my wife and talking about my family like this."

"You must be punch-drunk. You think I give a damn about trashy? I'm tired of going through this every time I call you. You need to have her understand that I don't want you, Lawrence. I'm glad you're off kicking her ass and not mine. Oh, and tell that ho if she calls my son a gangster again, I'ma burn a bullet in her ass and let her see who the real gangster is, trick."

"I'm hanging up. We don't have to take this."

"We?" she said in amazement. "Are you still shaving your balls, 'cause I swear you need some hair on them. Jabril is your son! Or did you forget you had more than one!"

"What about Jabril?"

"He's been getting into trouble lately, hanging out with the wrong crowd. And the other day he was arrested."

"Yeah, Robyn mentioned something like that to me."

"And you didn't think to call me?" Jaise said, confused. "We may be divorced, but we are still parents."

"Well, had you stayed and worked on our marriage and understood me, we wouldn't be going through this."

"This isn't about us. This is about saving our son!"

"All I can say is send him to live with me and I'll straighten him out."

"What?!" Jaise shouted. "You don't even call him. I have to call you and remind you when it's your fuckin' weekend, which over the last six months you have yet to keep. Let him live with you?" she said in exhausted disbelief. "You didn't even think enough of him to check your wife. Here she is calling my son a hoodlum, and I should send him to simply live with you, like he's a pest I need out my house? What the fuck is really good with you, Lawrence?"

"Is that how you speak to me now, like a homeboy? Is that show you're on called 'Ghetto Superstars'?"

"Fuck you."

"You lost that privilege."

"Look, what are we going to do about our son?"

"I already gave you my answer."

"You're his father, I'm his mother, and he's going to do what he needs to do. And you and I are going to raise him."

"I'm done raising him. He thinks he's as grown as I am."

"He's sixteen."

"Tell him that. And you know that all of this is upsetting my wife. So how about this: If you won't send him to live with me, then don't call me anymore. You get more alimony and child support in a month than most people make in a year, and if that's not enough to solve the problems and keep his ass off the street, then oh well, not my issue. The bank is doing my part. Now you need to do yours."

"I don't believe you."

"Believe it. Now I have to go. My wife has cooked dinner, something your gold-diggin' ass never did. I'm still paying the bill for the goddamn chef you hired." And he clicked off the line.

Jaise sat there staring off into space. Although she and Lawrence hadn't gotten along and he hadn't always done his part, never in a million years had she expected him to act like this when it came to their son. She swallowed the painful lump in her throat and did her all to smile as the driver opened the door and the paparazzi rushed to the car and began flashing their cameras in her face.

After stopping for a moment to speak with her magazine's photographers and giving them directives on what exactly she needed them to capture, Chaunci posed for a few pictures on the red car-pet and then headed toward the double doors of the mansion. She promised herself that she wasn't going to let anything piss her off. She'd already been featured in the entertainment section of the *Daily News,* with them calling her the one-minute diva. One minute she was a diva like no other and the next minute she was threatening to whup somebody's ass.

Chaunci grasped the sides of her skirt and lifted so that she wouldn't trip over the hem, while her fitted corset felt as if it were choking her waistline.

As she smiled once again for the cameras and paparazzi, she realized that the man walking in front of her was Idris. She'd just learned yesterday that he had been traded to the New York Knicks as their starting point guard. Her stomach flipped. She hadn't seen Idris since her senior year of college, and though she always knew that one day she'd run into him, she had prayed it wouldn't be anytime soon.

Chaunci tossed her shoulders back and acted as if she hadn't noticed him. But, once the French horns sounded and the hostess announced her name, she saw Idris watching her intensely. She quickly turned the other way and headed toward Milan, whom she'd just spotted.

"Chaunci?" Idris walked up behind her and she turned around. Immediately she felt a heated rush. Idris was six four and towered at least six sexy inches above her. He was the rich color of toasted almond or sunbaked brown. He reminded most people of Tyson Beckford, with the slanted eyes and charismatic smile.

He looked down at her and his chocolate eyes told her that she'd been missed over the years.

"Yes, I'm Chaunci," she said.

"I know who you are," he said. It was clear that he was search-ing her eyes to see if she had any inkling of who he was.

Chaunci averted her eyes from his. Even when they had been

lovers in college she had hated looking into his face because she was rendered powerless around him.

"It's Idris." He pointed to himself.

"I know who you are."

"Well, since you know who I am"—he looked her over—"can I get a hug?" he asked and pulled her to him before she could refuse. As Chaunci pressed up against his chest she could tell by the way he squeezed her and began to rock with her that she felt good in his arms.

"Wow, you're still beautiful." He stood back and looked at her. "Damn," he said more to himself than to her. "You really are breathtaking."

"Are you done?" She pointed across the room. "Because this conversation you're trying to have with me, I'm over it and I need to leave."

He looked at her strangely. "That's the nicest greeting you could think of after seven years?"

Chaunci paused and blinked. It was official this motherfucker was still bold and crazy, but she had something for his ass. She popped her clutch purse open. "My apologies, perhaps I should've greeted you with this." She slapped three hundred-dollar bills in his hand. "Now bug the fuck off." She turned to walk away, but before she could go too far, Idris grabbed her arm and turned her back to him.

"Wait a minute, wait," he said.

"I'm supposed to wait for you again?"

Instead of letting her go, Idris pulled Chaunci to a secluded corner of the room. "What exactly are you saying by giving me this money?" He paused. "Did you have that baby? You took my money and still did what you wanted to do?"

Every tear that Chaunci thought she'd cried out years ago filled her eyes, but she'd be damned before she let him see her cry. "Listen," she said, doing her best to sound beyond confident, "before I take my fist and fuck yo' big ass up, I'ma walk away from you."

He blocked her path. "Chaunci, I don't believe this."

"Well, believe this. Fuck you." She turned to walk away again and he immediately turned her back around.

"Look, I'm sorry. I messed up, I know," he said, "and the truth is I always wondered over the years." He stopped and shook his head as if he'd just been hit with a ton of bricks. "Listen, I need you to understand that I was a kid then."

"And I need you to understand colic, motherfucker. And fevers, and teething, and crawling, and potty training, and school, and parent-teacher conferences and shit." She poked him in his chest. "And I need you to understand how I stayed up at night and took care of our daughter while she was sick. Me, not you. And now that she's old enough to realize she has a daddy, she spends her days dreaming about your ass, thinking you are Mr. Fuckin' Mighty Man, while I'm stuck trying to explain where the hell you've been all these years."

"I didn't know."

"You didn't want to know."

"Chaunci, be fair here. I really need you to understand—"

"Okay, and I really need you to understand this: Get the fuck out of my face." She grabbed a drink from the butler's tray and walked over to where Milan, Jaise, and a few others were sipping champagne and enjoying the jazz band.

"Hey, girl. We need to talk," Chaunci said, kissing Milan on both cheeks. She nodded her head at Jaise and waved.

"Hi," Jaise said dryly as she eyed the room. "I'll be back."

Chaunci rolled her eyes as Jaise walked away. She looked at Milan. "Give me a moment, I need another drink."

As the songstress sang Phyllis Hyman's "Meet Me on the Moon," Milan sipped her white wine and drifted into a daydream.

"If I asked you to go with me to the moon, would you?" a voice whispered, interrupting her deep thoughts. "Or am I too late?"

Milan held her breath for a moment. She knew it was Kendu. Slowly she turned around and he was standing there. He was exquisitely beautiful, and her only regret was that he was somebody else's husband and not hers. She did her best to smile, after all, technically he wasn't the only one who was married. "I try not to think about those things," she responded. She smiled as she noticed Jaise and Chaunci had returned and were both looking at her strangely.

After a few minutes Jaise walked over and stood between them. "Kendu, where is your wife?"

"Jaise," Evan said as she walked over, "I'm here. You're looking for me?"

"Yes, actually, I was." She turned to Kendu and Milan. "Excuse me for breaking up the session. You can continue whispering to one another."

"Whispering?" Evan said, caught off guard. "Whispering about what?" She turned to Kendu.

Both Kendu and Milan were silent. "I'm listening," Evan continued.

Kendu ignored her and left her standing there as he headed toward the bar.

Evan tried to play off her embarrassment and chuckled. She looked at Milan and said, "Answer my question."

"What are you talking about?"

Evan pointed. "Let me explain something to you." She shoved her finger into Milan's face. "Kendu is my man, my child's father, and you need to stay in your miserable fuckin' lane. I've had enough of you hanging around. So what you better do—"

"Is get the fuck out my face!" Milan swatted Evan's hand from her face.

"Ladies," Jaise said, smiling at the cameras, "this is not the time nor the place. Let's have some class."

"You know what," Milan spat at Jaise, "I'm a little sick of your troublemaking ass. You started the shit and now all of a sudden it's 'Ladies, ladies.' Fuck you. Now, how's that for class?"

"Oh wow, that's an interesting twist," Chaunci said, laughing. "Milan," she now said seriously, "leave this crazy-ass chick alone. Trust me, in my two-thousand-dollar shoes I'm not dressed to throw."

"I got this," Milan assured her.

"You have what, Milan?" Evan rolled her eyes. "I'm so sick of you and this chick"—she pointed to Chaunci—"and your ghetto-ness."

Chaunci looked at Evan's glassy eyes. "You better get your high ass out my face."

"You don't need to be concerned about us being ghetto," Milan spat. "You need to worry about how much of this ghetto-ness your husband likes." Milan turned her back on Evan and spoke over her shoulder, "Pardon my back." She started to walk away.

Evan walked swiftly around and in front of her. "What exactly did you say, bitch?"

"Wait a minute." Chaunci stamped her feet. "Wait a damn minute. Did she, no, no, she didn't. Milan, let's just walk around this chick, because obviously she has lost her damn mind."

"Would you be quiet?" Jaise gave Chaunci the eye. "We need to calm down."

"Shut the fuck up and mind your business." Chaunci shot a quick and fake smile at a passing photographer and posed. After the photographer took the picture and walked away Chaunci turned back to Jaise. "You're the one who threw the rock and now you wanna act like, oh, let's just calm down?"

Evan pointed in Milan's face. "You could never be me."

"Exactly," Milan said, "because then I'd be on the outside look-ing in."

"I want you to leave!" Evan pointed toward the door.

"Kendu invited me. Tell him to tell me to leave."

"What the hell is going on over here?" Kendu stormed over, looking at Evan as if she'd lost her mind.

"Don't be looking at me like that. You better get ahold of this bitch."

"Don't call her a bitch."

"What would you like for me to call her? Tell her to get out," Evan said to Kendu while pointing her finger back in Milan's face.

"Or what?" Milan butted in. "What you gon' do? 'Cause you are talking entirely too much shit."

"I'm glad somebody agrees. I thought it was just me," Chaunci said snidely.

"Please," Jaise said, tight-lipped, "a crowd is starting to gather."

"You wanna fulfill your fantasy and try to beat my ass, is that it, Evan? If not"—Milan slapped Evan's hand out of her face—"then get your fuckin' finger outta my face."

"I know she didn't just slap my hand," Evan said as if she were asking the crowd encircling them a question.

"Evan, just let it go," Kendu insisted.

"Oh, you takin' up for her now?"

"Calm down," he said, "you're embarrassing yourself."

"Embarrassing myself!" Evan was floored, and as if she were under remote control she turned around, grabbed a drink from the passing butler's tray, and tossed every ounce of champagne into Milan's face.

The entire party seemed to screech to a halt. Milan blinked, and Yusef standing nearby could be heard to say, "What the—" Milan wiped her eyes and stood silently for a moment. Her mind rewound what had just occurred, and as fast as the drink had been tossed in her face she reared her hand back and slapped Evan so hard that Evan staggered back a few inches.

"Hurry, Carl!" Bridget yelled. "Get a close-up!"

Evan stumbled. After she regained her balance she took a swing at Milan but Kendu blocked it. "Stop it," he said as security rushed in and Evan started screaming, "Out! I want them out!"

One officer grabbed Milan and the other grabbed Chaunci. "Oh hell no!" Chaunci yelled. "You better get the hell offa me. If I'da beaten the bitch she'd still be on the ground."

"Hold it." Kendu looked at security. "This is my home. I have this under control."

"You're taking up for her again?!" Evan screamed while holding her face.

"Just calm down, Evan," Jaise said, grabbing her hand. "Let's just try and work this out. This is really causing a scene."

"At this point, I don't give a damn."

"Evan, believe me," Jaise said, eyeing the onlookers, "this looks good for no one's image. Please, let's just talk about this. Remember that when fights break out donations fly right out the door."

"Fuck all that!" Chaunci said, pissed. "And I want my goddamn check back too. I ain't donatin' shit!"

Yusef walked over and shook his head at Milan. "I can't take you nowhere," he said.

"Let's just go!" Chaunci snapped. "I've been thrown out of better places by worse people. I don't have to take this shit."

Milan rolled her eyes in disgust as she turned to Kendu. "I hope that baby she had is worth it!" And she stormed out with Chaunci in tow.

Once they were outside, Carl asked the ladies to tell the camera their feelings. "I can't believe this shit!" Chaunci spat at Carl. "She got me fucked up! That's how I'm feeling right now."

"Evan is just a phony asshole," Milan added.

"You should've whupped that bitch's ass," Chaunci said. "Like she owed you a man! Trick-ass video ho."

Jaise and Bridget walked swiftly over to Chaunci and Milan. "Ladies, can we talk about this?" Jaise said. "We need to straighten this out."

Chaunci looked her over. "This is what you do: Since you started the shit and now you're so interested in peace, tell the valet to get me my ma'fuckin' car. I'm ready to roll." She quickly turned to the right and then the left. "Valet"—she snapped her fingers—"I need my car please."

"Ladies, this can be worked out. Let's just calm down," Jaise insisted.

"Looka here," Chaunci said, "I don't know what you think this is or what you're really looking for, but this is as real as it gets. I'm pissed, and since you really don't know me, my suggestion to you is to get on."

"Chaunci, Milan," Kendu called as he walked outside with half of the party and every TV camera in the place following him. "Chill, time out, wait. Hold it."

"Chaunci," Idris said, walking over and grabbing her hand, "let me speak to you for a minute."

"Look," Chaunci said, snatching her hand back, "if you ain't the fuckin' valet don't say shit to me. Please. We're gone. Out of this mother . . . fuck . . . ker!" She wiggled her head and neck like a bobble head doll.

Yusef stormed over. "What in the motherfuck is you doin', Milan?!"

"You better get the hell out my face!" she warned him.

"All that free liquor in there and you got to show yo' ass? Da Truef can't get his drink on for an hour at least?"

"Milan, Chaunci," Kendu said, "Yusef, listen, please let me hollah atchu for a second."

"Are you crazy?" Milan snapped. "Really, have you lost it? You see how crazy that heifer is and you out here in my face? Do you want me to have to kill her ass? I swear I'm tired of being your best friend. Fuck it. I'm done. She can have you."

"You don't mean that."

"Don't tell me what I mean."

Kendu ignored Milan and turned to Yusef. "Look, man, I really didn't mean for this to happen."

"I understand, but you know women." Yusef attempted to sound sober. "So I tell you what"—he patted Kendu on the back—"if it makes you feel better I'll take that Crown Royal and Johnnie Walker Red to go."

"I can't stand your drunk ass," Milan snapped.

"Where the hell is the valet?" Chaunci stamped.

"Wait a minute." Idris attempted once again to calm Chaunci.

"If I recall correctly you're good at leaving," Chaunci said as her car pulled up. "So stay the hell outta my way!" She hopped into her car, and Milan and Yusef raced down the highway behind her.

"Spot-the-hell-on!" Bridget growled in glee. "I think I'm gonna piss in my pants. Nielsen ratings through the roof!"

The Club

Orange and white Japanese paper lanterns swung in the late-morning Manhattan breeze as the soft chiming sounds of Asian music filled the restaurant's rooftop terrace.

Although the producer preferred out-of-control shopping, cat fights, and high drama, there needed to be at least one episode where the women appeared to be working toward peace, even if afterward the claws came out.

Jaise and Chaunci were sitting in their seats with their legs crossed, watching the clocks, and waiting for their costars to show up. They'd grown tired of smiling at the cameras, making trivial conversation about the weather and politics. And instead of continuing with the bullshit, they each preferred to leave before one of them forgot that this was being taped for TV and a can of whup ass was suddenly opened.

After another half an hour went by, Jaise sighed. "I may as well take my sushi with me."

Chaunci snapped her fingers at the waitress and pointed to Jaise. "Can she get an empty bento box to go?"

Jaise laughed. "You are such a bitch."

"Can you, ah, add a 'Miss' onto that title of bitch please? It's a bit more elegant."

"I guess if it doesn't involve high drama, somebody else's man, or some new-money ghetto-ness you don't have anything to talk about."

Chaunci twisted her neck. "I am not the one."

"What did you just say?"

"I said," Chaunci said, twisting her neck again, "I am not the one, so you better check yourself before you wreck yourself."

"Was all of that necessary?"

"Are you serious? You came at me crazy and because I'm giving it back to you crazy there's a problem?"

"Look, I was just trying to make small talk with you, but that apparently is over your head."

"There you go again. What is your problem?"

"I don't have one."

"Oh, you have one," Chaunci insisted, "and if you keep talking slick I'ma make sure you recognize it."

Jaise arched her eyebrows and tapped the balls of her feet on the floor. She ran her hands over the gray leggings she wore, placed one hand into her hair and stared at Chaunci, who sat across from her in a pair of skinny-leg jeans, a tangerine Versace turtleneck, and gleaming black diamond earrings. "You know," Jaise said, "I really don't have anything against you. Actually, I'm a big fan of your magazine."

"So . . . what? You want a free subscription? Write a letter to the hardships department. Other than that I can't help you."

"I'm trying to bring this to a truce, especially since it seems we'll be doing brunch alone. Besides, it's not you. It's Milan I don't trust."

"Please, and your girl Evan is what? Perfect?"

"Practically."

"Yeah right." Chaunci chuckled. "That's a man-down situation."

"You don't have a reason not to like Evan. Especially since your girl Milan is trying to steal her man."

"Well, if he's there for the taking"—Chaunci rolled her eyes—"then that's his dirty ass. He knows he's married, and if he's stepping out on his wife then Evan needs to deal with him, not Milan. 'Cause the next time she tries to start a fight I'ma ghetto slide her ass."

"Wow," Jaise said as she started dipping her sushi in wasabi and soy sauce, "aren't you a fuckin' lady."

"Girl, look, I try to be fake and phony to keep up with you all," she said, picking up her spider roll with her chopsticks, "but it's tiring me out."

"Excuse you, I am who I am."

"And who is that?"

"A very classy," Jaise said, enunciating every syllable while putting special emphasis on her diction, "well-mannered, and understanding woman."

"Beyatch puleeze," Chaunci said, "you probably cuss more than I do."

Jaise laughed. "Well, what is it about Evan that you don't like?"

"What is it about Milan you don't like?"

"You never answer a question with a question unless you're talking to a man . . . But umm, it's not that I don't like Milan, but I do think the whole Kendu thing is suspicious."

"They're friends."

"Men and women can't be friends. Didn't you just write an article on that? I believe you did and you ended it with, 'Watch your man.' "

"You read that?" Chaunci smiled. "Yeah, I said that, but still in certain cases men and women can be friends."

"Yeah, you're right, when one of them is gay."

"And if they're not?"

"Look, I feel like any chick hanging around my man is either fucking him, has fucked him, or is setting up the game so that some fuckin' can take place."

"That sounds like insecurity," Chaunci said. "Although I feel you on that. But Kendu and Milan have been friends since they were kids."

"They are not kids anymore. Now on to you. Why don't you like Evan?"

"Let me see how I can put this nicely. The trick is crazy."

"Isn't that subjective? I could say that about Milan."

"Milan's cool. You have to give her a chance. But Evan, that bitch . . . Humph, I'm sorry but . . . I just can't pretend because I don't ever see me liking her ass."

"But don't you agree that some things have to be overlooked or we have to let some things go? I mean, the inability to do that is part of the reason why we're sitting here alone."

Chaunci took a moment to think about what Jaise had said and responded, "Yeah, maybe."

"No, not maybe. It's the truth. And by the way, that slick comment you made earlier about me being fake, don't think I didn't catch it. So for your information, I'm not fake. I just choose to keep my ghetto slide on reserve."

Chaunci laughed. "Oh really?"

"Hell yeah," Jaise said, "that's exactly what I wanna do to my ex-husband's new wife, grab that bitch by the roots of her fuckin' hair and sling her ass."

Chaunci gave her a high five. "Ghetto slide her ass until she flies."

"You are crazy, girl. I think I might like you . . . even though you think I'm fake."

"Really, I don't think you're fake. I just think you try too hard. Relax and enjoy, honey."

"That's the problem . . . ," Jaise said as she sipped her drink and her attention drifted toward the hostess, who'd just said, "Right this way, Mr. Mosley."

"I don't believe this," Jaise said barely above a whisper.

"What?" Chaunci turned around.

"Turn back around," Jaise said in a hurry, "before he sees you."

"Who sees me? Who are you looking at?"

"Trenton, my fiancé." Even for Jaise the white lie about Trenton's title in her life was hard to swallow, but still . . . he was her man. And yeah, they'd had an argument the other night and he hadn't been to her house since then, but his leaving for a few days was nothing new. He would often become enraged and used it as an excuse to storm out. Nevertheless, usually after Jaise begged and pleaded and left him a thousand messages, he would give in, take her off punishment, they would have bangin' sex, and all would be well with the world.

Sitting at the table and thinking her life was falling apart, Jaise watched Trenton pull out some bitch's chair and wondered why he'd never done anything remotely close to that for her.

"That's your man?" Before Jaise could answer Chaunci continued on, "And he's with another chick? Oh hell nawl, you better take your ghetto slide off reserve and let's go unhinge this negro."

"I can't do that. Suppose it's business."

"What the hell is he, an escort?"

"No, he creates video games and he meets with people from all over the world."

"Well, we need to go find out what the matter is . . . and just in case"—Chaunci rummaged through her purse and pulled out a small pair of nunchucks, a can of Mace, and a box cutter—"choose one."

"Would you put that away? All that shit is illegal in this state. You gon' get our asses arrested!"

"So, and? If you let a motherfucker know you ain't scared to go to jail he'll stop fucking with you. Didn't you read that article?"

"No, I did not."

"Oh my Gawd, you are way too sadity. Is that your man or not?"

"Yes." Jaise was barely able to speak above the lump in her throat.

"Then we need to pounce on dis pussyclot. Now let's go." She got up out of her chair.

"No," Jaise said, pulling Chaunci back into her chair by the arm. "Like I said, suppose it's business?"

"Then he can tell us that."

"I just need a minute to figure this out."

"What the hell are you figuring out?"

"I like to think before I react."

"Well, hurry up," Chaunci said, " 'cause I need to know where to put my earrings."

Jaise felt as if humiliation had baptized her. Drama was much easier to deal with when she didn't have a witness. Then she could sit back, observe, and figure things out on her own. But now with a camera crew salivating at her every move, and Chaunci doing her damnest to get the situation poppin', she was caught in a crossfire of not knowing whether to react on the attack or act like a lady, smoke a cigarette, and preach about men coming a dime a dozen.

"You're thinking too slow," Chaunci said, "and ya boy hasn't looked over here once, and come on, there's a camera crew standing here, and if it was just business, he would've noticed us, because he would've been paying attention to more than just ole girl. But he hasn't, so I don't know about you, but that says 'cheating ass' to me. Now, I don't know what you gon' do, but I'da split his wig to the white meat by now."

"That's disgusting."

"No, you being cheated on and tolerating it is disgusting. Kicking his ass is rewarding."

"I'm trying not to jump to conclusions."

Chaunci paused. "Oh, I get it. My fault." She started placing her weapons back into her bag. "You don't want to overreact, because you want to leave room to fuck Romeo again. So please forgive me for not attending to my business." She picked up her chopsticks and started eating her sushi again.

"Look, I'm not going to jump all over my man because I see him sitting there with a woman. She could be a business associate, and if I find out she's not then we're finished. Over. And he will be alone."

"He won't be alone, because he'll have home girl to keep him company." Chaunci stuffed her mouth. "I'm not mad at you though. You contradicting yourself like a motherfucker given what you said earlier, but hey, I'm sure when people see this on television somebody will relate. Hell, I'm the last one to judge. I know what it is to love a man who loves a few other people. And I have to admire you really."

"Admire me?"

"Yeah," Chaunci said with her mouth full, "you know how many unhappy hos woulda stomped over there, started a ruckus, and been back in the bed with that man by the end of the night? At least you're playin' your position. It's retarded. Whack as hell. And I pretty much think yo' ass is crazy, especially when you're too beautiful and too rich for the nonsense, but hey, who am I to guess the side effects of his dick?"

"You're going a bit far. I just know that Trenton has a lot of business associates and I'm not into making a fool of myself."

"Alright, well, call him, then," Chaunci said.

"Call him?"

"Yeah, tell him you were thinking about him and see what he says."

"And what is that going to accomplish?"

"If it's nothing he'll tell you he's at a business meeting and it's no big deal, but if he doesn't answer, if I were you, it would be a misunderstanding."

"Okay." Jaise swallowed. "You're right, I'm too classy for any other foolishness." Jaise threw her right shoulder forward and batted her lashes. "I'll call him."

As Chaunci sipped her drink, Jaise pulled out her cell phone and dialed Trenton's number. They watched him pull his phone from his inner jacket pocket, look at the number, and then slide the phone back.

Jaise called him again. This time he looked at the phone and sent her straight to voice mail. "I can't believe him," she said.

"Text him and see what he says."

Jaise texted him: "I need to speak to you. Pick up."

They watched him pull the phone from his pocket, read the text, and type something back.

Within a few seconds her phone beeped, letting her know she had a text message. I'M SLEEPING appeared on the screen.

She quickly called him back and he'd turned his phone off.

Jaise felt like a zombie, a frozen fool. She couldn't believe it. Tears filled her eyes. "Look, I'm not one for scenes, so I'ma go home and pack the things he has at my house."

"Straight," Chaunci said, "let's go. And donate the shit, so he doesn't have a reason to stop back by your house and get it."

Both women stood up and Chaunci placed a hundred-dollar bill on the table. "Brunch on me."

"Thanks," Jaise said, watching Trenton step away from the table. "Let's hurry. He just walked to the bathroom, so let's just go now." Jaise hated the feeling that had settled in the bottom of her stomach. It was the same feeling she'd had when she was married to Lawrence, a feeling of being nothing. She did her best to keep her eyes from sizing up the other woman as she and Chaunci walked by the table.

"Wait," Chaunci said, as they approached the exit, "I forgot something." She walked back to the table where Trenton's party was and stopped. "Don't I know you?" Chaunci smiled at the woman. "You look so familiar." She squinted her eyes.

The woman looked at her with pleasant surprise. "I don't believe so."

"Well, I'm Chaunci, and my friend over there is *Jaise.*" Chaunci yelled and motioned for Jaise to come over. "Come here. Doesn't she look familiar?"

Jaise could've choked Chaunci but she walked over reluctantly. Her eyes sized the woman up as she approached the table; her inner thoughts forced her to admit the woman was beautiful.

The woman looked at Jaise; it was obvious that she knew who she was.

Trenton smiled as he returned. "Katoya, who are your friends?" he said as he sat down and looked Jaise directly in the face, his smile turning into a look of complete and utter shock.

"Hey, Trent," Chaunci said as if they were friends, "I told Jaise I thought that was you. Give your man a kiss, girl. Don't be shy around me because I don't have a boo." Chaunci smiled while looking Katoya up and down. "You know how that is, don't you, Katoya?"

Jaise kissed Trenton on the lips and he dryly responded. She knew in her heart of hearts that this was the woman who had been crying on the phone. Jaise turned to Trenton. "I'm sure this is business." She offered the excuse. "So I'm going to skip on. Dinner's at seven, honey." She air kissed him.

"Y'all be good now, ya hear." Chaunci winked.

Jaise could barely walk as they exited the restaurant and boarded the elevator. Her knees were wobbly and her legs felt like willow branches. Once the doors closed Chaunci turned to Jaise. "Listen, I'ma give you some advice that I wish someone would've given me: Leave that motherfucker alone. Straight up. And if you choose not to, just know, accept, and understand, that he's fucking that bitch just as much if not more than he's been fucking you. So unless you're willing to settle for being disrespected, humiliated, and mutilated emotionally . . . again . . . then cut your losses and bounce. Otherwise," she said as the elevator doors opened and they stepped out toward the street, "use a condom." She kissed Jaise on the cheek, walked down the street, and disappeared into the subway station.

Jaise paced the corner until she was able to hail a cab. After giving her address to the cabby she tried not to cry, but when Carl, who'd slid into the cab with her, pointed the camera at her and asked her to express how she felt, tears slipped from her eyes and before she knew it the busy New York City streets went from a dance of traffic to a faded blur.

Milan

"I love to cook," Milan said, smiling at the camera as she cracked three eggs into a hot and oil-popping frying pan filled with red and green peppers and onions. "That's why you don't see any staff around here." She paused, almost gagging at the thought that she'd spat out such an outrageous lie. She didn't know how to cook, and Yusef refused to eat any of her experiments. "Yusef loves it." She waved away the burning smoke that rose from the pan. "I have him spoiled." She took a knife and cut off the burned ends of the omelet, then slid it onto a plate and garnished it with parsley.

Milan poured Yusef a glass of orange juice and hummed a Kirk Franklin gospel tune. She looked toward the bedroom and called, "Yusef, breakfast is finished, honey." Milan stood silent for a few seconds and then said into the camera, "Now, if you'll excuse me, I have to get dressed for a new volunteer position I'm starting at the hospital." She gave a Miss America wave to the camera and eased into the guests' bathroom. It was the only place she knew she would get absolute privacy.

She showered and dressed in her white nurse's uniform. She hoped that she would do okay, because she wasn't volunteering, she was actually starting a new job as an emergency room nurse. And although she might have a degree in nursing, she hadn't worked in a hospital since her internship in college.

"Hello, my name is Milan Hernandez-Starks." She stood in front of the bathroom's full-length mirror. "I mean Nurse Hernandez-Starks, I mean Nurse Starks. I don't know what the fuck I mean," she said, exhausted. She struggled to sound chipper. "Hello—I sound . . . so damn stupid." She sucked her teeth and gave up.

"You sure do," Yusef said as he tossed the bathroom door open without knocking and squeezed himself past Milan, not caring that the space wasn't big enough for the two of them. He slid his feet over the cold subway tile, stood over the toilet, and started to piss. "Where is you goin' today?" He shook his dick and flushed the toilet.

Milan frowned. Not only had he just pissed with the door wide open; he'd paraded in front of the camera naked. "You are so fuckin' nasty," she said under her breath.

"What, you don't piss?" he asked as if she'd lost her mind. "Yo' kidneys probably rotten than a motherfucker."

"Yusef, just be quiet."

"You gon' get enough of trying to shut me up." He looked at her white fitted nurse's uniform and overcoat. "What is you, Muslim?"

Milan rolled her eyes to the ceiling. "I start at the hospital today, Yusef."

"Doing what?" he snorted.

Milan whispered, praying that the camera crew and Bridget wouldn't hear her, "Remember I told you I applied for a nursing job?"

"You kidding, right? You tryna play me?"

"This isn't about you!" Milan said in a forceful whisper.

"Like hell it ain't." He looked up at the cameraman who stood in the doorway. "You a freak or some shit, lookin' at my dick!

What, you gay? What the fuck are you standing there filming me naked for?!"

"Hold it, buster!" Bridget interjected. "You don't talk to my camera guy like that! Go put some clothes on your ass if you don't want it filmed!"

"Trick, fuck you!"

"Yusef!" Milan said, surprised. "Don't say that."

"She should mind her business!"

"No!" Bridget pointed. "Fuck you, you porno freak! Hmmm," Bridget went on before Yusef could respond, "wouldn't that be interesting, a reality show with a buncha porno freaks? And sonny here could be the star!"

Yusef slammed the door in Bridget's face and turned his attention back to Milan. "You ain't going to work."

"Yeah, okay," she said sarcastically.

"Fuck that. I got my wrestling and I just invested some money in this trucking company, so we about to blow up again. My coach gon' see that I'm straight, and the next thing you know I'm back on my team and runnin' the fuckin' court."

"Okay, Yusef."

"Okay, Yusef, what? You tryna patronize Da Truef?"

"Listen, not this morning. I'm not going to argue with you. I'm tired and the day just started. I can't live another moment of this fantasy life with you. We have no money left."

"I have businesses. They just need a minute to get poppin'."

"There's no business, Yusef, and you're too high all the time to wrestle."

"Oh, so . . . suddenly you above Da Truef now?"

Milan ignored him.

"I asked you a goddamn question." He mushed her in the side of her head. "You think you better than me?"

She smacked his hand. "Do not fuck with me." She pointed in his face.

"You can beat me now? Da Truef is such a bitch that a chick

can kick his ass, huh? That's what you think of me?" He lunged his shoulders toward her. "I'ma punk in your Brazilian-ass eyes, huh?"

"My father was Dominican."

"Whoo, I'm impressed."

"Whatever," Milan snapped as her cell phone started to ring.

"You look stupid." Yusef laughed at Milan and said as she picked up her phone, "Fat, saggy ass."

Milan tried to ignore him as she answered her phone. "Hello?"

"Milan?" came from the receiving end of the phone.

"Yes." She took the phone away from her ear and looked at the caller ID. Not recognizing the number she said, "Who's calling?"

"Kendu."

"Oh." She paused. "What is it?"

"Listen, I have Evan here and we're calling to apologize."

"For what? She was just being herself," Milan snapped.

"And so were you," Kendu retorted, "but I've put up with it all these years."

"Funny."

"Look, we really would like you and Yusef to come over for dinner on Saturday."

"Oh hell—"

"I'm not taking no for an answer. We'll be serving steak and shrimp."

"I'm—"

"Allergic to shrimp, I know, so scallops will be prepared for you."

"Kendu—"

"We'll see you then." Before she could protest he hung up. She held the phone in her hand and thought about the invitation that had just been forced on her.

"Who the fuck was that?" Yusef snapped.

"Kendu. He just invited us over to dinner on Sunday."

"For what," Yusef laughed, "round two?"

"I can't stand you."

"Yeah, well, join the club. Now back to this job bullshit. You ain't goin'."

Milan snatched the bathroom door open. "The conversation is finished."

"Oh, you must wanna be fucked up." Yusef folded his arms across his chest.

"Would you go put some clothes on?" she said, tight-lipped. She looked at the camera. "I keep telling him I don't want to be an exhibitionist." She gave a fake chuckle.

Yusef slid a cigarette from the soft pack on the coffee table and lit it. Milan sighed as she placed her purse on her shoulder and slid her shades on. "Yusef, we need to talk when I come back."

He tooted his lips and blew out a blast of air. "I hope this ain't the same shit *we* keep fuckin' talkin' about every goddamn day." He looked at the camera. "And I mean, every goddamn day."

"Honey," Milan said, doing all she could to sound sincere, "but you don't even know what I would like to speak to you about." She forced herself to smile.

"Then what you wanna talk about, Milan, how you don't fuck me?"

Milan stopped dead in her tracks and looked at the camera. "Can you cut right here and give us a minute?"

"Nah," Yusef snorted, "ain't this reality TV? You said you wanted to talk."

Milan knew for sure that he was high.

Yusef continued, "Let's talk about how you got me jerkin' off every morning and shit?" He grabbed his dick. "You see this, huh?" He flicked the tip. "There was a time I couldn't keep you off the motherfucker. Now I don't even get to put it in your ass no more. And why is that? Huh? Why is that?"

"Ask your broke-ass pockets," she snapped.

"Oh, so what, you a whore now? You can only fuck me if I got some money? What kinda shit is that?" He looked at the camera. "Say this with me, kiss Da Truef's ass."

Milan sighed. "Like I said, I've been thinking about a few things and we need to discuss them."

"Oh, I see." He blew smoke toward the ceiling. "Now you wanna turn yo' back on Da Truef? What, Da Truef ain't good enough for you?"

"Why are you always so extreme? I just don't want this relationship anymore." Milan shook her head; she couldn't believe that she had just admitted that on camera. Image was everything and she was blowing the hell out of it.

"Oh, so just fuck Da Truef?" Yusef snapped. "So you been thinking." He mashed his cigarette in the ashtray. "Well, Milan, Da Truef been thinking too. Da Truef been thinking about how he don't even see you right now." He pointed his fingers like a gun. "You done fuckin' flipped, disappeared, and turned into some new shit." He turned back to the camera. "What you see here, America, is a magic trick, Milan-style."

"Yusef, like I said, this isn't working out. I'm tired and I can't do anything for you."

"You ain't never did shit for me, Milan!"

"Good, then it won't be too hard for you to move on."

"You want this to be over?" Yusef screamed.

"What, you missed the announcement!"

"Oh, now you usin' compound words—phrases and shit. *Did I miss the announce-ment,*" he mocked her. "If you wanna step, Milan, then leave. Bounce ya big ass outta here, but Da Truef ain't leavin'. You must've found some niggah who really wants your ass, but he won't last. I'll be sure to tell him that the big ass ain't worth all the drama."

"I can't believe I sacrificed so much to be with you. This is crazy."

"Sacrificed?" He cracked up. "Sacrifice something that makes a difference, sacrifice a goddamn sandwich, hungry ass! Must think you hot shit." He laughed. "Think you gon' get somebody else, when, how soon? Bitch, please." He flicked his wrist.

"Bitch?" Milan couldn't believe it. "Bitch?!" she shouted. "You called me a bitch?!"

"Yep," Bridget interjected, "that's pretty much what he said."

Milan pushed Yusef in his chest.

"What's the problem," Yusef continued, "I should've called you a fat-ass bitch? I knew it. Okay, fat bitch."

"You a bitch." Milan paused. "A bitch-ass, sloppy, triflin', sorry, wack-ass, lost-his-contract, non-ball-playin', crackhead asshole of a bitch! You're a useless-dick bitch!" She slapped his dick, which was now soft. "If I'ma bitch ya' cockeyed, cane-walkin', greasy-ass cookin' mama is a bitch, bitch!"

"Greasy-ass cookin?!"

"And your goddamn ADHD kids and their mamas are bitches, bitch!"

"Oh, hold it."

"I'm the one who put up with your sorry ass. I swear I shoulda listened to your son's mother who told me you weren't shit. She wasn't fuckin' crazy. She had good goddamn sense!"

"Now you listening to other motherfuckers about us, Milan? You know she hatin' on me and you!" He pushed her into a corner.

"Ain't nobody hatin' on us!" she screamed. "That bitch knew you weren't shit. It was me who didn't know!" She pushed him in the chest again. "Get the fuck outta my way!" She shoved past him.

"So people can tell you anything about me, right?" He snatched her around by the arm. "That's exactly why I just made you look like a fool on TV. You wanna pretend like you so much, but I just showed the world that you really ain't shit."

Instantly Milan stopped dead in her tracks and looked up in the camera. He was right. It was all hanging out now. A lump filled her throat and no matter how hard she tried she couldn't swallow it. After a few seconds of realizing that Yusef had set out to make a fool of her and she had fallen for it, she grabbed her keys and headed out the door.

Jaise

Jaise checked her online computer orders from her customers and then forwarded them to her warehouse manager. She thought about going to a few salvage yards and flea markets but quickly changed her mind and instead walked over to her fully stocked wet bar and popped open a bottle of Patrón, threw four shots back, and then chased them with chardonnay. She was tired of falling for men whose fucking her well equated to air.

Jaise wiped tears from her eyes as she pulled a Newport from the soft pack resting on the coffee table and lit it. She stared at the crackling flame and the rising smoke from the cigarette before she slipped the butt into her mouth and took a pull.

As tears continued to pour from her eyes, she wished that she could rewind time and take herself back to a place where she felt okay with being by herself. But after a few minutes she wasn't so sure that such a time had ever existed.

She heard Jabril's keys in the front door and quickly wiped away the tears. She held her wineglass in one hand and her cigarette in the other. As soon as her son walked in she felt like a lush. She was sure if she stood up she would fall.

"Jabril," she said, glancing at the clock, "what did I tell you about coming in this house so late? You're on punishment, or did you forget?"

He closed the door behind him and before he could respond Jaise yelled, "Don't slam my goddamn door!"

"What's wrong with you?" He frowned. "I just walked in the door and already you're startin'."

"You're not obeying my rules."

"Ma"—he pointed to the clock—"it's five o'clock."

"But you get out of school at three!" she screamed.

"What are you screaming for? I took a few minutes and kicked it with a li'l shortie. You buggin'!"

"Don't tell me I'm buggin'. I'm tired of ungrateful-ass men, and you growing up to be one, just like your daddy and just like Trenton."

"I'm not like neither one of them! And I don't appreciate you saying that to me, because I didn't do nothing to you. What you need to do is go base off at ole dude who treats you like garbage."

Jaise felt the dam in her eyes giving way. She was doing her best to hold it together and project her anger onto her son's behavior, but the truth was he hadn't done anything recently, well, not today at least, and he didn't deserve the way she was speaking to him. But who the hell else was there for her to take her anger out on, who had no choice but to take it? "Just go to your room!" she screamed, and before she could go on tears raced from her eyes and she was crying like a bumbling fool.

Jabril sighed as he stood in the doorway and watched his mother act as if she were losing her mind. "You know I hate to see you cry, Ma."

"What did I tell you to do?!"

"But you bring this on yourself. Why do you keep playing

yourself for these dudes? Screw him. So what if he has money if at the end of the day you feel like shit."

"Mind your business, Jabril," she said sternly as she wiped her tears again. "And don't cuss at me."

"Listen, you can put me on punishment, tell me to get out, whatever, it doesn't even matter, but you need to turn some of that anger on yourself, word up. 'Cause you acting like you don't even like you. This cat don't even speak to me. He don't even like me—"

"No, you don't like him. Either you don't want to be bothered or you're in his face about some nonsense."

"Yo, I'm not chillin' with no dude that treats you like a jump-off! You can tolerate that, 'cause I ain't. And when I see you ain't handling him, you right I'ma be in his face!"

"I'm grown!" She stood to her feet.

"Being grown ain't good enough if this is how you're actin'!"

"Who are you talking to like that?!" was all Jaise could think to say. This was the last thing she had expected. "Don't get slapped. I'm your mother."

"Then be my mother! Allow me to stop dealing with your issues so I can chill out and be your kid!" He stormed out of the room, flew up the stairs, and slammed the door of his room behind him.

Jaise sat down and sipped her drink. What Jabril didn't know or at least what life had not allowed him to experience yet is what it really meant to be broke—and broken—and humbled—and humiliated for love, and companionship, and lust. He didn't know how it felt to be on a new love high, with the perfect man, doing what you considered to be perfect things, only to see it start crumbling before your eyes.

Jabril didn't understand what it was to say to yourself and to everyone in your circle that you were done with foolishness and that you had learned so much from your first marriage, that the changes you had gone through were over. There was no way you'd ever be that desperate, or weak, or confused again; and you really believed this was the new mantra for your life.

So you dated and you met a man who did not spot the invisible suitcase sitting on your shoulder with the travel tags that read USED, ABUSED, MISHANDLED, and UNDER THE SURFACE FRAGILE.

This man was someone you thought was perfect and kind and wonderful. So you ignored his comments about not wanting any children. Hell, you already had one, and you ignored the fact that the guy didn't talk to your son. You knew plenty of women who separated their man and their children. It was your new normal. Your new rose-colored glasses.

And you believed it when he said you shouldn't be called a couple, because he didn't want the weight of a title. Certainly you could understand the reason that you should *act* together, but not really *be* together.

This also excused him for the times that other women called him and the days you didn't hear from him, because technically you weren't together. So again you accepted it, and the suitcase on your shoulder started to weigh down your neck, placing a choke hold on you.

More things happened. He cussed you, disrespected you, and it wasn't that he didn't like children; he just didn't like your son. You revealed too many of your secrets and had shown him the contents of your emotional luggage too soon, because now he used it against you and said he couldn't marry someone with so much unchecked shit. And you dealt with it because of course he was Mr. Right, right?

You became appreciative of his random acts of kindness. When he made love to you it was no longer a mutual thing; it was a favor, something he didn't have to do for you. And all the while the suitcase was steadily getting heavier and weighing down your chest, pressing on your knees, until one day you couldn't move, because you were shackled to a callaloo of old and new bullshit topped off with whatever slop he offered you.

Until today, and now you had no choice but to face his slapping you in the face. You hate that Jabril has been a witness to your being reduced to nothing, but this has suddenly become a matter of life or death. If you stay with Trenton you will be smothered and sucked lifeless, and if you leave you will be sore, open, packed with fresh wounds, but you will be alive, and you will survive. At least you hope so.

Jaise wiped the tears racing down her face and rose from the couch. She walked upstairs to Jabril's room and stood in front of the closed door. For a moment she felt like this was his house and not hers.

"Jabril." She cracked the door open, but he didn't answer. "Bril." She pushed the door open wider and found him with earphones on, nodding his head and scribbling on a notepad. He didn't notice she was in his room until she walked over to him and pushed the left earphone off of his ear and asked, "What are you doing?"

"Wondering why you in my room."

"Alright now, calm down the mannishness."

"Wassup, Ma?"

"Look, I'm not perfect, right."

"Right."

"That was a statement."

"Oh, my fault."

"Anyway, as I was saying, I'm trying to deal with issues that I have."

"Just stop chasing this dude, Ma, and you'll be straight."

"How do you even know it's about him? I could just be feeling this way."

"Ma, the only time you bug out like this is because of Trenton. And I'm just fed up with you being in tears."

"I know."

"So what he do? He cheated on you?"

Jaise didn't answer.

"That means yes. I hope you know he didn't just start doing his thing."

Jaise sat silently for a moment. Was it that obvious? "You stop worrying about me," Jaise said. "You just make sure you know how to treat the girls, you understand? If you don't like a female, leave her alone. Don't lead her on, sleep with her, and make her think that one day you'll be with her only. It's better that she know the truth than believe a lie. Treat women like ladies. We like to be loved, taken care of, and appreciated. Remember that."

"I know all of this, Ma."

"Well, I'm just reminding you. You treat them the way you would want a man to treat me, understand?"

"Yeah, Ma, I got this. How you think I stay so popular with the honeys?"

Jaise laughed. "Boy, please. Now I'm going downstairs to pack up Trenton's shit. The Salvation Army will be here in a few days."

"Yeah right." Jabril twisted his lips. "You won't be giving his things away."

"I'm serious."

"Okay, Ma, if you believe it so do I," he said as his phone rang. "Excuse me," he said to Jaise, while pointing to the phone, "Brilly-Bril need to get this."

"I can take a hint," Jaise said as she walked to Jabril's door. She watched him spit game on the phone before she walked out quietly.

Chaunci

After a day spent taping frivolous conversations and pretending that she was buying real estate in the Fijis and a car that she never left the lot with, Chaunci needed a break. A nine-inch Zulu-warrior Mandingo–dingaling of a break.

There was no way she could contend with another night of not having her erotic soul rocked. She needed an orgasmic high like a weed head needed a joint. So she decided to take Edmon up on his standing invitation for her to use the keys he'd given her last year to his place.

Chaunci stepped out of a taxi, stiletto heels first. The rain splattered against the rhinestone ankle straps as she entered the lobby and sauntered up to the elevator to Edmon's penthouse suite.

Quietly she crept into his minimally designed, Asian-themed space, where everything was immaculate and in its place. His bleached hardwood floors were so clean that you could eat off them.

Chaunci knew if she had her timing right Edmon would be in the shower, as he always was at the same time every night. He had a stringent routine—from his early five a.m. rise to his six a.m. run through Central Park, his noon lunch, four p.m. workout, seven p.m. dinner with instrumental jazz in the background, his nightly chapter reading of a Baldwin classic, and then before he retired for the night his ten p.m. shower.

The only difference in his schedule tonight would be Chaunci joining him under the rain spout.

Careful not to scare him, Chaunci called his name. "Edmon."

She could hear him sigh, a grateful sigh, but a sigh nonetheless. "You're late," he said as she watched his silhouette behind the frosted glass. "Three days and a wasted pair of front-row Sade and Hill St. Soul tickets late."

Damn, Chaunci thought, she'd forgotten about the concert. "Baby," she said as he opened the shower door, "I'm sorry. Forgive me."

Chaunci could tell by the look on his face that at the same time he loved and he hated her nonchalance. It drove him crazy.

Chaunci dropped her trench coat, with nothing underneath, to the floor and stepped into the shower. Immediately Edmon lifted her by her waist and pressed her back against the steamy flagstone. The way he sucked her nipples let her know that he missed them. She closed her eyes, and as Edmon entered her, Idris filled her mind. Imagining Idris made Edmon's touches electric; actually it made his touches disappear and melt into a lovemaking memory where Idris knocked her creamy walls down as if he were fighting for his life or dying to make life, depending on how one looked at the river of cum they exchanged with each other. Prepared to call Idris's name, Chaunci opened her eyes as Edmon gripped his massive hands into her back and whispered, "I love you."

After they'd made love in the shower they lay in the bed and Chaunci said, excited, "Edmon, I finally got the Jay-Z and Beyoncé interview I've been wanting, and do you know I'll be the first magazine to publish their wedding pictures?"

"Didn't they get married a couple of years ago?" he said, unimpressed.

"About a year, give or take, but they don't grant this type of interview."

"Okay, baby, that's nice. I'm glad you were able to play with that."

Chaunci was taken aback. "Play with that? Do you remember how bad I wanted to do this interview?"

"Don't insult me, of course I remember."

"I'm not the one being insulting. But then again, why should I expect you to have any regard for what I'm doing—"

"To avoid a disagreement," Edmon said, "let's drop this and talk about something else?"

"No, whenever it comes to my magazine you always want to change the subject. Damn, everyone doesn't want to own Viacom or have fifty percent of the stock in American Express. Believe it or not some people have other goals."

"And I respect that. Otherwise I would not have given you the money to finance your magazine. Let's not forget that."

"I didn't forget that, but apparently you were okay with investing money even though you think that *Nubian Diva* is frivolous."

"I never said that. I just think that there are enough glamour, beauty, and how-to-braid-hair magazines. Black women need something else to do other than read another piece of paper, editorial, or whatever you wish to call it, on how to spend all your baby daddy's money on designer brands instead of saving it for generations to come."

"I can't believe you just said that. *Nubian Diva* offers women a helluva lot more than designer digs. We discuss finance," she said as if she were counting on her fingers, "men, children, things that matter to all women, not just materialism."

"If you say so," he said dismissively.

"Do you even read the magazine?"

"I glance through it."

"Have you ever read anything I've written?"

"I read the article you did on me."

"I can't believe that you would invest in something you don't even care about."

"Listen, you're pushing me. I did it so that you could experience success. Okay, there I said it. Can we drop this now?"

"Wow," Chaunci said more to herself than to Edmon, "I don't believe this."

"Why are you so sensitive? I really don't want to argue, so have you made up your mind where you want to spend our honeymoon?"

"I've been so busy getting high off of success that I haven't had the time to give it much thought," Chaunci said as she twisted her chocolate diamond engagement ring around her finger.

"Are you having second thoughts?"

"What would possibly make you think that I would ever have second thoughts?" she said sarcastically. "Why, I like being your little lady."

"You seemed pissed," Edmon said. "Are you?"

"Not at all, I'm just reveling in our time together."

"And what is that supposed to mean?"

Chaunci simply turned her back and let her silence answer the question. She didn't exactly know what the shit meant. All she knew was that she'd met Edmon when she was a struggling freelance writer, working part-time at a law firm, with a baby, no daddy, stacks of bills all over the place, and student loans doing a job on her credit rating. Nevertheless, she was determined to follow her dreams of writing full-time. While freelancing she was asked to write a story about Edmon Montehugh, the most eligible black man at the time.

She'd had a tough time landing the interview, but she knew if she nailed the story it would do wonders for her résumé, so after much persistence she nailed it and they clicked. The story was wonderful, but it was more than that, it was their chemistry. Edmon felt like a breath of fresh air. Finally Chaunci was able to speak to a man who didn't complain about his ex-wife, children's mother or mothers, his life, the white man, or Mexicans taking all of the jobs away. He was intelligent, a gentleman, and he handled his business.

Chaunci took the chance and told him about her dreams to own a magazine, and within two weeks he had given her the money to make it happen. Then a month later he unexpectedly proposed and Chaunci instantly said yes.

An hour later when Chaunci turned back to Edmon, he was knocked out asleep with a coating of slob on the side of his mouth. Chaunci eased out of the bed, put her trench coat on, and carried her stilettos in her hand as she walked out of the apartment.

As Chaunci locked the door, a voice came from behind her and scared the hell out of her. "We would appreciate it if you would stop leading us on a goddamn cat-and-mouse chase just to find out who the hell you're screwing!" She turned around and it was the producer, Bridget, and the camera guy, Carl.

Chaunci was instantly pissed and rendered speechless. She rolled her eyes and continued about her business. She was exhausted by the time she caught a cab home. As she prepared to cross the street to her apartment building, she hesitated for a moment; she could have sworn that Idris was leaning against the wet brick of her building.

"You can't be fuckin' serious," she said with contempt as she stepped in front of him. "How did you get my address?"

"Just know that I have it."

"Why are you here?"

"I rang the bell and *our* daughter told me you weren't there"—he hunched his shoulders—"so I waited."

"I don't know what the fuck for," she said, waving him off, "because as far as I'm concerned you and I don't have a daughter."

"How many times do I have to apologize?" He walked close to her and the seduction of his cologne caused her to lose her footing for a moment. Idris caught her hand and helped her to regain her balance.

"I'm never going to accept your apology," Chaunci said, "so you can stop."

"You can't expect me to walk away, again?"

"I don't see why the hell not! You don't know Kobi and she damn sure"—she poked him in his chest—"doesn't know you."

"What the hell is it going to take to make this okay?"

"Okay?" Chaunci snapped, hating that emotion was starting to make her voice tremble. "Make this okay? Here's what is okay: If you keep getting in my damn face, I'ma make it okay for you to pay child support, because after that hundred-and-twenty-million-dollar contract the Knicks just gave you, you can afford it. So my suggestion to you is to stay the fuck outta my way! Now make that okay." And she slammed the glass entrance door behind her.

The Club

Evan hoped the boom mic couldn't pick up the rapidity of her heartbeat. She placed her right hand at the base of her neck, her quick-paced breathing made her palm rise and fall while she drifted into deep thought of what Aiyanna and Kendu had been laughing about for more than an hour. As she became convinced that they were probably laughing at her, the maid dropped a piece of china and it shattered to the floor, scaring Evan out of her daydream.

The maid looked at Evan and hoped she wouldn't lose it, as she had been known to. When Evan said nothing the maid quickly cleaned up the mess and disappeared into the kitchen.

"I think I'll be nosey," Evan said, smiling at the camera as she eased down the hall toward Aiyanna's room, only to find Kendu closing the door behind him.

"What were you two doing?" she asked him.

"I read her a book. Is that okay?"

Evan's heart wrenched. She was torn between spittin' in his face, bursting into tears, or both. As the bell rang and the maid announced, "Mr. and Mrs. Starks have arrived," Evan suppressed her anger.

Kendu turned from Evan and walked into the great room where Yusef and Milan were standing.

"My man," Yusef said as Kendu headed toward him and they exchanged a brotherly hug and handshake.

"What's good, man?" Kendu asked. "How's the holiday season coming along?"

"You got it," Yusef responded. "You know how it is, buying a buncha shit for my kids." Milan shot him the evil eye, knowing he hadn't even paid child support in months. "And my wife wants to spend all of my money."

They both laughed as Kendu walked over to Milan and Yusef was greeted by Evan.

As Kendu and Milan embraced, Milan hated that she was instantly lost in his scent, and in the way her skin felt against his as he squeezed her a little too tight and too close. "Thanks for coming," he said, holding her hand a moment too long.

"Only for you," Milan whispered as she turned to Evan and handed her a bottle of Cabernet. "How are you?"

"I'm well." Evan smiled. She and Milan gave each other light hugs and air kisses on each cheek. "You look really cute." She looked at Milan's Louis Vuitton wedge heels and said, "The shoes are fabulous."

"Thank you," Milan said, looking around. "I've always loved this place. I swear your estate is magnificent."

"Yeah." Yusef nodded his head in agreement. "I was just telling Milan that we gon' start construction on an estate like this. The only problem is trying to find enough land in Manhattan where we can put a helicopter pad, feel me?"

"Yeah, bruh, sounds nice," Kendu said.

"Well, you know how I do it."

Milan felt like slapping the shit out of him. Apparently he

didn't have a single bone of embarrassment over the obvious lies that slid like butter off his tongue. She wanted to tell him to shut the fuck up; they'd just gotten in the door and already he was lying. But because she knew he would take that opportunity to embarrass her, she changed her mind and looked back at Evan. "Dinner smells wonderful."

"Oh, the chef really laid it out," Evan bragged as they all walked into the dining room and took their places at the table, where chilled glasses of Dom were waiting for them. "I told him that this was sort of a peace meal, you know."

Milan nodded.

"Listen, Milan," Evan said, grabbing Kendu's hand and slyly draping his arm around her, "I know we have had our share of misunderstandings."

"Yeah we have," Milan agreed.

"Misunderstandings?" Yusef laughed. "Shit, the last time y'all were together I just knew somebody was gon' get they ass beat. And Evan"—he sucked on the toothpick he'd stuck in the corner of his mouth—"you may have stayed skinny over the years, but my girl here," he said, gripping Milan's shoulder as if he were feeling for a muscle, "don't let that tight waist and flat stomach fool you. Did you see that ass? Large like a ma'fucker." He looked at Kendu as if he were expecting an accompanying laugh but he didn't get one. Nevertheless Yusef carried on. "Serena Williams don't have shit on Milan. Fa'real, dawg, Milan mighta whupped yo' li'l ass to the ground." He shifted the toothpick to the other corner of his mouth. "I ain't sayin' but I'm just sayin' you mighta wore an ass whippin' that day. Feel me?"

Embarrassment flooded Milan's face. "Why did you have to say all of that?"

"All of what, Milan? I was just making a statement that you ain't to be fucked with. What, Da Truef can't even take up for you now?"

"No, he can't," she quipped.

"Ungrateful ass. Can't help yo' ass out for shit."

Milan ignored him and looked back to Evan. "Look," she said, "we need to try and get past all of the arguing and nonsense. We're together all the time now and we need to learn to get along."

"Exactly," Evan agreed. "I mean, we're too classy for this kind of foolishness. And we don't need all of this negativity."

"So," Kendu said, "let's raise our glasses to friendship, love, and a renewed vision of what beauty really is."

They clinked their glasses. "Cheers!"

During dinner and some light chatter about the weather, politics, and sports, seemingly out of nowhere Kendu started to laugh.

"You ai'ight, bruh?" Yusef looked at Kendu with one eye closed.

"Yeah." Kendu grinned. "I was just thinking of something."

"Oh ai'ight, you better tell us what to hell the thought was, because the way you started laughin' to yourself, I thought you had a split. I was 'bout to say we can light that up in the driveway right now." He shook his head to the side for emphasis.

Milan blew air out the side of her mouth.

"What?" Yusef attempted to whisper. "I said something wrong again?"

"What was so funny?" Milan said to Kendu, ignoring Yusef.

"Remember when we were all broke?"

"Like it was this morning." Milan smirked. "What made you think of that?"

"This linguine. I remember at Morgan the closest we got to shrimp and pasta anything was some damn shrimp-flavored ramen noodles."

"Hell yeah," Milan said, falling out laughing, "and to spice it up we used to put hot sauce in it."

"You ate that?" Evan frowned.

"He never made that for you, Evan?" Milan asked, surprised.

"No." She looked at Kendu and playfully rolled her eyes. "He tried though." She looked back to Milan. "But I specifically told him when you get it a little more together then you step to me."

"Wow, well, obviously"—Milan slyly rolled her eyes toward Yusef—"I didn't have that much discretion."

"So what are you saying?" Kendu asked. "You ain't like my noodles?"

"No." Milan laughed. "I'm just saying that you were a cheap ass. Every time I came to your room I didn't want you fixing me a ten-cent pack of noodles."

"You shouldn't have come hungry."

"Whatever, you didn't say all that when you had me tutoring you in math and you couldn't pay me."

"That's what the noodles were for."

"You have always been cheap. When we were kids and I begged you to take me to Astroland you would never buy hot dogs or cotton candy from the concession stand."

"Hell no, you know how much money I spent winning you those big-ass prizes?"

Milan laughed so hard that she fell back against her chair. She wiped the tears from her eyes. When she looked at Kendu everyone else in the room seemed to disappear. "Knott, remember when you were pledging?"

"Knott?" Evan frowned. "Who is Knott?" She looked confused.

Milan sat up. She'd been thrust back into reality. She smirked and said, "What?"

"Who are you calling Knott?"

"Kendu," Milan said, taken aback. "I've always called him Knott."

"Really?" Evan arched her eyebrows. "Knott?" She turned to Kendu. "Since when did you pick up a nickname that your wife doesn't know about?"

"It was a name I had as a kid. My friends from the block gave it to me because I always claimed to have a knot in my pocket," Kendu said.

"A name from the block?" Evan turned back to Milan and snapped at her with a tinge of sarcasm in her voice, "You do realize he's not on the block anymore?"

"No." Milan returned Evan's dash of sarcasm. "I thought for sure your spending habits had him out there."

"Ding." Yusef stuffed his mouth. "Round one. My money goes on the big girl. Hey yo." Yusef turned to the maid who had just come into the room. He pointed to the Cabernet they brought and said, "Homegirl, crack this open for me, it's 'bout to be on and crackin' in this piece." The maid opened the wine and Yusef looked at Evan and Milan.

"Chill," Kendu whispered to Evan.

"Don't tell me to fuckin' chill."

"You pissed, huh, Evan?" Yusef said, sipping his drink. "But I feel you, 'cause I'm sittin' here like, these ma'fuckers gotta lotta damn memories: kids and shit, Astroland, cheap-ass noodles. What the else was y'all doing? Playin' kiss a girl, get a girl?"

Kendu looked taken aback, and Milan snapped, "Please, we're childhood friends, that's it."

"Well, a whole lotta them ma'fuckers end up on the playground bustin' cherries, so what exactly is you sayin'?" Yusef said.

"Good question." Evan slightly rolled her eyes.

"Don't let him get you hyped," Milan said to Evan as she pointed toward Yusef. "If you're pissed this is not who you wanna follow, trust."

"Pissed." Evan playfully waved her hand. "Girl, please. I know for a fact that you and Kendu are best friends, especially since—"

"Since what?" Milan crossed her legs.

"Let me put it this way, I wish I could be like you, relaxed and just let myself go. But with this man"—she pointed her thumb toward her Kendu—"not."

Milan sat there for a few minutes. She wanted to cuss this bitch out. But she changed her mind, especially since the thought entered her head to drag Evan across the table and whup her ass for the old and the new, but that, too, soon became a passing thought. Then she looked at Kendu, who'd just said to Evan, "Let me speak to you for a moment." And she chose to shut up, because she knew if she opened her mouth that anything was liable to come out.

"Excuse us." Evan smiled as she and Kendu walked into the kitchen. Once they disappeared from sight, the camera guy zoomed in on Milan and Yusef. "Tell the camera, how did that make you feel?"

"I don't feel any kind of way." Milan gave half a grin. "Evan will always be exactly who she is."

"Listen," Yusef snorted, "this is how I feel about the situation, and Da Truef is gon' try and be as diplomatic as possible. No matter how you slice it, them two"—he pointed toward the hallway—"is some bougie motherfuckers."

"How you gon' say something like that sitting at their damn table?" Milan snapped. "Oh my God." She waved her hands.

"Me?" Yusef looked at Milan as if she'd lost her mind. "You were the one who stole on this chick in her living room just a few weeks ago. All I'm sayin' "—he looked into the camera—"is that the food is free and I spent my last dollars on this wine"—he tapped the bottle—"and I ain't leavin' till it's gone. So, what I think, or better yet what I feel, is this: My wife better act right, cool out, and if she wanna light Evan's ass up, all I need is a minute to get full, get me a steady buzz goin' on, and then if she want we can jump the broad. Feel me?"

As Kendu and Evan walked back toward the table, Milan said, "Shut . . . the . . . fuck . . . up."

The camera zoomed out and allowed Evan and Kendu their space to retake their seats at the table. "We had to tuck our daughter in." Kendu arched his thick eyebrows.

"Listen, Evan," Milan said, attempting to return the conversation to a decent level, "The other day Bridget suggested that we take a trip to bring the New Year in."

"Oh, girl, please." Evan flicked her hand. "Not. I want to bring my New Year in with my husband and our child."

Milan hated the feeling of a verbal knife entering her chest. She cleared her throat. "I can understand that, but you never know. Maybe a tropical island someplace. An escape from winter, just the girls. It just might turn out to be fun."

Evan hesitated. "Maybe." She looked toward Kendu. "What do you think?"

"I think you deserve to go."

Evan smiled. "He is always so sweet." She pecked him unexpectedly on the lips.

"Give me a kiss." Yusef looked at Milan.

"A little later," she whispered and patted his hand. "I don't wanna pull down my pants in front of company."

"So," Kendu said, attempting to get past the exchange that had just happened between his guests, "Yusef, since you've been off the court, what've you been doing?"

"Trying to convince Milan to let me get on her back and shovel snow." He cracked up laughing.

"Oh-kay," Evan said, and they all finished their meals up quietly.

The evening lasted for another hour before Yusef and Milan prepared to leave. "Thank you so much for inviting us," Milan said.

"Yeah, this was fun," a half-drunk Yusef agreed. "I'ma go to the car." He pointed toward the door. "I think the driver just pulled up."

"Mommy! Mommy!" Aiyanna yelled at the top of her lungs. "Come 'mere quick!" she cried. "I just had a bad dream."

"Thanks for coming, Milan," Evan said. "But the boogey man never goes away."

"Take care, Evan." Milan waved as she watched the cameras follow behind Evan.

Kendu walked Milan to the door, and as soon as Evan was out of their sight and the double mahogany doors that led to the bedroom quarters were closed behind her, Milan turned swiftly around and said, "What the fuck is your problem?"

Her sudden change in disposition and her flaring attitude caught Kendu so off guard that he automatically took a step back. "Huh?"

She pointed her index finger admonishingly in his face. "I have enough fuckin' problems. I don't need for you to be coming on to me!"

Kendu closed and locked the doors to the entryway where they were standing, blocking them off from the rest of the house. He walked up so close to Milan that her mouth was practically kissing the base of his neck. He leaned over her and looked down into her face. The sweet essence of his cologne was drowning her. "I can't undo the pain my choices may have caused you. And either you understand that or you don't. But I wasn't coming on to you. I was holding a conversation with you."

"Whatever, Kendu. I forgot you'd joined the church of the self-righteous."

He chuckled a bit. "Know what, just say it." He looked Milan in the eyes. "You have something that apparently you've been wanting to express, at least all night, so say it."

"I just don't like the shit you did."

"Why? Tell me." As she was about to speak he placed his index finger at the center of her lips. "And don't lie."

"All those memories . . . remember," she said mockingly, "when we were broke."

"This isn't about us being broke. Try again," he said matter-of-factly.

"And noodles . . ." She twisted her neck. "Remember that."

"This damn sure ain't about noodles."

"You didn't have to recall the shit in front of your wife."

"You're concerned about my wife?"

"I don't give a damn about her ass."

"So get to the point."

"I'm at the fuckin' point."

"You know what, Milan, let me hit you with this real quick—"

"No, let me—"

"Interrupting me is a bad habit. Stop it. Now, we've always been cool. Always. I could tell you anything and you know you could tell me anything. In college I enjoyed your company like you were my sister, but after we made love you could no longer be like my sister."

"The problem was you were fucking me and Evan."

"But I was with her first."

"And I was pregnant first!"

"You were pregnant?" Kendu paused. "Why didn't you tell me that?"

"What, it would've been the tiebreaker? Kendu Malik, please, I had an abortion, so it's fine."

"I don't believe you did that. You could've told me that." He shook his head in disbelief.

"And what would you have said?"

"To give me a minute."

"I didn't have a fuckin' minute then!"

"So what do you have now? I'm here. I'm listening."

"I have nothing to say."

"You have a lot to say. So what? Wassup?" He paused and seeing that she didn't respond, he carried on, "See, your problem is that you're in love with me, and this whole shit, this reality show, this shit with Yusef, this shit with Evan, and this holier-than-thou routine, this shit is an act."

"What are you talking about?"

"You know what I'm talking about."

"What, how much Evan loves you?"

"Please, Evan doesn't love me. Evan loves what I represent."

"So what? She's with you for the money?"

"It's more than the money. It's about the power, the ability to have access to so much, and the high it gives her. If she could nut off having the world at her fingertips she would . . . hell, maybe she does. But so what? I can't be her knight anymore."

"So what are you telling me this for?" Milan wasn't sure why, but tears had welled in her eyes. "I don't see where any of this is my business."

"Just tell me you love me, and you want me, because in a minute you gon' explode and I can't love you back if you burst into pieces." He pressed his lips against hers. "Tell me you love me," he whispered, "so I can tell you back."

"I can't do that." Tears slipped between her lips. "I can't."

"Tell me."

"Knott."

Kendu licked the outline of her lips. "You're the only person I still let call me that."

"Knott." Milan found herself pecking him back on the lips repeatedly.

"Tell me you love me in three words."

"I can't."

"You too fuckin' hardheaded," he said as they started to kiss, slowly at first and then rapidly and repeatedly, swallowing each other's breaths and liquidating their thoughts of needing to have the other, yet knowing the reality.

"I'm not going to be your mistress." Milan broke their kiss. "I love me too much to play background to Evan again. Besides I have a husband."

"Do you love him?"

Milan took a step back. "I gotta go." She attempted to walk away and Kendu pulled her back to him.

"When you start running from me?"

"When you start coming on to me?" Milan squinted her eyes and snapped, "I have enough problems. I don't need to be your reject bitch."

"I'm not Yusef."

"Look, I really have to go."

"Talk to me. What the hell is your problem?!"

"I'm miserable!" she practically screamed. "That's what the fuck the problem is, and I'm tired, I'm so fuckin' tired."

"But you don't have to be."

"Milan!" Yusef screamed as he had the driver lay on the horn. "Bring ya ass. You know Bobby Brown's reality show *Gone Country* is about to come on, and if I miss that shit it's gon' be a problem!"

"Misery's calling." Kendu opened the door and nodded toward the car.

Milan stepped out the door and within a matter of moments she and Yusef were driving away.

"You coming to bed, baby?" Evan walked up behind Kendu and kissed him on the neck.

"Evan." Kendu was startled. "What are you doing?" He turned around and spotted the camera and the boom mic hanging over his shoulder.

"Shhh . . . let's just finish this night in peace. Make some beautiful love." Evan wrapped her arms around him. "I want you, Kendu."

"Stop it." He turned to face her, while watching the camera in his peripheral vision.

She grabbed his hands. "Please don't do this."

Kendu snatched his hands back. "I said stop it."

"We have to work through this. You're just mad," she said in a panic. "You're just upset, but we can do something about this. We can."

Kendu shook her. "Evan, what the fuck!" he said frantically. "You're driving me crazy! Do you hear yourself? Do you? When are you going to stop crying and begging me? Damn, just leave me the hell alone or, better yet, act like I don't even exist." And he turned away, brushing Carl on the shoulder as he passed him by.

Evan stood there for a moment before walking down the hall and through the French doors to the back of the property. The buzz she'd acquired from her nightly cocktail of Vicodin and alcohol slowly faded away. She walked to the edge of the ocean, the crescent moon bathing her back; she continued to walk out into deeper waters until the bottom began to dance from beneath her feet. Not wanting to venture too far, Evan turned around and headed back toward the shore. Once she'd returned to the pebble-laced sand Evan studied how the moon scribbled calligraphy on the rising water and marveled at what it would be like to be buried in such beautiful waves.

Jaise

"I have reached a point in my life," Jaise spoke into the camera, as she placed clear tape over the opening of a cardboard box she had marked SALVATION ARMY, "where I don't tolerate nonsense from men." She stacked the box on top of another. "You see," she said, taking a deep breath, "when you're cried out and you realize you deserve better, it becomes a cakewalk for you to move on."

Jaise stopped talking and seemingly out of the blue started singing Aretha Franklin's "Respect." It wasn't necessarily her jam; it's just that she was spitting out so much bullshit, that she was losing her train of thought.

Jaise pushed back the custom drapes in her living room and watched the sprinkling of snow falling from the sky. "I'm thinking of buying a home in Scotland. I hear the winters there are fantastic," she said for no rhyme or reason other than to say something that sounded ridiculous and expensive.

The phone rang just before she could make her next unsolicited comment. She quickly looked at the caller ID: Trenton. Her heart raced and her palms began to sweat. Immediately she knew she needed to be calm and hold a decent conversation. No going off and no cussin'. She went to reach for the phone just as Jabril raced into the room. "This chump is on the phone!"

"Alright, Jabril, he is still an adult. Show some respect."

"Yeah, ai'ight, you want me to tell him you cold on his mark ass or you wanna cuss him out for yourself?"

"Don't start minding my business."

"See, I told you he would be back."

"It's just a phone call."

"Yeah, right, all I know is if I wake up in the morning to take a leak and see an extra toothbrush it's gon' be a situation."

"Give me the phone." Jaise snatched it from Jabril's hand.

Jabril stood there while he and the cameras watched Jaise closely. She turned her back to them and spoke into the phone, "Hello?"

"What the fuck," Trenton snapped instead of saying hello. "What was all of that?!"

"That was my son telling you that this is over, we're through. We need some space."

"Yeah," Jabril said in the background, "a lot of it."

Jaise covered the receiver. "Don't you have something to do, Jabril? It's Saturday, go outside." She reached for her purse and took a hundred-dollar bill out. "Go do something."

"I thought I was on punishment."

"Go!"

"Yeah, ai'ight," Jabril said as he walked backward out the front door.

Jaise returned to her phone conversation. "What did you just say, Trenton?"

"You heard me. Never mind your disrespectful-ass son, why would you call my phone and leave me all kind of crazy-ass messages about coming to get my shit or you're donating it?"

"You know why."

"So what are you saying, Jaise? You really want us to be over, you really want me to go? Because I will and you know it. Here I was feeling bad about you seeing me at a business meeting with Katoya, hoping and praying that you didn't think that the brunch date was more than what it was, and when I wake up and make up my mind to call you and explain, I check my voice mail and you're acting like a psycho."

Jaise was boiling on the inside; she was beyond sick of his lies. "I'm no damn psycho! And you're lying." Jaise knew her intentions were to stay calm, but fuck it, all bets were off. "You were at brunch with that skanky bitch, and I know you're fuckin' her!"

"You're delusional." He laughed.

"Oh, I'm delusional, so how come when I texted you, you told me you were sleeping and I was in the back of the restaurant watching you kiss that trick in the palm of her hand?"

"First of all she's French, and that's how they greet one another!"

"That bitch's name was Katoya. Her ass is from the goddamn hood! Liar!"

"Well, if I'm lying and you seem to know the story from beginning to end, then why should I keep talking? You seem to have it from here."

"Trenton, please."

"And here I just came back from taking my mother to church and was on my way over there."

"It's Saturday."

"So, she goes to prayer meeting on Saturday, your point?"

"You know what. I don't have time for this. Your ass was caught, and instead of you being a man and admitting it so we can work through this, you act as if I'm a fool, like I don't have eyes. Like I don't have feelings! Like I'm just supposed to sit back and tolerate this shit!"

"Look, I don't have to lie to you. And the truth is if that's what you thought, then that says to me that you really don't trust me and maybe, hell, maybe I need to be gone for good and give you some space to think. Your son certainly didn't make it a secret that he wants me gone. So maybe I need to take the hint and leave."

"All I said is that we needed to talk about this," she said evenly, doing her best to control her emotions.

"Talk about what? I told you it was business, but the truth of the matter is, yeah, I was attracted to Katoya. I noticed that she was nice looking but I felt drawn to her because I love you so much and you're stressing the hell out of me. You don't trust me and you're constantly accusing me. It's as if you don't appreciate who I am. With as much money as I have I can have whatever woman I want, but I chose you. But you . . . you cause me grief and I didn't feel that with Katoya. She made me laugh, made me feel appreciated, and she certainly didn't make it a secret that our relationship could've been more than business. But do you know what I did and what I said to her? I told her I loved you, and look what I get in return? Nagged."

Jaise rubbed her temples. "You should've gone to church with your mama so you could stop lying."

Trenton snorted. "I rebuke you, Satain!"

"Yeah, you're just the person I need to come and lay hands on me."

"See." He paused. "This is the bullshit that keeps me from proposing. The moment I think I can build a life with you, you act ridiculous. I'm over here being honest with you and you're calling me a liar. I mean, really, where are we going with this?"

"I can't believe how you're turning this around and blaming me when you're the one who owes me the explanation."

"I don't owe you an explanation. Didn't you tell me I had until noon to get my things? So as far as I can see what you're telling me is that we're not together, so it doesn't matter."

"It doesn't matter?" she said dubiously.

"Exactly," Trenton said for confirmation. "You said it, I didn't. So, you know what? I agree with you and Billy badass over there. I think this is indicative of us needing some space."

"Space?"

"Yeah, your mistrust of me is really getting to me and I can't deal with it. I need a minute to catch myself. And since you say that I'm with somebody else, three's a crowd. So, I'ma do my thing and you do yours. You have a son and you need to get him together before you start trying to change me."

Before Jaise could comment her doorbell rang. She was so caught up in the mixture of hurt, pain, and pisstivity of what Trenton had just said that she didn't think twice about snatching the door open without asking who was there. She simply assumed it was the Salvation Army, so she pointed to the boxes without ever looking up.

Jaise continued on with Trenton. "Let me tell you something—"

"I'm not doing this with you, Jaise," Trenton said sternly. "Good-bye." And he hung up.

She immediately called back and his voice mail picked up. "I don't believe this shit!" she screamed, throwing her phone across the room.

"Ah, should . . . I come back?" a male voice floated over her shoulder. "Or do you welcome all your guests this way?"

Jaise jumped. She'd forgotten that quickly that she'd let someone into her house. She anxiously turned around and noticed it was Detective Asante. "You scared me!" She folded her arms under her breasts.

"I'm sorry, I didn't mean to frighten you."

"What are you doing here? He just left and he's in trouble that quick?! I told him that he had one more chance and I was gon' kick his ass all over this goddamn earth!"

"Well—"

"I tell you what, I hope you brought two pair of handcuffs because when I'm done busting him up, you gon' need to charge me."

"Listen, your son isn't in trouble that I know of."

you here for?" Jaise said, hating that her mind n how fine the detective was, especially since she dumped less than five minutes ago. There was no this fuckin' easy. Surely her constant dead ends with me. reduced her to being a floozy.

"I just came to drop off an invitation to you. I run a youth empowerment group called Each One, Teach One—"

"And?"

"And I wanted to extend the invitation to your son. Every week we have someone different, usually a hip-hop star, come and talk to the group about being positive, staying focused, and believing in dreams."

"Umm-hmm." She looked at him suspiciously. "Do you drop by everyone's house that you arrest and let them into your community activism? What you tryna get credit for, lowering the recidivism rate? Or is this a tax write-off?"

"Run that past me again."

"Understand this: Jabril is not going back to jail, and just because I'm doing this million-dollar housewives shit"—she pointed toward the camera operators, who were smiling at the complete contradiction she was living—"doesn't give you permission to come seek a donation from me."

Detective Asante shot Jaise a look that instantly let her know he didn't appreciate her sarcasm. "I didn't ask you for a donation." He stepped into her space. "I wanted to inform you of something uplifting for your kid, because I felt like he needed it."

"He needed it? Do we look like we need uplifting?" She pointed around her house. "Do you see how well we live?"

"And what does that mean when your son is out throwing illegal tantrums because he's trying to get your attention?"

"Don't tell me about my son!" She pointed into the detective's face.

"Look, maybe this was a bad idea. I just thought you'd be interested in being part of the solution."

"Are you saying that I'm part of the problem?" Jaise placed her hand on her hip.

"I'm saying you need to lighten up." He stepped closer to her.

"Excuse you, Detective?"

"Why are you so tense—?"

"How about you arrested my kid. That's enough for me to be tense." She tossed her neck in motion.

"What he did was illegal. He needed to be arrested. So you need to calm down."

Jaise fanned her face, and if it wasn't for a sin and a shame she'd unbutton his shirt and run her hands through his chest hair. Jaise took a step closer to him and their eyes combed each other's bodies.

"Look," Detective Asante said as he quickly stroked her cheek, "no foul, no harm." He took a step back. "But I will leave this with you. If you would stop being so tight and relax, then you might actually see when someone really means well."

"Well, who is that? Somebody looking for me?" A voice came from behind Detective Asante. Jaise looked up and Trenton was walking in her front door.

"You don't knock?" Jaise hated that her judgment was suddenly clouded.

"You wanna introduce me to your friend?"

"No."

"Oh," Trenton said, taken aback, "so you don't give me five minutes to be outta your life before I'm replaced?"

"I don't replace, I upgrade." Jaise gave Trenton a snide smile. "Trenton, this is . . ." She pointed to the detective and suddenly realized she didn't know his first name.

"I'm Bilal." Detective Asante shot Jaise a look and then held his hand out to Trenton. "How are you?"

Trenton left Bilal hanging and looked at Jaise. "So you into gang members now. I see he has a gun on his hip."

Detective Asante laughed slightly. He walked over to Jaise. "Remember what I said." He kissed her on the forehead before he turned to leave.

A chill shot through Jaise's body as she watched the detective disappear from her sight.

"So what the hell was that?" Trenton snapped.

As Jaise turned around, suddenly she felt on top again. Trenton seeing Bilal had melted him back into the palm of her hand. At least for this moment she could take a deep breath and relax. "I'm not dignifying that," she said as she headed up to her bedroom with everyone following her.

"What the hell do you mean? So were you seeing him this whole time? Have you been using me?" Trenton slammed the bedroom door in the camera crew's faces.

"Good question, Trenton," Jaise said walking into her closet and pulling out a tight-fitting black spaghetti-strap dress and pumps. "Considering you've been using me."

Jaise stepped into the shower. She could hear him talking to her through the water and steam, but she ignored him, doing her all not to laugh.

"You're not going any-damn-where, Jaise!" Trenton demanded.

"Oh yeah," she said, stepping out of the shower, naked, with water dripping over her smooth brown skin. She could tell by looking into Trenton's face as well as at the mountain rising in his pants that he was turned on. He walked over to her and held her hands. "Why are you doing this?" he asked softly against her neck and kissed her lightly. "I get it." He kissed her collarbone. "I understand that you were hurt. And I know I acted like an asshole."

"Whatever, Trenton. You take me for granted and I'm tired of it." She loved the way his roaming hands felt all over her body.

"No, I care about you, I really do." He caressed her breasts. "But I don't want you to go. I want you to stay here with me and we're going to work things out. Okay?" He eased down her belly and started sucking her inner thighs.

Jaise could no longer take it. She was always weak when her pussy sat in Trenton's face.

"You gon' leave?" He licked her soaking wet clit.

Jaise didn't respond and the only sound that could be heard was his tongue lapping between her thighs.

"Answer me." He sucked her clit, causing her knees to buckle.

No answer, only moans.

"You want me to stop?" He licked her melting cream.

"No."

"You still want us to part?"

Silence.

"Answer me." He licked.

"No." Her voice trembled.

"And I don't want you seeing that man again."

"Yes, baby," she said as she started to cum. "Oh yes."

After Trenton licked, sucked, and ate Jaise's cream he carried her to the bed, where he lay on top of her and pushed his dick in. Usually Jaise would wince from pleasure, but this time instead of feeling his sweet hardness all she felt was the weight of his body.

He lifted Jaise's legs over his right shoulder and she watched him pleasure himself while she thought about how she was falling back into the same black hole again. Suddenly she couldn't breathe and she needed him to hurry up and finish so she could put her mixed emotions and feelings in check.

"Oh baby!" she screamed in an effort to hurry him along. "Get that pussy!" She watched his face contort as he stroked faster. "Damn, work that big dick. Shit, this dick is so big."

"It's that big, baby?"

"The biggest."

"Bigger than that niggah's?"

Jaise didn't answer, because although she didn't know, she doubted it. Besides, Trenton wasn't the biggest; he was average. It was his money and the possibility that he would be able to help her maintain her comfortability that made his Johnson seem like a boulder. "Let me ride you," she said.

"Yeah, you wanna feel that dick, don't you? Grrrr . . ."he growled, and Jaise curled her lip in disgust. She'd just fucked him the other day and she had no memory of his ever doing this. It was obvious he had his women confused; growling must've been what the other chick liked.

They switched positions and within a matter of minutes of her bucking her hips, she looked into his face. "Grrr," he growled again, and then as if God had finally answered her prayer the mountain deflated and a river of warmth was running between her legs.

"If you would learn how to act, I would wait for you to cum sometimes," he said as he rose from the bed and went into the bathroom.

"Excuse me," the Salvation Army worker said to Jabril as he walked up the brownstone stairs, taking two at a time, "do you live here?"

"Yeah, why?"

"We're here to pick up a donation someone called us about earlier."

"Oh, I got you," Jabril said as he opened the door and showed the worker where the packed boxes were. Trenton may not have lived there, but he had tons of things. Jabril smiled and even helped the worker tote boxes to the van and when he was done, he tipped him. "That's for some needy family." He smiled before returning inside to the entertainment room, where he grabbed the remote and flopped down on the couch. He placed his feet on the coffee table, channel-surfed, and started spitting a rhyme stuck in his head.

Just then Trenton walked past him with a beer in his hand, no shirt on, and a pair of Joe boxers with smiling faces all over his ass.

Jabril was speechless. Trenton walked over to the couch, sat down, and placed his feet beside Jabril's on the coffee table. "Let me tell yo' punk ass somethin'," Trenton said. "I don't like you. And when you get eighteen you leaving this motherfucker." He pointed into Jabril's face. "I'm the one hittin' ya mama off, so I run this here spot. And the next time you get arrested I'ma make sure your mama leaves you there."

Before Jabril could open his mouth, Jaise was standing in the doorway. She threw Jabril a look and said, "I got this." She threw Trenton his clothes. "Get out! And don't ever come back."

"What?" Trenton was caught off guard.

"That's my child," Jaise said, "and I will not have you talking to him any kind of way."

"If you don't go and sit your desperate ass down and behave you will find yourself manless."

"I became manless when I met you."

"Now you hittin' below the belt, Jaise. Don't call me beggin' "—he stood up—"because you know this is over, right?"

"Did you just get the motherfuckin' hint, or what?"

"I tell you what," Trenton snorted, "I'ma leave when I get good and goddamn ready to." He flopped back down. "If you want me to leave, you'll be moving me and this damn couch."

Jabril rose to his feet. "I will throw you and this couch out!" He grabbed Trenton by the arm.

"Let me tell you somethin'!" Trenton turned around as if he were going to run up on Jabril.

"Try it," Jaise begged, " 'cause we jumps motherfuckers up in here. So bring it and we gon' whup yo' ass!"

"Please bring it on!" Bridget cringed. "I'm about to piss all in my pants."

"Ma, you ain't got to argue with this wanksta," Jabril said, shoving Trenton out onto the stoop, causing him to leave a trail of clothes and one of his shoes behind him. "And don't bring yo' ass back!"

"This is some bullshit!" Trenton screamed, as Bridget and Carl rushed to the door to film him walking down the snowy street with nothing but his underwear on. "Trick!"

"I got your trick!" Jaise opened the window and threw the remaining shoe directly at his head.

"Don't let me see you again!" Trenton screamed.

Jaise watched Trenton disappear from sight and then she looked at Jabril. She knew that a thousand thoughts were running through his mind.

Wrapped like a cyclone in a plush white terry-cloth robe, with nothing underneath, Jaise stood before her son, knowing she had to explain the best way she could that although she was his mother, she was also a woman, and the woman in her was what was so fucked up. "Listen, I'm trying, okay?" She felt tears bubbling in her eyes again. "And I really need you to swing this with me. I'm not perfect, and I know you've seen me dogged and fucked up, crying and carrying on. And I know I spent most of your life telling you not to be like the men I keep choosing, but I'm trying to get this right . . . I am . . . So," she continued, tears sliding down her cheeks, "I just need you to give me a chance."

"You don't have to cry, Ma. You know I got you."

She wiped her eyes. "I know, but I owe you more than my fucked-up choices and bad timing."

Jabril said, "I understand, Ma."

Embarrassed, Jaise quickly headed upstairs to her master bedroom, where she slid to the floor and once again cried herself into oblivion.

After a few hours of succumbing to misery Jaise heard a light knock on her bedroom door. She wiped her eyes and the loose snot with the back of her hand. "Yes?" she yelled through the crack.

"Ma," Jabril said, "I'm 'bout to roll, ai'ight?"

"And when are you coming back?"

"A few hours. I just wanted to take this li'l honey to the movies, I mean the library."

"Yeah right. Just behave and be safe."

"Peace," he said. Jaise heard him walk away, and then a few minutes later she heard him coming back. "Ma, maybe you need to go out and have a drink, on me." He slid twenty dollars under the door. "I'll hollah!"

She could hear his feet thumping down the stairs as she smiled and laughed at his gesture. "That boy," she said to herself.

Jaise opened her bedroom door and the camera was pointed directly in her face. She knew she needed to say something about what had gone on today, but she didn't want to talk about it too long, so she simply said, "Anything you see me do, don't try it at home." She closed her door again and sat on the edge of her bed, watching the clock and waiting for the camera to disappear.

After a few hours, when everyone had gone, Jaise swore she could hear an echo of her own voice. "Hellooo . . . helloo . . . hellooooo," she said. "Who is it?" she answered. "Okay." She cleared her throat. "I'm really walking a tightrope here. My son is right. I need a drink."

She took out the black dress she'd teased Trenton with earlier, slipped on her three-inch Ferragamo heels, and adorned her ears with three-carat pear-shaped rose-colored diamonds and her wrist with a matching tennis bracelet. Afterward she made up her face with a hint of blush, MAC lipstick, and smoky eyes.

On her way out she slipped on her short-waisted mink coat, grabbed the keys to her pearl white Bentley, and left.

The Blue Mirror supper club in Jersey had quickly become Jaise's favorite spot to hang out on lonely nights. It was intimate, classy, and the various jazz bands that played on the makeshift stage were always on point.

Tonight Chandra Currelley and her band were singing and playing their lovely and timeless classics.

Jaise sat on a stool at the bar, sipping a glass of white wine with her eyes closed while she drowned in the music. The more Jaise tried not to think, the more her mind became flooded. And just when she thought she'd mastered it, that all her thoughts and worries about being alone, about God answering prayers, and about moving mountains, were silenced, she heard "It's lovely to see you again" drifting softly over her shoulder. Jaise instantly knew who it was. "Are you following me?"

"I could ask you the same thing."

"But my answer would be no. Can you say the same?" she asked snippily.

Bilal laughed slightly and Jaise couldn't help but notice how sexy his laugh was. "Listen," he said, "you're too beautiful for everything that comes out of your mouth to be sarcastic and rough."

Jaise swallowed. She hadn't even turned around and looked in his face yet, because she knew if she did it would be all over, and she was tired of being so damn easy. "So what you're saying is you like your women weak?"

"No. But the beauty of a woman is her stern softness. Her ability not to take any shorts, yet be a lady about it. So I don't know what ole boy or whoever did to you, but don't let him take you away from you." He turned her around to face him. "Understand me?"

Not knowing how to respond, Jaise said, "Would you like to dance?"

Bilal's smile lit up the place. "My pleasure."

Chandra's sultry voice serenaded them as Bilal held Jaise and she laid her head against his chest. "I'm so tired," she whispered as she ran her hands along the collar of his starched lavender shirt.

"Tired from what?"

She sighed. "I'm tired of stopping and settling, and hoping that one day I'll meet the one."

"But you have to be patient and allow that to happen."

"It's like I see these women and they look so happy with their men and their children . . . and I'm just like, Can't I have some of that? Why do I have to go through hell just to get to heaven?"

"Because you haven't learned to yield. God likes patience."

Did he just say 'God'? she thought. This was the first man she'd ever dated who had mentioned God outside of the bedroom. For a moment Jaise didn't know what to say.

"Are you alright?" Bilal swayed with her as the live jazz band's music continued to play in the background.

"Oh . . . yeah . . . I'm here, I'm okay," she said, realizing that she was steadily being hypnotized. "So since you seem to know these things"—she gave a nervous chuckle—"then . . . you tell me, how do I yield?"

"It's easy." He turned her around and brought her back to his chest. "You simply exhale. You don't ask why, you don't get upset when a situation doesn't work out, you move on."

"Interesting."

"You're a beautiful woman, Jaise. Allow yourself to be loved, instead of being so hard-pressed to give your everything."

Jaise stopped dancing long enough to look into his face. "How do you know I give my everything?"

"Do you?"

Jaise didn't answer. Instead she started dancing again.

"Just enjoy the simple things."

"Is that what you do?" she asked him. "Is that why being in your arms feels so good?"

"That's a question you have to answer."

"I just keep thinking . . . that life was much simpler when I was living in a basement apartment giving rent parties."

"That's funny. You giving a rent party. I can't imagine."

Jaise hummed while she and Bilal danced quietly through the next couple of songs. "You sing?" Bilal asked Jaise. "My grandmother used to hum like that, and she had a beautiful voice."

"I used to sing when I was a kid. Nothing serious."

"I want you to sing for me one day."

"Hmm, maybe I will."

After they finished dancing they sat down, shared a few drinks and more conversation.

"You are too funny." Jaise smiled. "I never imagined my night would end like this."

"Well, I'm glad it did, considering how you were going off on me earlier this evening."

"I'm sorry, I was just going through some things."

"Alright." He smiled and she realized he had dimples.

"Well, I hate to leave," she said, looking at the clock, "but I have to get home."

"I understand. I'll walk you to your car."

Bilal held the door open and rain was pouring down. "Wait a minute." He took his suit jacket and covered her hair with it. "Where's your car?"

She enjoyed the scent of his jacket. "Right out front."

"After you," Bilal said as he walked Jaise to her car and opened the door for her to slide in.

"Do you think," Jaise said, pausing to watch the rain wash over him, "we could maybe do this again?"

"Whenever you're ready," Bilal said. "You come and get me. No pressure, and on your watch. How's that?"

Jaise couldn't believe it. Was this a joke and this mofo's pregnant wife was due to come riding down the street in a minivan with a six-year-old kid screaming, "Get away from my daddy, tramp!" Or was this real and Jaise had simply been watching too much TV?

She looked at his left hand, something she hadn't done all night. No ring, but in this day and time, what did that mean? "Are you married?" She squinted her eyes.

Bilal took a second too long to answer, and Jaise sucked her teeth. "I knew it was some bullshit," she spat.

"Bullshit?" He arched his eyebrows.

"Bull . . . shit."

Bilal looked taken aback. "Since you had it pegged then why did you ask?"

"Because for a moment there you seemed sincere. But I knew this was too good to be true. So tell me, does your wife know you're standing here trying to bed me?"

"Bed you? I don't sleep with every woman I meet. I have to love a woman first. You should try that, it would eliminate so much hurt."

"And that means what relative to your wife and kids?"

"Now I have kids?"

"How many and how many mamas? I knew you were too fine. Listen, let me just go home. I've been down this track and I ain't comin' back."

"Well, what track is that?"

"Sorry-ass men like you! You're married and you don't even have the decency to wear your ring. You have three or four kids all over the place, and all night long you've been in my face. Is that why you're all the way over in Jersey, so you can mac across state lines. Pathetic! You probably have Connecticut sewed up too! A tristate player. I'm so tired of men and their shit." She wiped invisible sweat from her brow.

"You done?" Bilal arched his eyebrows. "Or should I give you a few more minutes to assume and make a fool of yourself?"

"Oh, now you've turned to insulting me?"

Bilal leaned into Jaise's driver-side window, softly cupped her chin, and spoke against her lips. "I'm not married. If I were it would be my pleasure to wear my ring. I don't have any children, and if I did I would never deny them. And I'm in Jersey at the Blue Mirror because I like it here."

Jaise felt stupid.

"Now, if my treating you like a lady and enjoying your company is too good to be true for you, then you need to raise your standards." He stepped away from her car. "So, I tell you what, when you get it together and you're okay with being treated well, you let me know." He tapped the hood of her car, walked away, and disappeared behind the swinging glass door.

Jaise sat there for a few minutes and looked up the stretch of Elizabeth Avenue. Her eyes skipped from one building to the next. She thought maybe she owed Bilal an apology, but then again, maybe she didn't. She started her car, took off down the street, and watched the Blue Mirror become a distant memory.

Chaunci

Chaunci looked at the creases along Edmon's brow and knew that he was pissed. It had been two solid weeks since she'd last seen him, and not until now while they sat at the restaurant's dinner table, did she remember that she'd forgotten about the date they'd made with the florist.

Chaunci sucked the corner of her lip, and before she could decide what she should say to break the ice, Edmon said, "Don't give me any fuckin' excuses as to why I was waiting for you and you didn't show up. Therefore, to avoid any and all confrontation, on Monday we have an appointment with a wedding coordinator."

Chaunci hesitated. "I won't be able to make that."

"Why not?"

"Because Monday, Wednesday, and Saturday are my days to be taped, and any other day besides those I'm either at the office, with Kobi, or stealing five minutes of some me time."

"Selfish shit." He tapped his fingers on the table. "So what am I, an afterthought?"

"You're the one who didn't want to be on the show."

"I want to marry you, not be your costar."

"Then you've gotten what you've asked for."

"I don't understand why you would want to do something so cheap, ridiculous, and shallow anyway."

"That's enough, Edmon."

"No, I'm serious. I gave you much more credit than wanting to be a talentless and desperate reality star." Edmon stopped himself mid-sentence. Chaunci looked in his face and her eyes ordered an apology. "All I'm saying," he continued on, "is that I didn't give a nice share of my money to you for you to be frolicking around like some cable TV D-lister."

Chaunci couldn't believe it; she was reduced to utter silence.

"Fuck it," Edmon continued on, "I may as well say it in laymen's terms since you're sitting there with a blank look on your face. The shit is stupid. And it's taking up way too much of your time."

It finally clicked. This was why Chaunci couldn't let her guard down long enough to love him. He was too judgmental, too demanding, and if something didn't fit into his pristine world, then, like he'd just reminded her, there was no need for it to exist. "You are way out of line," she said, doing her best to rein in her temper, because the next stop after cussing his ass out was flying over the table and fucking this yuppy motherfucker up.

"I'm not out of line, I'm tired. Do you know how I feel sitting here? I'm the one who rescued you and supported your dream. Not the other way around. And here I am feeling like—like—you're the man and I'm the damsel in distress."

"Fuck your chauvinistic ass."

"Damn, well, at least I know I'm not the only one you make a habit of cussin' out," Idris said, sliding a chair over from the neighboring table and sitting down. He held his hand out to Edmon. "Idris Lawson, my pleasure."

Chaunci couldn't believe it. It must be a full moon because she'd just cussed one asshole out and now she was making her way to reading two in one night. "Am I going to have to call the police on you?" Chaunci asked Idris.

"Call 'em," Idris said, taking out his cell phone. "And while we're waiting on them I'ma order me something to eat."

"Who is he?" Edmon frowned.

"Tell the man," Idris said to Chaunci, "who I am."

"I'm not telling him shit."

"Well, then tell me why I've been calling you for weeks and you've been ignoring me."

"What the hell is going on here?" Edmon looked at Idris.

Not wanting to make a scene, Chaunci did her best to maintain her composure and said, "Before I tear this motherfucker up, you better get out my face."

"Alright, you need to leave," Edmon demanded.

"Do I look like I scare easily? Man, please." Idris looked back at Chaunci. "I wanna see my daughter."

"This is Kobi's father?" Edmon was obviously shocked. "You told me you had no contact with him."

"I didn't," she said, "until Evan and Kendu's charity event. And now much like a bedbug this motherfucker won't go away." She turned to Idris. "Didn't I pay you your three hundred dollars back? Didn't I? I thought so," she said, answering her own question. "Now leave me the hell alone!"

"Is everything okay?" The hostess walked over to their table and gave Chaunci a nervous smile.

"Nah," Idris said, "I ain't ordered my food yet. I'll have the rosemary shrimp and scallops. Oh, and some pork chops. I haven't had that in a long time." The hostess took Idris's order and walked away. "So, while we're waiting," he continued, "give me a time and a date."

"Understand this"—Chaunci tucked her clutch under her arm—"I'm not giving you shit." She rose from her seat. "As far as I'm concerned you don't exist." She walked toward the exit.

"Chaunci!" Edmon called, walking swiftly behind her.

"Leave me the hell alone!"

Chaunci stepped out the door and hailed an oncoming cab, slipped in, and was gone.

The Club

The evening sun was the color of crisp amber and its reflection made streaks of crimson on the melting and muddy snow piled on the curb. A homeless man was leaning against it and rattling the GO GREEN metal garbage can with his feet as the bus doors opened and Milan stepped off, her hobo Coach bag sliding off her shoulder and the hem of her garment bag dragging on the ground. She walked over to the homeless man, dropped fifty cents in his Styrofoam cup, and went into Luca Luca boutique.

Milan was thankful that she was early because she didn't want anyone to question why her clothes were in a bag and instead of designer digs she rocked a nurse's uniform.

The last thing she needed was for the producer to question why she was riding a city bus with the common folks. The whole point to the show, along with it being an investment for Milan, was to make America jealous, and she had yet to give even a plain Jane a reason to salivate.

When she walked into the boutique she was greeted by the store's manager, as the rest of the staff busied themselves in the background preparing things for when the cameras would arrive. Milan ignored the strange look the store manager gave her as she looked down at her white opaque stockings and biscuit-toe nursing shoes. "Can I use your restroom?" Milan asked quickly as the manager continued to study her feet.

Caught off guard, the manager responded, "Of course, yes. Yes, of course." She escorted Milan to the back, where the bathroom was a slither of existence and could easily be lost among the sea of clothing surrounding it. "Help yourself," the manager said as she opened the bathroom door.

As Milan hurried to get dressed, she had no time to dwell on how her paycheck wasn't even enough to purchase one of the boutique's blouses. Doing her best to outrun her thoughts, she quickly zipped up her hip-hugging black Zac Posen jeans and slid on her tangerine V-neck sweater. Her four-inch Manolos enhanced the pep in her step as she looked in the mirror, shook her hair out, and popped her lips together. Soon she was stepping out from the back of the boutique to the front, where Kendu was now sitting in one of the cream leather chairs, leafing through a magazine and glowing like a piece of beautiful black art.

Milan leaned against the door frame and stared at him. From past experience of placing her lips there, Milan knew there was a tattoo of a clawing lion on his left pec, the number thirty-six on his forearm, the brand of Omega Psi Phi on the back of his right shoulder, and in the space between his left thumb and index finger was a flying eagle.

He wore a black sweater and a pair of baggy jeans. On his left wrist was an iced TAG with a diamond link bracelet draped over it, and on his feet were black Marc Jacobs leather sneakers.

"Shopping?" Milan asked, finally calming the butterflies in her belly and giving Kendu a half smile as she headed toward him.

"Damn . . ." He sighed in amazement. He put the magazine down and stared at her. He could tell that she was nervous by the way she kept leaning from one foot to the other.

He stood up and without hesitation or obtaining her permission he curled his index finger into one of Milan's belt loops and pulled her directly in front of him.

"Where is your wife?"

"On her way." He placed his hands on her hips.

"Then why are you here?"

"She forgot her wallet, and since I was on my way into the city I told her I would drop it off."

"Oh . . ." Milan nervously smiled, feeling his hands roam all over her ass. She turned toward the staff, who were too busy to pay the two of them any attention, and then back to Kendu. "Don't you think this is a bit much?"

Kendu hesitated. "Tell me to stop." He pulled her even closer to him. "I need you to tell me to stop so I can do it. Otherwise I can't help myself." Without thinking twice he placed kisses along the violin curve of her neck.

"Okay," Bridget said, bolting into the store, "I want a camera at every angle."

Milan looked toward the door and she knew guilt was written all over her face.

Kendu quickly walked over to Evan, who was just entering the boutique, and handed her wallet to her. "Have a good time," he said.

"Milan," Chaunci said as she walked over to her friend, "we need to do lunch ASAP."

"Why, wassup?"

"You will not believe the shit that has been going on with me."

"May I have your attention, please?" Bridget clapped her hands. "This is how we will do this. The attendant will place a pile of clothing on the counter and either you buy it or act as if you are buying it. Everyone has to stand next to the cash register for a mock total. Understood?" She snapped her fingers. "Okay then, let's begin."

Chaunci and Milan stood back and watched Jaise and Evan begin to pick out clothes and stack them on the counter.

"What is your problem?" Bridget asked Milan and Chaunci. "Snap, snap."

"Listen," Chaunci said, looking at Bridget as if she were crazy, "you are getting on my nerves. Every time I turn around you are in my business. Do you want us to do the show or are you auditioning?"

"Okay, ladies," Jaise said, walking out of the dressing room with an obviously too-small and definitely not-the-right-color puke green dress on, "let's retreat to our corners." She pointed to the cameras. "This is supposed to be a shopping spree not the WWE."

"Please don't mention anything about the WWE," Milan said wearily.

Chaunci looked at Jaise. "You would be okay if you would let those who don't get along, not get along."

"Whatever," Jaise said dismissively, and turning around in her dress she asked, "How do I look?"

Evan cleared her throat.

Milan did her best not to snicker. "Girl, you look . . . sooooo . . . sharp."

"That dress is so hot," Chaunci said. "You're on fire."

"Oh good, I might get it." Jaise returned to the dressing room.

"That trashbox looks stupid," Milan said.

"Trashbox," Bridget mumbled and scribbled a note on a piece of paper.

After an hour of the women continuing to browse the boutique and doing their best to keep the bickering at bay, one of the boutique associates walked over and said, "Ladies, we would love for you to be the first to try out our new spring swimline collection."

"Oole, I need a swimsuit," Milan said, taking a black lace bikini from the woman's hands. "Oh, this is really cute."

"I'm so over this," Chaunci complained. "Milan, hurry up so we can catch a cab out of here."

Milan, Evan, and Jaise all went into the dressing room with bikinis in their hands. Milan was the first to come out and show hers off. "Girl, you look cute," Jaise said as she handed back the one she had to the associate. "I don't like this," Jaise said. "Milan," she called, turning back to her, "that looks really nice on you . . . Oh wait"—she turned to Evan, who'd just come out of her dressing room—"you two have on the same bikini."

"Oh, there must be some mistake," Evan said. "I don't wear plus size."

"Would you give it a rest?" Jaise snapped at Evan. "She looks fine."

"I forgot that subpar was right up your alley." Evan rolled her eyes.

"And that's your friend." Chaunci laughed. "Yeah, okay. Back to you, Milan. I think you should get that."

"I think you should too," Jaise said, staring at Milan. "What is that?" She pointed to her left breast.

"What are you talking about?" Milan looked down. "It's a tattoo."

"Of an eagle?" Jaise asked and then answered her own question. "Yeah, that's an eagle. I've seen a tattoo like that before."

"Yeah, on Kendu," Evan said, doing her best to hide her shock.

"You have matching tattoos with Kendu?" Jaise asked. "So anybody up for coffee?" Jaise attempted to change the subject.

Evan laughed. "So typical and so pathetic." She shook her head. "I have had enough of you. When did you get that? Last week, after you came to my home and realized that my husband actually loves me?" She stepped up close to Milan. "Don't you have a husband? Then why are you trying to get with mine? You're nothing to him. You need to wake up and see that."

"Evan," Milan said, brushing her off, "I don't have time for your jealousy. We got the tattoos in college. They mean nothing. Hell, if you want one, help yourself. I wouldn't give a damn." She turned to Chaunci. "Maybe we need a drink with lunch."

Evan felt heat washing over her body. She needed another pill in order to calm down and treat this peon like the nothing she was. She snatched Milan by her shoulder to turn her back around. "I tell you what," she said, pointing her finger in Milan's face, "your friendship with Kendu is over, you desperate, low-class bitch."

"Focus, Carl," Bridget said. "Focus."

Evan continued, "I am sick of you pretending like you are so important when you aren't shit. Nothing. If Kendu really wanted you he would have married you. But you weren't good enough."

This was the second time Evan had slid an invisible knife into Milan's chest.

"What happened, Milan?" Evan continued to jab at her. "Did he fuck you and leave you for me? Is that why you're so desperate to always be around? Was Yusef your second choice and you didn't even get that right?"

Milan looked Evan directly in the eyes. "I'm not going to cause a scene," she said evenly, "because what I have to say is quite simple: If you have a problem with me being in your husband's life, ask him why it's so important to him for me to be there. Ask him how well we really know each other. Ask him. I dare you." She took her cell phone out of her purse. "Ask him how he feels about me. Can he ever see not talking to me, seeing me? Ask him. Otherwise shut the fuck up. Because if I wanted him, I'd have him. And in a minute if you keep talking shit, I will be seeking to take him back."

Milan stood silent for a moment and when Evan didn't say anything in response, she looked her up and down and said, "Now stay away from me."

"Can you redo that line?" Bridget said, as if the argument had been scripted. "But this time, stand real close to her and look up into her face, point your finger, and tell her just how much you will kick her ass."

Milan and Evan ignored Bridget. "None of what you said fazed me," Evan said, laughing. "If you are such a staple in Kendu's life, then why aren't you his wife? I mean, hell"—she snickered—"impress me."

"I'm done." Milan walked back into the dressing room and quickly changed. "I've had enough."

"About damn time," Chaunci said as they walked out of the boutique together.

Bridget clapped her hands as they left with the door swinging behind them. "Perfecto! You ladies are naturals!"

When Them Jones Come Down

(A month later)

Milan

Milan was overcome with exhaustion as she sank into the last seat on the subway train next to an old man who smelled like old and hot piss. Usually when there were no other seats left she would've stood on the train, but this morning she couldn't. She'd worked a double shift, hadn't had any sleep in close to twenty-four hours, and if she didn't sit she was due to pass out at any moment.

As the train began to chug along, Milan looked out the window past the graffiti-covered bridge and at the neighborhood she'd grown up in. She wondered how much it would cost to live there again.

She hated to think about how her paycheck didn't even begin to cover her expenses. Her credit cards were hundreds of thousands of dollars behind, she and Yusef owed back taxes up the wazoo, and there was no way, since she hadn't been paid yet for being on the show, that she could continue the façade of being a millionaire's wife when the money had run out. She couldn't wait for Friday so she could have the momentary high of having a nice sum of money in her hands, before she had to divide it up among her bills and fall even deeper in the dumps.

The only thing paid in full was the apartment, but the tax liens stopped her from being able to sell it, and the money she made from working barely covered the fees for the building. She couldn't win for losing.

Yusef refused to do anything other than dream, talk about a wrestling career, and map out a failed plan of how he was going to prove to a coach who wouldn't even take his calls that he deserved another shot at playing ball again. Milan knew she was the only one dealing with reality, so when Yusef started staying out all night getting high, she became proactive. Since her material items were all she had left and she didn't want him stealing her shit, she'd leave him twenty dollars on the dresser every morning, and she held no ill feelings because at least when he was gone she was at peace.

Her head pounded with a migraine and her feet ached. She'd been working the emergency room all night and she wanted nothing more than to crawl into bed, wrap up in her goose-down comforter, close her eyes, and drift to sleep.

Before she knew it she had nodded off and was awakened by the homeless man knocking her on her sleepy ass as if a ghost had forced him from his seat and was making him flee the train. He never said "excuse me" or "pardon me, ma'am," as all the contents of her purse splattered across the floor of the train.

No one on the train offered to help her pick up her belongings, and except for a few wide-eyed children no one looked to see what had happened to her. She quietly picked up her things and sat back down in the seat. As the train arrived at the next stop and more people boarded, Milan couldn't believe her eyes. She saw Yusef with his arm draped around another woman, who looked as bad, if not worse, than he did. When the two of them sat down a few seats away from her, it was obvious that they were both high.

"Yeah," Milan could hear Yusef scream, "I'm Da Truef, baby. Number twenty-three on the New York Knicks, and any day now I'm expected to get a new contract."

Truthfully, Milan didn't know how to feel. Was Yusef being here with another woman the North Star she needed? It wasn't that her husband was sitting with his arm draped around another woman; she didn't care who he showed affection to. This was bigger than that. This was about reading the writing on the wall and seeing that the curtain had fallen, the spotlight had died, and her ride to fame and fortune had ended. This was the moment when she realized there were no more dreams and all she had left was real life, and real life was kickin' her ass.

The next stop was hers and she exited through a back door far away from Yusef and the woman, who both stayed on the train.

The winter wind cut across Milan's face and sent chills through her. She swore she was going to start wearing her furs on the train, because her hooded Burberry peacoat was no match for thirty-degree weather.

After the two-block walk from the subway she arrived at the all-glass entrance to her building with her face frozen and her eyes feeling like slits. She'd noticed some of her neighbors looking at her strangely, but she'd grown used to the double takes and questionable glances, especially since more times than not she was seen with a camera crew following her.

"Milan!" Bridget yelled. "We've been waiting on you. We haven't filmed you all week. You've been working too much," Bridget said as she and the camera crew boarded the elevator with Milan. "In a moment everyone's going to think you're doing more than charity work at the hospital. We called to confirm your status there and they refused to give us any information."

Milan ignored Bridget as the cameras started to roll on their way to her apartment.

"I hope Yusef is here. Perhaps he'll start banging his chest and calling himself Da Truef again, 'cause other than that your ass is boring."

"Excuse me?" Milan snapped.

"I don't mean any harm, you know," Bridget said. "I mean, boring in the best possible light."

"I'm sure."

"You know you're my favorite." She patted Milan on the arm. "But this is all about a second season."

Once Milan arrived at her apartment, she noticed something odd about the door. There was a padlock on it, a pink paper that read ORDER TO VACATE THE PREMISES, and a court-ordered foreclosure notice taped to her door like an advertisement.

"Get a close-up," she heard Bridget say behind her.

Immediately Milan's head started to spin. She snatched the papers off the door. There was no way they could be foreclosed on. The apartment was paid for. Yusef swore that he paid cash for it at the closing. It was his wedding gift to her, a place of their own. On their honeymoon night he handed her a white box with a red bow on top and inside was a pair of keys to their four-bedroom, five-bathroom, exclusive apartment with a terrace and a stunning view of the New York City skyline. She saw the paperwork, the apartment was in her name . . . There was something wrong . . . This couldn't be. She leaned against the wall as the drumbeat in her head turned into a tuba. Unpaid taxes. Tax liens. Fuckin' taxes. She couldn't believe it. She sent them checks every month . . . every month . . . There must be some mistake. There had to be. There had to be a way to clear this up, because after this . . . there was nothing left.

Suddenly the cameras and a smiling Bridget seemed to fade from her vision as she focused on what she needed to do next. She took out a letter from the IRS she had in her purse. She pulled out her cell phone and started dialing their number. Then she quickly hung up and decided that she needed to run to the bank instead. If she could get copies of the checks she had sent them, then she could show the IRS that they'd made a terrible mistake. And besides, where were the letters from them letting her know they were taking her home away? They couldn't just invade her life like this. Certainly they had to give her notice. Hell, even Yusef had given her notice that their life was about to be fucked up.

Milan hustled down the long and cold New York blocks with Bridget and the camera crew galloping behind her like a team of Clydesdales to Chase Bank.

"May I help you?" A smiling young man walked over to Milan as she entered the bank and extended his hand.

She was oblivious to his gesture as she said, "Yes," more as if she were talking to someone from space than to someone standing before her. "Umm." She did her best to hold back the tears threatening to spill from her eyes. "I have a problem here." She handed him the paperwork. "This can't be so."

The young man scanned the papers. He glanced up at the cameras and then back into her face. "Ma'am, we have nothing to do with this. This says foreclosure papers due to tax liens. You need to go and see a lawyer, not a bank employee."

"I don't have any money for a lawyer." She shook her head. "But . . . I pay my taxes. I mean . . . we're behind, but I pay them what I promise every month."

"Perhaps it wasn't enough," the young man said sympathetically.

"It was." Milan did her all not to cry. "I know it was."

"Well, I really don't know," he stammered, "what you want us to assist you with."

"I need copies of my checks so that I can prove to the IRS I was paying my taxes."

"No problem."

Milan followed him to his desk, where he pulled up her account on the computer. "Who is Yusef Starks?"

"My husband. He's on the account as well. It's a joint account."

"Well, ma'am"—he turned the computer monitor around toward her—"it appears that Mr. Starks has written . . . let's see here, ten thousand, six hundred dollars in bad checks."

"What?!" Suddenly Milan felt out of breath. "No." She shook her head. "I was depositing money in this account every month."

"Well, we're prosecuting the two of you. This is a joint account, so you two share equal weight."

"What did you say?" she asked as if the bank employee had suddenly started to speak Greek.

"I'm surprised you're not in jail." The employee quickly turned on her. "This is a crime!"

"A who?"

"Banks are in enough trouble in this economy, and we don't need thieves ripping us off!"

"Thieves?"

"You owe us ten thousand-plus dollars and we want it!"

"I need help," she said distantly. "I don't have anything left."

"I'm calling security. I'm sure there's a warrant out for your arrest."

Black was all Milan could see as her palms started to sweat and she felt as if she needed air. This was wrong, it had to be. This shit was crazy. Yusef was a lot of things but he wouldn't destroy her like this, not when she was trying to save what little they had. Milan turned her head from side to side. On one side she saw the bank employee looking through her with the phone to his ear, and on the other side of her was a smiling Bridget and a beaming Carl. It was official: She was the walking dead.

Milan looked toward the bank's picture window and she could see an oncoming bus. She didn't know what bus it was or where it was going. All she knew was that she needed to be on it, because somehow and some way she had to outrun the falling sky.

She bolted out of the bank with the doors swinging behind her and made it just in time to hop on the bus and leave the bank employee, the overweight security guard, and a beaming Bridget and camera crew standing there filming her as she disappeared into thin air.

It was well into the evening when Milan walked the chilly and ghostly concrete that surrounded the Astroland amusement park, which was closed for the winter. Bits of snow fell from the sky and melted on her head, as she stuck her fingers through the holes in the metal gate and gazed in on the place that encompassed so many memories. Despite how barren it was, Astroland was where she could travel back in time, to a place and a space where all that mattered was having enough nerve to ride the Cyclone roller coaster and how big a stuffed animal you could win.

She smiled and laughed as memories of great times ran through her mind, and then it hit her, the difference between now and then. All she had in her purse were three dollars, a MetroCard, and a cell phone with a dying battery.

She tried without success to hold in the cold tears that continuously slid down her cheeks, and before she knew it she was sliding down the gate, crouching to her knees, and barely able to raise her voice above a whisper.

"So this is it?" A voice invaded her moment of desperation as she crouched on the sidewalk. "You just walking around like you have nothing . . . nobody . . . like life is just shit, huh?"

Milan didn't look up. She knew it was Kendu. It had to be. Who else would know where to find her? "How'd you know I was here?"

"I know you."

"So you have ESP now?"

"Nah, Bridget ran to our house and filled Evan in. I overheard."

"Oh, so now my life is a bunch of he said, she said." She shook her head. "Bridget is the fuckin' worst. No matter what goes on in my life . . . she sees it as ratings."

"And when it airs the people who'll be watching will see it as TV. So what's the problem?"

"The problem is it's my goddamn life!"

"You signed it away for reality TV."

Milan had gone from feeling desperate to being pissed. Kendu was horrible at being sympathetic. He was strong, and he expected everyone else to be the same way. Though he was a good friend, he was terrible in the pity department. "You're so fuckin' inappropriate." Milan laughed in tearful disbelief as the back of her thighs started to feel numb from the cold concrete.

"I'm inappropriate," Kendu said, taken aback. "You're sitting on the ground in a three-thousand-dollar coat carrying a thousand-dollar bag, looking like somebody stole all your fuckin' candy, and I'm inappropriate?" He arched his thick eyebrows. "Okay."

"I didn't ask you to come here and rescue me." She stood up and pointed to his chest. "I don't need you!"

"You need somebody."

"And you're it? Furthermore," she said, wiping her eyes, "I have your number, and if I didn't dial your digits then what the hell are you sweatin' me for? Don't be worried about me. Worry about that looney-ass wife of yours."

"Evan is at home. You the one on the ground."

"Would you get the fuck out my face, please? Because in a minute I'ma reach up there"—she looked at him towering over her—"and check your fuckin' chin."

Kendu laughed. "You don't have a reason to be jealous of Evan."

"I'm homeless." Milan squinted her eyes. "And you really think that at this moment I give a damn about that gold diggin'–ass tramp? That's between you and your pockets!"

"Listen, I'm not about to argue with you in the street. Let's go—"

"Let me tell you something you don't—"

"Look, we can talk about this inside."

"Inside where? Did you forget that quick that I'm homeless? I can't believe Yusef would do this to me."

"Yusef?" Kendu asked, surprised. "You share in some of the responsibility. Besides, it's not as if I didn't tell you not to marry him."

"You are really on your own sack right now. You can marry who you want and I can't?" She rubbed her temples. "This is crazy. I need to find me someplace to live, not stand out here and go back and forth with you. Who gives a fuck anymore what you do and who you do it with! Stay and make more babies with the bitch. What do I care?! This is not about me loving you and what decisions we made and didn't make. This is about my life being tossed to the wind. About me losing everything, everything!" she screamed at the top of her lungs as tears ran like a marathon down her face. She tried to speak but the words started to crumble in her mouth. "I have nothing but the clothes on my fuckin' back and three dollars in my pocket! Do you hear me?! There is nothing left! Nothing! I took my goddamn life, married the Jinn, and I got the hell my hand called for . . . so oh well." She wiped her eyes. "Milan is a big girl and I am okay by myself . . ."

Kendu walked over and wrapped her in his arms.

"Get off of me," she cried into his chest, doing her best to push him away. "You don't give a damn. Just go on and leave me alone, please. I can't believe that I don't even have a place to live."

Kendu held her in his arms. "Milan, you know I'm not good with this crying shit. All I know is that I'm here and I'm not leaving you."

"What? You gon' be homeless with me? 'Cause I'm *not* going to Sag Harbor with you."

"I wouldn't take you to Sag Harbor. I have someplace else that I go to. Ai'ight?"

"I guess—" She cut herself short, deciding that whatever else she had left to say wouldn't change her situation.

"What?" He looked at her, knowing that she'd cut herself off.

"Just say it, Milan. Otherwise you gon' be hintin' at this shit all night."

"Kendu, why is everything so fuckin' cut-and-dry with you? Sometimes I want you to wallow with me, even if it's for five minutes, give misery some company."

"What, you want me to say some soft-ass shit? Some poetry?" He attempted to make her laugh. "You know Common is my boy. I could spit some rhymes."

"Never mind, Kendu. Just take me to the homeless shelter."

Kendu laughed. "Come on and just get in the truck."

The leather seats in Kendu's Escalade heated the back of Milan's thighs as she sat looking out at the New York City traffic, wondering when the night had become so loud. This was the first time she'd ever heard it speak and remind her of all the things she had misused, abused, and simply taken for granted.

Now she was stuck knee-deep in a pile of shit wondering why she never thought to keep some money tucked away. It was evident that karma was an unforgetful motherfucker, because this was obviously payback for accepting Yusef's hand in marriage based on his NBA contract.

"Kendu," Milan said, noticing they were in SoHo, "why are we here?"

"I come here when I need to get away."

"Get away from who?"

"My life."

"And what am I supposed to do here?"

"Stay here, and in the morning I'll give you some money. We can go see my lawyer, pay the bank their money, and then see what else we need to do. After I handle the taxes, you want the apartment back or you want me to sell it?"

"I don't want the apartment," she said, reluctantly. "Do whatever."

"Why do you sound like that?"

"Like what?"

"Unsure? I mean if you want to live there it's on you, just tell me."

"No, I don't want the apartment. It's finished, sell it. I just want my things out of it." Milan shook her head and her hair bounced over her shoulders. "I don't even know, like"—she paused, tears trembling in her throat again—"if I want this."

"Want what, Milan?" He sighed.

"Why are you sighing and shit? See, I can't. I can't do this. I haven't even moved in and already it's a problem. I just need to find me someplace else to go."

"You have three dollars, where you going?"

"Knott, do you understand that I just left a situation where I was riding high off another man's shit, and now I don't have anything. Look, I know I didn't tell you, but I'm not volunteering at the hospital, I work there as an emergency room nurse—"

"You? Work?"

"What the hell? Why does everyone act like working is a crime? I went to college, I have a degree. I have a nursing license—"

"Yeah, but you used your degree to snag an athlete."

"Is that why you're here?" she snapped.

"I could be a garbageman and you would love me."

She hated that he was telling the truth. "You really think you're the center of my universe!"

Kendu looked at Milan as if she'd lost it. "I'm not doing this with you."

"You never hear anything I say. I appreciate your being here, but I feel like I'm spinning my wheels. I can't go from one man to the next, because I know me, and it's only going to take a few moments before I'm pretending that all of this is mine."

Kendu laughed and then he kissed Milan on the forehead. "You won't have to pretend, baby, 'cause this ain't your shit. You know how much I paid for this spot?"

"Why is everything so fuckin' funny to you?"

"Because you so goddamn extra and dramatic. We've been sitting here ten unnecessary minutes. I can understand that you feel fucked up, but relax, I got this."

"That's the problem."

"Ai'ight, I tell you what, 'cause I will not argue with you. I'm tired, I'm hungry, and there's a game on. The building is four seventy-five, I'm on the twenty-first floor, and when you get over whatever you're going through, tell security I was expecting you."

"I can't believe you're so insensitive! My life is shit and you're trippin' because I won't come spend the night with you?"

"What? Are you looking for me to beg? You know me better than that. And the truth is, you knew Yusef was smoking that money up and you chose to shop instead of building you a stash. What do you want me to do about it? Pretend like your bad choices didn't exist?"

"Forget I said anything."

"No, you need to hear this. Because on top of your money being gone, you decide to do some show that requires you to spend more dough while your finances are in the toilet. Did that make sense, Milan? Be serious. This is a joke. You and your husband wasted all of your money and guess what? Bloomingdale's, Saks, Tiffany's, and the drug dealers ain't gon' give that shit back.

"So, look, call one of your girlfriends and see if they'll throw a pity party with you. And maybe Bridget'll host it, because I'm not. Now, like I said, if you would like to come upstairs, you have the address. Otherwise sit yo' ass outside and cry." He kissed her on the lips. "Peace." Kendu hopped out of his truck and started walking up the block.

Milan sat there crying. "Shit!" She slammed her hand on the dashboard, causing the alarm to start screaming.

Instantly her migraine returned. A half hour later the cold from the outside had snuck in and the truck alarm continuously set and reset, keeping Milan's nerves on edge. She wanted nothing more than a glass of wine and a warm bed, and unless she was willing to camp out at a local church or go to a mission she was sinking in shit's creek.

"Fuck it." She reluctantly eased out of the truck and the alarm started going off again. "Shut up!" she yelled as she headed toward the industrial loft building whose entranceway was so prestigious that it smelled like money, and once she boarded the restored freight elevator it said even more.

Milan reached Kendu's floor and noticed that the door to his apartment was cracked open. She walked in and her eyes couldn't help but roam in delight. Painted concrete floors, exposed rafters and ductwork ran across the twenty-foot-high ceilings. There were floor-to-ceiling windows everywhere, and all of the furniture was white and black with touches of red. Original, signed Malik Whitaker and Lee White paintings adorned the walls, and Kendu's football jersey hung above the concrete fireplace in a mahogany frame.

Milan could see the back of Kendu's head and the back of his muscular shoulders as he sat on his black leather sectional with no shirt on.

Milan closed and locked the door behind her and then walked around the extended side of the sofa, where she did all she could to fight off the second and third glances she took at the tattooed lion clawing sexily over his left pec.

"Oh, you were just going to leave me outside?" Milan sucked her teeth, ignoring her desire as she walked past Kendu and sat across the room from him on the end of the chaise.

"What? You needed some blankets?" He sipped his beer, never taking his eyes off his seventy-two-inch flat screen, where ESPN was airing a Raiders and Jets game. "Damn!" He suddenly jumped up and shouted at the TV, practically spilling his Heineken on the floor as some of it swooshed out the top of the bottle.

"Oh, so you just don't give a fuck?" Milan complained.

"I offered you some blankets." Kendu sat back down. "What more you want? I can't stop it from snowing." He sipped his beer again. "Yes! That was a good catch, baby!" he screamed at the game, as the Jets' wide receiver scored a touchdown.

"So, you don't even offer me anything to drink?"

"There's the fridge." He pointed to the side.

Milan was pissed. "What do mean, there's the fridge? I can't believe you said some shit like that to me!" She folded her arms across her breasts.

"Yo, you ungrateful as hell."

"Whatever."

"What do you want me to say, Milan?" Kendu placed his beer on the floor. " 'Cause you're getting on my nerves."

"Fuck it then, if I'm getting on your nerves, never mind."

"You know what?" Kendu's chest jumped and his biceps thumped. "What you need is your ass kicked." He rose from the couch, got her a beer, and walked over to the chaise, where he saw tears sitting at the base of her eyes. He hated to see her cry because it melted him every time. "Look," he said, standing between her legs, looking down into her face. "You need to relax." He unexpectedly ran his hand down her neck and over her cleavage. "Just for tonight, chill, because there's nothing you can do about your situation right now."

"But I don't have anything." Tears streamed down her cheeks. "For the first time in my life I don't know what to do. I owe the IRS money. The bank is after me."

Kendu squatted to his knees and looked directly into Milan's eyes. "I wish I could tell you the answers, but I can't. I don't even know what the hell I'm doing with my own life. All I know is that after fighting and battling with fucked-up choices, that sometimes I have to come here and lay still, chill, and just say, 'Not today. Today, I'm straight, and nothing else exists. Period. I'll deal with it tomorrow.' "

"But I don't know how to do that." Milan eased up close to Kendu and wrapped her arms around his thick neck. "I try to just sit"—she massaged his neck with her fingertips—"and be quiet, but all I keep hearing," she said, drawing her face into his, "are all of my problems screaming in my head." She tried to fight it, but she felt like her lips had a magnet for his, so she kissed him, and he responded.

"Let me show you somethin'." He started unbuttoning her uniform top, kissing every ounce of skin that was revealed.

"I feel like I just wanna run away, like to the sky, maybe." She lay back on the chaise as his now-loose belt buckle clinked, his tongue ran up and down the center of her body as he slowly undressed her.

"Let me take you there." He pulled her panties down with his teeth, revealing her feminine beauty.

"Kendu." She placed her hands on his face as her back arched and her hips matched the rhythm of his lips as he licked her creamy slit, until all Milan could do was beg for more.

Kendu loved the smell of her, the way her clit melted to jelly and her sweet flesh rubbed the evidence of her pleasure against his face. He loved the way her erotic cat smothered his lips and the way her thick thighs encompassed him. He bit her clit slightly the way he remembered she liked it, and then as if he were preparing for a monstrous wave, he took his heated and luscious tongue, placed it at the base of her cherry, and within seconds her drippings were coating his throat.

He kissed her all over her ass, hungrily licking between her cheeks. Then he dropped his pants to the floor and before he lay on top of her Milan sat up and began caressing his shaft into her mouth. His dick was so big and so filling that she had to relax the back of her throat to take him all in. She licked and she sucked all of his unending inches, until Kendu's pelvis began to contract and he blessed her lips with his liquid gifts. Immediately he was hard again, and Milan lay back and opened her world up to him. Loving the feel of her full breasts against his chest he pushed them both together and rotated his sensually gripping sucks from one chocolate nipple to the next.

Milan lost control and for the first time ever she let it all go. Her issues and problems had no room and no space in this place where she so desperately wanted to be. She watched Kendu with her eyes wide as he sat up and kneeled, rubbing himself in her wetness. His dick was so big that if he didn't use it all now, he would have enough to save for later. His had always been the prettiest dick she'd ever seen.

Conscious of his size and confident that she hadn't had any dick like this, Kendu slowly pushed in his cock, and with every inch he could feel it becoming smothered with more and more of Milan's vanilla icing. He loved the thickness of her sticky pond, and with the size of her hips and the way she was starting to twirl them, he knew that when they were done both would be unsure about who had whipped whom.

"Damn, baby, wait," Milan said, unable to catch her breath.

"You really want me to wait?" He slid his dick out, slid down her belly, sucked her dripping juice, and then all at once pushed his dick back in. "You really want me to wait?"

"No," she gasped, as he starting fucking her so hard that her ass jiggled and jumped. Milan could feel her walls expanding and collapsing every time Kendu went from the top of her pussy to the bottom.

She continuously lost her breath as she did her best to hold on for the ride. Her head was spinning and a bomb was ticking. She placed one leg on the floor-to-ceiling window and the other she wrapped around his waist. She loved how he felt inside of her, letting her know with every stroke that she was going to take this dick and she was going to take it as often as he wanted to give it to her.

Her stomach began to tighten and she could feel her orgasmic bomb preparing for explosion. Milan knew at any moment she was due to drench his dick with payment for his generously helping to ease her pain. "Kendu!" she screamed. "Oh damn . . . ummm . . . baby, baby, baby . . ."

Kendu could feel Milan's warm milk drown his manhood as he plummeted in and out of her, causing her to belt out what she had bottled up inside of her all this time: "I love you."

Before he could think of how he needed to respond, especially since he wasn't the best at formulating his thoughts into words, his blessings exploded into her.

A few minutes into catching their breath, Kendu kissed Milan on the lips. "I don't want to only be friends anymore."

"I know." She kissed him.

"I just need you to understand that I got some shit going on . . ."

"I know . . ."

"And with my daughter." He shook his head. "I'm scared as hell to be away from her."

"I thought she'd gotten better. She hasn't been sick in a while."

"She has gotten better, and that's why I've been thinking I need to really leave Evan now. But I can't leave all at once. It's gon' take a minute."

Milan placed her finger against his lips. "Shhh, this is the place where you come to chill, remember?"

After a few hours of making love off and on and moving from the chaise to the center of the bed, Kendu lay asleep, while Milan lay with her head in the center of his chest and stroked his pecs with the tip of her index finger. She hated that she loved him so intensely, because she knew it was a distraction from what she needed to be doing, which was working on getting her own life together. Her life was in disarray, yet she'd awakened feelings in herself that she'd been able to hold at bay or at the very least place in perspective for the last few years, and now she knew she couldn't deny her love anymore.

She didn't like Evan. That was no secret. So fucking her husband didn't rock Milan's core, but what did was the reality that she would be at the bottom of Kendu's short list, and there was the chance that she would end up in the same predicament that she was in with Yusef, where all her hopes, dreams, and desires rested on what he did and how he could afford for them to live.

"Go to sleep," Kendu said groggily as he turned over and ran his fingers through her hair. "Stop thinking." He kissed her. "We'll take care of it in the morning. My lawyer's already on it. So get some rest, 'cause Johnson"—he pointed to his dick—"gets up early in the morning."

"Johnson is already up." Milan slid down his chest. She stared at his dick and then kissed the tip. "Look at all this dick."

"Yeah, you right." Kendu nodded. "Look at all that dick."

"You're so arrogant." She laughed.

"And you love it."

Evan

"I need you to stop fucking with me," Evan said to no one in particular, as she stirred Aiyanna's oatmeal as she'd been doing religiously for the last hour. Tears were aching the back of her eyelids, but she was beyond crying. She felt strangely out of her mind. Not manic, not hyped up and wanting to fight, but she felt her sanity leaving and her mind on the brink of taking her someplace she'd never been before.

At first she thought she could swing with Kendu saying the bare minimum to her, acting as if they were barely roommates, as long as he didn't leave her. But she'd been noticing more and more how he would disappear for days and weekends and she could swear he'd come back with the faint scent of Chanel No. 5 lingering on his body.

"Aiyanna!" she yelled, and a few minutes later Aiyanna skipped into the kitchen.

"Sit down and eat your breakfast before the bus comes."

Aiyanna started shaking her head and swinging her ponytails. "Mommy, I don't like your oatmeal. I only like it when Chef John makes it."

"Shut up, Aiyanna, and eat the shit before you pay for being grown." Evan pointed her finger at her.

"I'm not eating that. It always makes me sick. And I haven't been sick in a while. I don't want to be sick again."

Evan trembled and her eyes began to blink repeatedly. She had to be mistaken because certainly Aiyanna wasn't talking to her like she was the mother and Evan was the child. Maybe Aiyanna needed to be reminded that she wasn't too young or too old to get her ass kicked. "You working on being fucked up," she said, grabbing Aiyanna's face and pressing her fingers deeply into her cheeks. "Do you know what I've been going through to prepare this for you?" She took a spoonful of the oatmeal and shoved it into Aiyanna's parched mouth. "And you have the nerve to tell me what you're not going to eat? You want me to kick your ass, Aiyanna?!" She shoved oatmeal into her mouth again. "Huh?"

Aiyanna was too scared to cry as the oatmeal that she refused to swallow poured out the sides of her mouth. As Evan went to shove another spoonful into her mouth, the school bus blew its horn. "You're lucky," Evan said, squinting into Aiyanna's eyes, "and unless you want your daddy to leave because you're being a bad ass and not listening to me, then you better do what the fuck I tell you to. You understand me, little girl?" Aiyanna couldn't hold it in anymore and her tears rolled over Evan's knuckles. "You understand me?" Evan repeated.

Aiyanna nodded.

"You better, and if you even think about telling your father, I will beat your ass and make sure he never sees you again."

"Bridget," Carl whispered as he secretly filmed Evan, who was so caught up that she hadn't even heard the camera crew come in, "I don't like the look of this."

Bridget smiled. "Shhh, this is a producer's wet-goddamn-dream. This screams Emmy!"

"But she's gone too far," Carl said, obviously distressed.

"You are to film, not play therapist."

Carl looked taken aback. He knew Bridget liked drama, but this was too much. So instead of verbally intervening he dropped a piece of equipment, forcing Evan to turn around as Bridget stared daggers at him with her eyes.

Evan jumped. "Bridget, Carl"—she nodded and looked at the other guys in the camera crew—"how long have you been standing there?"

"Not long." Bridget smiled. "Aiyanna's school bus is outside."

Evan took a paper towel and wiped Aiyanna's mouth. "Go!" She kissed her on the cheek and whispered in her ear, "And remember what I told you."

Jaise

"Ma," Jabril said, "why do I have to pull my pants up?"

"Boy, you better pull 'em up," Jaise said, tight-lipped, as she parked in front of the YMCA, "or I'ma hurt you."

Jabril laughed. "Ma, I'm taller than you."

"And I will still kick yo' tall ass," she said, taking her keys out of her Range Rover ignition. "Now come on."

As they walked up the block Jabril looked at the building they were headed toward and said, "The YMCA! Oh hell no, my boys can't see me in here!"

"You cussin' in my face?"

"I'm sayin' though."

"You're not saying a thing. Now come on."

As they walked inside Jaise hoped the nervousness she felt didn't show on her face. She arched her back as her fitted jeans rode her plump behind and the waist of her blue mink jacket rested on her hips. Her thick MAC lip gloss weighed heavy on her lips as she walked up to Bilal and smiled. "My son and I—"

"Holy shit," Jabril mumbled. "Ma," he said, tight-lipped, looking at Bilal and realizing who he was, "you tryna set me up?"

"Shut up." She turned to him and then back to Bilal. "We were invited to an empowerment group, and I came to see who was speaking."

Bilal smiled and nodded at Jaise. "Really? You came to see who the speaker was going to be?" He looked toward Jabril and held his fist out for a pound. "Wassup?"

"You got it?" Jabril said nervously, then turned to his mother. "Ma, can I speak to you for a minute?"

"Excuse us," Jaise said. She and Jabril stepped to the side. "Yes."

"Ma, what's going on here? You tryna get me arrested? Is this one of those Scared Straight programs or something? You not gon' leave me here, right?"

"Jabril—"

"Ma, I learned my lesson."

"Okay, it's not like that," Jaise said as she spotted Jay-Z walking onto the stage. Jaise pointed. "This is why I brought you here."

"Jay-Z?! Dang, Ma, for real?" He looked toward the gym, which was filling with people. A group of young ladies walked past them. "Excuse me"—Jabril popped his collar—"but the honeys are callin'."

"I bet they are," Jaise said as she walked back over to Bilal and smiled. "I hope the invitation still stands."

"It does."

She looked him over. He was so beautiful that it didn't make sense. Jaise bit her bottom lip in hopes that she would be able to speak without blushing. "I apologize for the way I acted the last time we saw each other."

"Apology accepted."

"I just—"

"Look," Bilal said, "stop explaining yourself and just be yourself. Now come on"—he took hold of her hand "—let's go on and enjoy the show."

Jaise was in heaven watching Jabril throw up his hands and wave them in the air as Jay-Z rapped. It was as if he remembered he was sixteen and could relax and enjoy himself. There were no worries about what his father was doing or, better yet, not doing. No concerns about Robyn saying something inappropriate or jealous hearted. There were no disturbances at all. Simply a day out chillin' with his moms.

"Ma!" Jabril said when the concert was over. "That was the truth! Yo that was hot."

"It was hot, son?"

"Man, please. I just might come back."

Jaise hugged him tightly and Jabril started coughing. "Ma, please, I can't breathe."

She playfully mushed him in the head. "Funny."

"Ma, you can't be doin' all that huggin' and stuff in public. You never know it might be girls walkin' around here tryna be my bust-it babies."

"You better watch your mouth."

"Psych, I'm just playin', Ma."

"You better be," she said.

Jabril looked at Bilal. "Mr. Asante, you ai'ight for a pig, I mean a jake. I mean, you straight. You seem to be okay is what I'm trying to say."

"You know we have a basketball league. I'd like to see you try out."

"Oh no, no sports," Jaise interrupted. "I have seen my share of athletes go down the drain."

"Well, something tells me Jabril just may be different." Bilal smiled at Jaise.

"Exactly, I'm glad somebody recognized," Jabril said as a group of girls walked by. "Excuse me."

Jaise couldn't help but smile. "This was fun," she said after they had found themselves talking about everything under the sun. Jaise couldn't remember when she had been so turned on simply by the words coming out of a man's mouth. "I would like to see you again," she said to Bilal, slyly pinching herself to make sure she wasn't sleeping.

"Yeah?" He gave her a sexy grin. "I would love to see you again."

"Really?" Jaise giggled like a schoolgirl. She knew this was a bold move, but seeing that no one was around she mustered up the nerve to try it. Jaise placed her arms around Bilal's neck and kissed him, and he responded with a gracious and soul-stirring kiss that sent chills, sweet dreams, and sparks through her. The kiss was so intense that Jaise found herself tossing her head back into the palm of his hands as he ran his fingertips through her hair. Breaking their kiss, Jaise said, "Why don't you stop by later?"

"Nah, not yet." He smiled.

Jaise couldn't believe it, an obvious invitation to pussy and here he was turning it down. "And . . . why not . . . ?" She hated to ask but she needed to know.

"Because I would like us to see where this is going first, before I start coming by your house after a certain time at night."

"And how are we supposed to know where this is going?"

"We'll feel it." He kissed her again.

Jaise stared at him. She thought for sure the last man like this was dead. "Good-night." He kissed her on the forehead.

"Good-night," she said, doing her best to keep her legs from buckling as she walked toward the exit. Jabril was standing outside. Once she got to the door she realized Bilal was standing there watching her. She turned to wave bye and threw every ounce of motion into her ocean. When she arrived at her car, she and Jabril slid in and Jaise leaned her head back and closed her eyes. "Please," she whispered to herself, "let him be the one."

Chaunci

Chaunci's posh Times Square office had the perfect view of a *Millionaire Wives Club* billboard with a picture of her standing beside Milan, rocking a fierce wide-brim hat with attitude to match. The picture had been taken before the show began taping, and she wondered if the photograph were to be taken now, would they each smile?

Chaunci's Prada heels clicked as she walked across the tiled floor, decked out in her Norma Kamali teal power suit. She smiled for the camera as they taped her at the office.

"Good morning, everyone," she greeted her staff and sat down at the head of the conference table in her oversized black wing chair. The straight skirt she wore rose slightly up her thigh as she crossed her legs and undid the three buttons down the middle of her suit jacket.

"I would like to discuss a few things for our upcoming issues. I've been thinking about adding a book review section. Any thoughts?"

"I think it's a wonderful idea," Jeneen, one of the staff writers, commented, leading a few of her colleagues to join the discussion.

Chaunci could hear them chatting away, but her mind started to drift as thoughts of Idris distracted her.

Doing her best to refocus on her meeting, Chaunci joined in the discussion with her staff. They moved on from the book review idea to the upcoming cover choices. Once they were all done Chaunci smiled and said, "Thanks, everyone, we'll meet again next week." As she walked out of the conference room her secretary said to her, "You have a stack of mail on your desk, a certified delivery that came a few moments ago, and a special delivery that's waiting for you as soon as you walk into your office."

"Thanks, Danielle," Chaunci said, pushing the double doors to her office open to reveal an array of red and white fully bloomed roses that were set out all over her office. A smile lit up Chaunci's face. She couldn't believe it. She loved flowers. She just didn't know who they were from. She looked up at Bridget, who said, "Is this from the mystery man?"

Chaunci ignored her and read the card: "I'm sorry. Love you and miss you, Edmon."

Chaunci blushed, sat down at her desk, and began sorting through her mail. She noticed that the certified letter was from Manhattan Family Court. Anxiously she tore the envelope open. Her heart pounded as her eyes scanned the letter: a court hearing . . . Idris . . . asking for visitation.

Chaunci couldn't believe it. She wanted to cuss and scream, but she couldn't get the words to come out. Instead tears rolled down her face as the letter slid to the floor. She could hear Bridget gasp as she picked up the letter and read it, but at the moment there was nothing Chaunci could do. She was paralyzed and couldn't move.

Jaise

"Where are you going dressed like that?" Jabril said as he walked into his mother's room without knocking and sat on the edge of her bed. "What kinda clothes are those?"

Jaise stood back and looked at herself in the full-length mirror. She wore a fitted chocolate Yves Saint Laurent halter dress with a V that dipped down the front, showcasing her abundance of cleavage, and caressed her hips like a second layer of skin. The bottom of the dress had two splits on the sides, showing off her Tina Turner legs, and her stiletto heels enhanced her heart-shaped bottom. "I thought I looked nice."

"You look ai'ight"—he waved his right hand from side to side—"but, for real, for real, Ma, you like thirty-five years old and you don't need to be dressing like you're young and everything. All of that you got hanging out," he said, pointing to her cleavage, "that isn't necessary. And where are you going anyway? On a date?"

"Yes, is that okay?"

"I hope it's not Trenton."

"No, it's not."

"Oh, well, I guess maybe you can go then. But, then again, who are you going with?"

"Bilal."

"The cop?"

"Yes."

"Where is he taking you?"

"Out to dinner. Wait a minute." Jaise caught herself. "Why do I have to explain this to you, and why are you asking me so many questions?"

"Just asking." Jabril folded his arms across his chest. "Can you bring me back something to eat?"

"I'm not coming back right away."

"That's cool, just bring it back in like an hour."

"Jabril—" Before Jaise could go on, her doorbell rang, and the nerves in her body settled in her stomach. "Oh, goodness," she said, looking at herself in the mirror again, "how do I look?"

"Well, personally, I think you need to put on a blouse underneath that dress."

She waved her hand. "Never mind, just get the door."

Jabril grumbled, "I have to wait for my food *and* answer the door. Just treat me like a slave."

"Shut up," Jaise said, popping a peppermint in her mouth, "and do what I just told you to do."

Jaise took a series of deep breaths as Jabril opened the door. When she heard Bilal asking Jabril how he'd been, she walked out of her room and made a grand entrance at the top of the stairs. No matter what Jabril said, she knew she looked fabulous and her confirmation was Bilal stopping mid-sentence and stroking his chin. He was dressed to the nines in a gray Armani evening suit and square-toed wing tips.

Jaise smiled. "Mr. Asante, good evening."

"Good evening, Ms. Williams, you look radiant."

"And you as well."

"Oh my God," Jabril groaned.

"What you say, Jabril?" Jaise asked, walking down the stairs.

"I said y'all look hot." He shook his head.

Bilal held out his arm and Jaise took hold. "Good-night, Jabril."

"Good-night?" Jabril frowned while walking her to the door. "You mean good-night until tomorrow morning? So when am I gon' get my food?"

Jaise ignored him as she started looking around for where Bilal's car was. "Bring me a double cheeseburger," she heard Jabril say from behind her.

Bilal removed his keys from his inner suit pocket and pressed the remote for his car alarm. Jaise heard the alarm disarm but she didn't see his car. She prayed like hell that he didn't have the remote for show and his car was actually the city bus pulling up to the curb.

"Bilal, sweetie," she said as gently as possible, "where is your car?"

"Right here." He tapped the hood of a block-long Deuce and a Quarter, rusted green with a faded black ragtop. He opened the door and it practically fell off the hinges, just missing her feet.

"Oh hell no," she mumbled. "What is this?"

"Something wrong?" he asked, smiling.

"Ahhh . . . you know what?" She thought about how he was a cop and his income was more than likely limited. "We can take my car." She pointed. "I think I see a leak or something under there." She pointed to the liquid by his front tire.

"Ma," Jabril called from behind her, "that's his ride? Oh hell no." He cracked up laughing. "I betchu glad Bridget isn't here to see this. Call me, Ma, if you need me to bring my scooter and come get you."

"Close that damn door!" she growled.

Jaise could hear Jabril laughing as he closed the door.

"Look," Bilal said, "if you don't want to go out, let me know. No hard feelings."

"No," she said, "it's fine."

"You sure?"

"Yes," she said as she slid in, "I'm positive."

Jaise sat in the car doing her best not to look around or pay any attention to the sagging vinyl ceiling liner that was touching the top of her head. "You might want to place your hand up there to hold that up. Otherwise the foam underneath might start snowing on you."

"No, this is fine—ahhh!" Jaise screamed and whipped her neck around. "What was that?" she asked as Bilal started the car.

"The engine."

"Geezus."

"Bilal, sweetie." Jaise cleared her throat. "Why are we in the drive-thru for Crown Fried Chicken?"

"What, you rather have Burger King?" He smiled, and she could've slapped the shit out of him. Certainly he was too fine to be this cheap. Already this was the date from hell.

"I think ahhh, I'll pass," she said. "I'm not really that hungry."

"Are you sure? You know what? I'ma get a bucket anyway."

A bucket. Jaise looked around. Maybe this was some shit that Bridget had planned, Bilal was going along with it, and some-how—some way—and somewhere this was going to turn out to be a joke. Oh, wait a minute, maybe—maybe—this was an episode of *Hell Date.* "Bilal, honey," Jaise said in a soft voice. "You know I don't really like practical jokes. I really hate when people pull those."

"Okay, baby. Well, I don't tell jokes. I mean, I like to laugh, but not at someone else's expense."

Jaise felt like screaming, because obviously this motherfucker was serious.

Bilal placed the order and a few minutes later he received an oversized plastic bag, which he placed directly in Jaise's lap. "Hold this for me, baby."

"Sure." Jaise arched her eyebrows and mumbled, "Why the hell not."

"You say something, Jaise?"

"Oh no, I didn't say a thing."

Jaise could've sworn that Bilal's car had hydraulics the way it bumped up and down and then took off like a bat out of hell while they were driving into Harlem. This was crazy. Never in her life, not even in high school, had she experienced any shit like this. When they pulled up in front of the concrete box that Bilal insisted on calling a club, she knew right away she was dumping his ass. Forget it. He was nice, extremely fine, and he was the only man who made her wet simply by the words that came out of his mouth, but if this was what he was working with, she didn't want it. "What is this?" Jaise struggled not to frown.

"It's a cool spot. They have live blues, and remember you told me you would sing for me?"

"I could've sang for you after we had dinner at Tavern on the Green. We didn't need to come here."

Bilal tilted his head to the side and gave Jaise a sexy grin. "You go in here, we have fun, and believe me there is more where this came from. Loosen up, I promise you'll like it."

Jaise hated that all he had to do was smile and she was putty in his hands.

Bilal grabbed the bag from her lap and Jaise noticed three grease spots on her dress. "Hold your head down for a minute, baby." Bilal started dusting bits of yellow foam residue that had fallen into Jaise's hair. "It's out now."

Before Jaise could think of what to say or how she should feel, Bilal walked around the car and opened the door. Jaise could see that he was holding the door up so that it wouldn't hit the ground and drop off. She clutched her purse to her chest like an extra heartbeat as she walked in. The place was called Lucille's, and apparently it was a chicken and waffles joint. They supplied free waffles, dollar shots, and the customer supplied the chicken.

"Bilal," the owner, Lucille, called out to him. Lucille was about sixty with hair dyed the wrong shade of red for her brown complexion. She was what most people would call big-boned, but she had bird legs. She kissed Bilal on the cheek. "Nice to see you remember an old woman. I almost divorced you." She had a serious South Carolina drawl.

Bilal laughed. "You too much, Lucille." After placing the plastic bag on the counter he placed his arm around Jaise's waist. "Lucille, this is a dear friend of mine, Jaise."

"Nice to meet you, honey, and welcome to my place. Have a seat." She pointed to the bar stool. Jaise started to ask would a table be too much to ask for, but seeing that there were only a few and the place was packed, she decided against it and instead when Bilal pulled out her bar stool she sat down.

Bilal unbuttoned his suit jacket and laid it on the stool next to him. "I know this is different for you."

Jaise attempted to laugh. "Oh no, I dine like this all the time."

Jaise blew air out the side of her mouth as live blues played in the background. Lucille took their chicken and placed it in a white bowl next to a stack of homemade waffles. She gave them two plates, cutlery, and two shots of White Owl.

Jaise watched Bilal begin to eat his chicken. There was so much grease on the plate that she could feel her arteries clogging just from the sight. She did her best to take her mind off the food, but the waffles smelled too inviting.

"Forget it," Jaise said under her breath. "When in Rome, or better yet the ghetto . . ." She took one of the wings from Bilal's plate and covered it with hot sauce.

"How you gon' take my wing?" Bilal laughed. "And the last wing at that? I didn't take any of your waffles."

"You can have some," she said, breaking off a piece with her fork and placing it to his lips. Bilal looked her dead in the eyes as he slid it off her fork with his tongue. Jaise almost lost control. She had to fan her face just to bring herself back.

After a while of eating some of the best cardiac-clogging fried chicken and sweetest waffles in the world, Jaise forgot about being

174 · *Tu-Shonda L. Whitaker*

dressed in a five-thousand-dollar dress with grease spots, two-thousand-dollar shoes, and carrying a fifteen-hundred-dollar handbag. She didn't even think about how she'd ridden in a car that looked as if a broke-down Foxy Brown and Shaft should be stepping out of it.

All Jaise could see was this man sitting next to her whom she was feeding from her plate. The very man who was making her laugh, genuinely laugh, and making her forget everything that had ever haunted her. Not even her father had been able to chase this many demons away. Jaise leaned over and graced Bilal with a soft kiss.

"Sing for me," he whispered against her lips.

Jaise eyed both sides of the small and dim one-room juke joint. She could tell that not much had changed in this place since Lucille had opened it in the seventies, yet Jaise felt nervous. It wasn't that she couldn't sing. She'd been able to sing since she was five, and sang at her grandmother's funeral and brought everybody, including the pastor, to their feet. Oh, she could sing, but she'd never in her life felt as nervous as this. "Alright," she said shyly, "I'll sing."

Bilal winked his eye at the piano player as Jaise eyed the people in the place. Different people had been singing all night, some blues songs they created on the spot and others, songs that were classics. And those who didn't sing danced until their heart was full.

Jaise stepped onto the makeshift stage, which was a wood platform set about an inch off the floor. She whispered her song selection to the pianist and stepped up to the mic. "I'm a little shy, y'all," she said, laughing as she addressed the audience.

"That's all right, sugar-doll," one of the old men in the audience yelled, " 'cause big daddy is just the one to work all that shyness out of you."

"Hush, Willie!" Lucille said. "Always got somethin' nasty to say." She looked at Jaise. "Sing, baby."

Jaise sucked in a breath and on the internal count of three she opened her mouth and pure bliss floated through the air. She had the sultry voice of Aretha Franklin with a killer range. She looked at Bilal and sang "Natural Woman."

Jaise sang like she had never sung in her life. Couples slow danced across the floor, and though the place was full, the only person Jaise could see was Bilal.

Jaise didn't know what to make of what she was feeling. She didn't believe in love at first sight. It was too sappy, too fairy-tale, too much like Cinderella. She didn't have that kind of faith, but she knew that something was different. Her heart beat a little faster when she was around him, her smile grew wider, and her blush a little higher. Maybe love at first sight didn't exist, but she had no doubt at this moment that paradise did.

When she was done, everyone who wasn't already standing stood to their feet and clapped feverishly.

Before Jaise could say thank you, she heard a familiar voice saying it for her. "Thank you, thank you." She turned and there was a crying Bridget, walking out of a blackened corner with Carl, pointing a mini video camera at her and wiping his eyes. "That was beautiful," Bridget said. "I had no idea that following you around would lead to this, but that was beautiful. Carl," Bridget said, sniffing, "mental note: When they edit this, play *As the World Turns* music right here."

Jaise shook her head, astonished at the lengths Bridget had gone to. Jaise walked offstage and into Bilal's embrace. "Now, that was beautiful," he said.

"Thank you," she said as they began to kiss passionately. "Thank you."

Milan

It was déjà vu. Karma. A life full of desolate boomerangs that would set Milan up to have an affair with Kendu for the second time in her life, yet with no real possibility of their ever being together. When she had decided to leave Yusef she had plans, but ever since she had become Kendu's mistress . . . again . . . she hadn't followed through with any of them. If anything, she felt herself slowly accepting the role she'd become known for: the waiter. Waiting for him to come over, waiting for him to find the right moment to leave his everyday life and be with her, waiting for him to leave his wife, waiting, waiting, and more fucking waiting. Denying herself and doing everything on his time because this was the only way to perfect the role she'd been assigned to play.

She was tired, tired of always feeling like his wife's understudy. If Kendu didn't love Evan, then he needed to leave the bitch, and if he didn't want to leave her, then Milan had to be a big girl about it and realize that once again she had brought the ruckus on herself. So as she lay next to him, his broad chest and hard stomach pressed into her back, she decided that it would be the perfect time to test him and see just how far he'd be willing to go to make her happy.

Milan knew Kendu loved to be awakened with his dick being sucked. It was a freaky thing she liked to please him with. He was more than filling, and sucking him required a certain technique; otherwise the thickness and the length of his Johnson would cause her to gag.

"Shit, baby," Kendu said, his eyes still closed, and his hands running through her hair. "That feels so good." The slurping sounds of her mouth were a beautiful melody, like a Picasso painting turned into music. Once Milan was done and Kendu had complimented her skills by calling her name and filling her mouth with salty rain, he flipped her over and returned the favor, by eating her from the back wall of her dripping sex. Kendu's tongue was a python, so it never took Milan long to cum, and within a matter of minutes they were joined as one, their heads spinning, their bodies dancing, and their mouths making promises that neither of them could keep.

After they'd graced each other with orgasms and had taken their morning shower together, they lay back on the bed and Milan noticed Kendu watching the clock. This was his routine; at first it seemed mundane, then it was aggravating, and slowly it had become heartbreaking. In the beginning he would spend tranquil nights with her, then he started coming at around midnight, after Aiyanna was asleep, making love, and then leaving before six in the morning so he could return home before Aiyanna awoke for school.

It was now five a.m.

Milan stroked the hair on his chest. "Kendu, I was thinking that we should go away."

"Go away?" He slid his hands over her ass. "Go where?" He peeked at the clock.

Milan could feel him easing toward the edge of the bed, so instead of continuing to trace along his eightpack, she lay on top of him. "I've always wanted to tour my namesake in Italy."

He looked at the clock again. "I don't know when I'll be able to do that."

"Why not? You're out on injury, and I can take a few days off. Surely you can take some time and spend it with me?"

"Milan," he said, exhausted, his eyes reflecting the electric red from the digital clock. "I can't do that right now. Maybe in the summer, when Aiyanna is out of school."

"What, are we taking her?"

"No, but I have to make arrangements with Evan."

"Why?"

"What do you mean, why?" He was clearly aggravated at the question. "She's Aiyanna's mother, and you know that Aiyanna is always sick. Suppose the doctors get a breakthrough and I'm not here?"

"Yeah, suppose, Kendu." She rose from the bed and started slipping her clothes on.

"I'm not leaving my daughter." He sat up and draped the sheet across his lap.

"I didn't ask you to leave her. I just asked you to love me! Talk to me at least. I'm sick of guessing how you feel and what stage we're at. I feel like Zorro's sideline ho and shit. I can't compete with this," she said more to herself than to him.

Kendu sighed. "You don't have anything to compete with. You know how I feel."

"Yeah, Knott," she said sarcastically, "the wind told me."

"What do you want me to tell you, Milan? That I love you? You know that. You've always known that."

"And how is that?"

"Because I told you that already."

Milan laughed. She couldn't help it. "You haven't told me you loved me since the day before you married that bitch. Now, somehow I'm supposed to hold on to that same 'I love you'? That motherfucker had a 'but' at the end. 'I love you, *but* she's pregnant. So what's the 'but' now? I love you *but* the baby is sick? You think I want that type of love, really? Spare me the goddamn grief, please."

"You know what? I can't do this right now," Kendu said dismissively. "I have to help Evan get Aiyanna ready for school, and then we can continue this discussion, alright?"

"No, Kendu, it's not alright. I'm fuckin' tired!"

"Tired of what, Milan? You can't set up expectations for me. You knew I was married. You and I have always had this understanding."

"What understanding?! That I should be second, excuse me, I mean third. Well, shit, if you count football, fourth. I don't want that anymore."

"Milan, do you know the turmoil I'm going through right now to be here with you? My daughter is chronically ill, and I'm over here with you chillin' in a damn hideaway, like this shit is cool. Well, it's not, and if something happened to my kid I would never forgive myself for this."

Milan blinked. She felt like he'd put a gun to her head and pulled the trigger. "Well, Kendu," she said, now completely dressed in fitted jeans, a periwinkle sweater with a leather Louis Vuitton belt around her waist, and pencil-heel ostrich boots, "stop coming back and you can end the turmoil. And as far as your sick kid, it's awfully funny how whenever you're home she's not sick, but when you stay away too long she's back on the critical list. Yeah, you better go home so you can see if your doting wife is giving your kid a nightcap of Pine-Sol and piss."

"I don't believe you said something like that."

"Well, I said it." She grabbed her leather jacket and stormed toward the door. "Now, there's your excuse to leave me the fuck alone."

"Milan," Kendu called out to her, "wait."

She pointed at him as her hobo Louis Vuitton bag slid down her arm. "No, you fuckin' wait!" And she slammed the door behind her.

"You better have a good reason why you are at my front door on the very day that I took off to sleep in." Chaunci yawned as she opened the door and Milan stepped into her two-story apartment.

Before Milan could answer, Kobi, who was dressed for school, came running toward Milan with her bookbag flopping up and down on her back. "Ms. Milan!" She hugged Milan around the legs.

"Kobi! How's my little girl?"

"I miss you."

"And I miss you."

Kobi started to laugh. "Ms. Milan, remember sometimes I would come to your house and you used to burn your food and Mr. Yusef would say, 'Da Truef, Da Truef, Da Truef's tongue is on fire!' "

"That's enough, Kobi," Chaunci warned.

"I'm just saying that Mr. Yusef was funny, Mommy. Ms. Milan"—Kobi turned back to her—"did you know that Mr. Yusef is homeless now? Me and Anty Dextra see him all the time, with a coffee can, telling people that they can get his autograph for three dollars."

"Go!" Chaunci pointed. "Go and tell Anty Dextra that it's time for you to go to school—"

"Mommy—"

"Now!"

Kobi held her head down. "Bye, Ms. Milan. I guess this is one of those 'Kobi's too grown' moments. Now I have to go to school."

"Bye, Kobi." Milan walked over to her, kissed her on the cheek, and said, "Have a good day at school."

"I apologize for that, Milan," Chaunci said.

"Girl, please, out of the mouths of babes come the truth. Besides, she's adorable." Milan followed Chaunci into the kitchen where the chef was preparing breakfast.

"Will you be dining with us?" the chef asked Milan.

"I'm not really hungry," Milan said.

"She'll be staying," Chaunci interjected. "You have to eat something." Chaunci turned to Milan. "I know I'm beautiful, but I know you didn't come over here just to look at me."

"Will you be dining on the terrace this morning, Ms. Morgan?" the chef asked.

"Yes." Chaunci smiled. "We'll be on the terrace."

The early morning spring air was incredibly warm as the golden sun shone into their faces. They sat down at the mosaic-tile bistro set and placed white linen napkins in their laps. A few minutes later the chef dressed the table with fresh fruit, croissants, orange juice, coffee, bacon, and cheese omelets.

Chaunci sipped her coffee. "So what's up?"

"Girl, you know Prada came out with some fly red patent leather shoes and a matching bag?" Milan sipped her orange juice from a flute glass.

"What?" Chaunci frowned. "You didn't come over here to talk about Prada."

"I can't just come over now?"

"Of course, but you didn't *just* come over. You have a reason, so what's going on?"

Milan sighed. "Okay." She placed her glass on the table and began eating her omelet. "If I tell you something, I don't want you to judge me. I just want you to listen."

"What are you going to tell me, that you're having an affair with him?"

"With who?"

"Kendu."

"Didn't I ask you to listen?"

"I'm listening."

"And how do you know it's Kendu?"

"Because I remember how you looked at him the night of the charity gala, and I knew then that either you were sleeping with him or you would be. It's just that when Jaise called it, I denied it and checked her. But I knew the truth."

"Jaise? So you were discussing me with Jaise, that bitch? What, are you two friends now?"

"She's okay, and no, we're not friends, and we weren't discussing you. I was more or less defending you. Look"—Chaunci sighed—"would you just tell me what you have to say?"

"Well . . ." Milan hesitated. "You're right about me and Kendu."

"How long?"

"About a month. When the apartment was foreclosed on he came and got me, and the place where I'm staying in SoHo is his spot, where he goes to get away."

"Get away and what? Have an affair with you?"

"There you go, passing judgment," Milan said, sucking her teeth.

"I haven't passed judgment on you just yet. I need to see how far in the valley you are first."

"Iyanla Vanzant may write a column for you, but I don't need you practicing her relationship tips on me."

"I'm sure. Now go on."

"I just wish he would leave his wife."

"Did he tell you he would?"

"Not in those words exactly, but he loves me."

"Oh, I see, umm-hmm."

"And you know his daughter is really sick."

"Sick, huh? Umm-hmm."

"Would you stop that?" Milan snapped.

"You asked me to listen." Chaunci popped a piece of bacon in her mouth. "I'm listening."

"I'm just saying that this is hard to deal with. I have a lot going on."

"Did you tell Kendu how you felt?"

"Yeah, we had an argument this morning, and I told him I was just tired of loving him and it's always a conjunction at the end."

"What, I love you *but* I have a crazy-ass wife, a sick kid, and I need you to stay in your place just until the right moment comes and I can, what"—Chaunci tapped her bottom lip—"leave?"

"This is why I don't like to confide in you."

"Oh, girl, please. You knew I was not going to babysit you, especially when you're wrong."

"Kendu and I were friends before he ever knew Evan."

"Then he should've married you. But the moment he took on a wife was the moment you should've fallen back. All the way back." Chaunci laughed. "You know that's some shady shit you're doing, though, right? How can you sleep with your costar's husband? I don't like Evan either, but damn."

"But it's not like we planned it, it just happened. You know what? Forget it, just drop it."

"What, is that code word for 'I'm pissed with you for telling me the truth'? Please"—Chaunci rolled her eyes—"you know I don't care if you get mad. I mean, you're still my sistah girl, and if any of them bitches come out of their faces wrong, you know I'm armed, but I like to fight battles I can win. And if Evan finds out and loses her mind on your ass, I'ma get in it, but I'ma be slow gettin' there."

"You don't understand, everything is not black-and-white."

"Milan, this is crazy. Do you plan on looking at yourself, or are you too focused on upgrading your choice of the male species? From one athlete to the next?"

"It's not like that with us. We are in love."

"Do I need to get a tape recorder so I can play back how you sound?"

"He really doesn't want to be married to Evan."

"Then he needs to divorce her, not fuck you. If he's so concerned about his ill daughter, why is he rendezvousing with you?"

"You are being way too critical. Listen to me, he loves me, but the shit is complicated. He comes to the loft between the hours of eleven and about five-thirty or so, and then he leaves to go back home to be with Aiyanna and so forth."

"Okay, so not only are you not worthy of being the wife, or him leaving his wife—the very wife that you claim he doesn't love—he now has you on a schedule? That's some rotten shit."

"You're only saying that because you don't really know him."

"I don't want to know him. I don't need to know him. You are my friend and all I'm saying is this: I'm sure he loves you or he feels something, but, and there's the conjunction, he is attached to his life with his wife. Even if she is causing him drama, he likes to be in the midst of it; otherwise he would leave. And he has enough money so that everyone could go their separate ways and financially be okay. This isn't your average run-of-the-mill 'who's going to get the house or pay the mortgage' type of thing."

"He's not leaving, because of his daughter."

"If his daughter is so sick and he can't be without her, how does he find time to have this affair with you—"

"But—"

"Let me finish. You need to set some standards. You have hopped out of one man's bed and straight into another's. Stop that. If this man loves you, then he'll understand that you have some things to do for you. He's taking care of his business. You need to think about yours, because apparently you didn't fall on your ass hard enough, and if losing your marriage, your money, and your home wasn't enough for you to wake up and see that you need to take care of yourself, then you have more issues than I thought."

"And you say all that to say what?"

"Get your shit together."

Both women were silent for a moment. "So you think it's that easy?" Milan asked.

"I know it's not. But when Kobi's father left me I had to get over that, so I know what it is to love a man who has a lot of other things going on. But I also know what it's like to have your own."

"So you don't ever want to love again?"

"I have Edmon."

Before either of them could say anything they both fell out laughing. "You're wrong for that, and you have the nerve," Milan said, "to talk about me?"

"Girl, Edmon and I have an understanding."

"What, that he's pussy whipped?"

"It's more than that."

"Like what, because I already know you don't love him."

"I do love him. I'm just cautious about it."

"And why is that?"

"Because she who loves least controls the relationship. That's why I'm able to sleep in and you're stressed."

"True, but he who has more money certainly has an upper hand, and that, my dear, is why you're marrying Edmon."

"Not true. I'm marrying Edmon—"

"Because at thirty it's the thing to do."

"No," Chaunci said, "because he will be a good husband and a wonderful provider."

"Still scorned, huh?"

"I am not scorned." Chaunci sucked her teeth.

"Oh, okay, I see."

"I mean I loved Kobi's father, 'loved' being the operative word."

"You need to stop. Now, we're girls, so tell me, do you still love him?" Milan held her index finger up. "And don't give me no article, page four, under the 'I'll never love again' section of your magazine bullshit. Tell me as your friend, do you love him?"

Chaunci sighed, and her heart filled her throat. She hated that she'd been put on the spot. Because to say she still loved Idris after all these years would somehow feel as if she was admitting defeat. "I haven't been pining over him all of these years or anything. I just made up my mind that I had a mission and I couldn't let anyone get in the way."

"Is that a yes?"

"I can't bring myself to say yes."

"You just did."

"No, I didn't. If I admit that I love Idris, then that would be like saying that it's okay the way he treated me. It's okay that he paid me three hundred dollars to get rid of my daughter, because he saw my pregnancy as a problem. It was okay for him to do all that he wanted to me because no matter what I would be there for him. Well, no, it's not okay."

"So you're in love with him and you're scared?"

"It's a little more complicated than that."

"No, it's not. Love is simple. You love him. It's the other shit that's complicated."

"I can't just have him swing back into my life as if what he did was cool."

"Maybe he's a different person. Have you spoken to him since the gala?"

"Too many damn times. He showed up here one time. I saw him at a restaurant another time. I feel like he's suddenly everywhere."

"Does he want to see Kobi?"

"Yes, he does, but no, he's not."

"Why? Don't put her in the middle of that. My mother did that to me and it was horrible."

"Look, when you're a single mother raising your baby alone, and you've already been through the shitty-ass diapers, the teething, day care, and all that other stuff and you finally get to a point where you think you can handle everything on your own, the last thing you need is for the deadbeat to become Daddy the Superhero and decide he should stake claim."

"That's between you and the deadbeat, not the kid, not Kobi, who deserves her daddy. And maybe, Chaunci, he's a different man now. Perhaps he's changed."

"Then why is he taking me to court?"

"To court?" Milan said, surprised.

"Yes, can you imagine the nerve? As much as black men hate 'the man' telling him what to do, he takes me to court."

"He wants to see his daughter. Why don't you talk to Idris and maybe you two can come to some type of agreement. If I were you I'd rather work something out with him on my own than have some damn judge who considers me another case telling me what to do with my child."

"Idris can go to hell! I had to take my child to a damn lab for a blood test because of him. Do you know how humiliating that is?"

"Don't mess around and walk out of the courtroom crying. Just talk to Idris."

"Fuck him."

"With all that anger, you probably will, and soon, too." Milan laughed.

Chaunci sucked her teeth. "I'm not sleeping with him ever again. Not that I have any bad memories, and unless he fell off, he knew how to hit it. But his knowing how to groove says nothing to me about what type of father he would be."

"Well, I think he and Kobi deserve a chance to find out."

"Look at you trying to give me advice."

"You need to take some of my passion, mix it with your determination, and give the man a chance."

"Umm-hmm, what-the-hell-ever, now finish telling me about these Prada shoes."

Milan didn't return to Kendu's place until late in the afternoon. She was determined that she was going to pack her things and start looking for a place of her own. Maybe even stay with Chaunci until she found one, because there was no way she could stay here. She looked at her watch and realized that she had a few hours left to get her things together before Kendu showed up again.

On opening the door Milan was surprised to see Kendu sitting there with a beer in his hand and smoke rising from the cigar in the corner of his mouth. The beautiful sight alone started chiseling her resistance away.

Kendu mashed the cigar in the ashtray and placed the beer on the table. He stood up and walked over to Milan. "We need to talk."

"Kendu—"

"If you still hate me and you're thinking about leaving me I'll understand, but I have thought about this all day and I need you to know that I love you. I love you like crazy, until the shit is sick. I have never experienced anything like this, and I know that I take you for granted, and I apologize for that, but I can't apologize for wanting to be with my daughter."

"I'm not asking for that. I know she's sick."

"It's more than that, though. Listen, before I was adopted I lived in like ten other homes, and I thought there was no one in the world who would love me, who looked like me or wanted to be around me for long. I mean, hell, all I had of my biological family was their last name. But I never knew who I was. Did I have my father's nose, my mother's smile? My grandfather's laugh? What did I have? I always felt like the kid who could be given away. And don't get me wrong, I love my adopted parents, but when Evan got pregnant and I thought about how I was finally going to have someone in this world who belonged to me, who resembled me, who was related to me, I felt like, yeah, this has to be it."

"Did it hurt me to leave you alone?" He pulled her close. "Hell yeah, but I had to be a man and I had to claim my family. I had to, because I couldn't have my kid feeling like I did."

"So what happens in the meantime?" she said as he pressed his forehead against hers.

"I don't know, Milan. I know I'm not lying to you. I know that

I love you and that I am going to leave Evan, but I just need a minute," he spoke against her lips.

"I don't know how many more minutes I have left." She slid her arms around his neck.

"Then just give me now," he said as they started to kiss passionately and he laid her on the bed. "Just give me right now."

Evan

It was official: He was having an affair. The two private eyes she'd hired had both told her the same thing: From around midnight to five in the morning he was spending time with another woman. They hadn't identified the woman, but they'd been able to get a few pictures, one with the two of them kissing and the other with them making love, the woman's back pressed up against the window with the New York City skyline illuminated behind them.

Instead of crying Evan smiled. The pictures let her know that she wasn't going crazy. It was Milan, the bitch who once again was destroying her life. It had been the same thing when they were in college. Milan fucking Kendu behind her back. No one thought she knew, because she one-upped Milan's ass and had a baby. But now what was she to do? Kendu wouldn't touch her. He didn't like her, he didn't want her, and he had the nerve to tell her so. He didn't see his cheating when they were in school as detrimental to how she felt back then; he could see only himself and how he felt now.

But she couldn't lose him, that was no secret, and since begging him hadn't worked, Evan could think of only one thing left to do. She had to do what her stepfather loved for her to do when he wanted his "special girl, really bad." She had to pretend to be the very person Kendu must've wanted her to be: Milan.

After she had swallowed her daily cocktail of Vicodin and alcohol, Evan's head was spinning as she struggled to draw a mole above her upper lip with black lip liner. The hazel contacts she wore irritated her, and she couldn't seem to shade the circle in without smudging it. After giving up on having the perfect beauty mark, Evan moved on to fingering her two-thousand-dollar infusion weave that draped jaggedly over her shoulders.

"Who'd you dress up like a slut for?" she heard her mother's voice whispering in her ear.

"Daddy wants me to wear this dress and perfume," she responded. "I don't like it when he wants me to dress up. I don't like the nasty things he does to me."

"So what do you want him to do? Leave? You want us to be out in the street with nothing? You selfish little bitch! You know you like it . . . you know you like it! You do! You do!"

"Stop it!" Evan screamed, banging her fist on the mirror and causing the glass to crack and spread like a spider's web. She shook her head and relaxed her shoulders. She had to get her thoughts together in order to pull this off.

A few seconds later she sprayed Chanel No. 5 all over her body and then she slid on a sleeveless fitted black dress. Her new eagle tattoo shimmered against her cleavage. She slid on black satin elbow gloves, placed her black garden hat on her head, and allowed the small veil to drape directly over her eyes. Finally she was beautiful.

She stepped out of the bathroom and watched Kendu as he lay sleeping in their bed. Evan eased into the bed next to Kendu and ran the tip of her index finger between the indent of his muscular pecs.

Kendu opened his eyes as he lay between sleep and wake. "Milan," he whispered. "Damn."

"Shhhh." She placed her index finger over his soft lips.

Kendu opened his eyes wide and looked down. "Evan . . . ?"

"No." She shook her head. "It's Milan."

Kendu's heart pounded in his chest. He looked down at Evan, stunned. He couldn't believe his eyes. She almost looked like Milan: the contacts, the hair, the mole above her lip. The perfume.

But then again, Evan wouldn't do something like that. Not Evan, she was too vain. This was a coincidence. It had to be.

Evan didn't have time to wonder what he was thinking. She could tell by the sound of his voice that he wanted her to stop, but she couldn't. She ran her tongue down the center of his washboard chest.

He looked down at her. "Evan, get up."

"No, not Evan." She licked the tip of his dick and swallowed him whole.

"I said stop. Now get up."

She sucked in her inner cheeks and by the way his eyes rolled to the back of his head she knew she had him right where she needed him. "Shhh," she assured him. "I need this—we need this."

"I said stop." Kendu paused. Her tongue tricks were ridiculous, and he wished he could control his hard-on, but he couldn't. "Stop." He gripped the back of her head and slipped his thick and heavy dick from between Evan's lips. "No."

As he turned away and rose from the bed, Evan grabbed his hand. "You don't mean that. I need you to put it in."

Kendu looked at her and wondered, *Did she even know who she was anymore?*

As he backed out of the room Aiyanna was running in the door from school. "How's Daddy's girl?" he said, sweeping her into his arms and slyly closing the door on Evan, who was kneeling on the floor.

"Is Mommy mad?" Aiyanna asked.

"No, baby," he said. "I tell you what, how about if I get the chauffeur to take you to Granny's house so Daddy can talk to Mommy a little bit."

"Daddy, we're supposed to go out to dinner, remember?"

Evan rose from the floor and looked in the mirror. She hated herself. She hated what she'd come to be, so she picked up the scissors and started cutting her hair, until it fell like snowflakes. Patches of hair were everywhere. "You stupid bitch!" she snapped at herself. "You stupid bitch!" She started slicing her arms with the scissors, carving S.B. in them. Afterward she started punching herself, repeatedly, until all she could see was blood running over her eyes.

Evan heard Kendu convincing Aiyanna that he needed to do something for her, that he had to take her somewhere. The same speech that her father had given her when her mother had a nervous breakdown and never came back again.

Evan felt light-headed and fell to the floor, but she had just enough strength to pick herself up and grab her car keys. She staggered through the French doors of the bedroom to the outside, got into her car, and placed it in gear.

"Evan!" she could hear Kendu screaming behind her, as she headed toward the highway.

Evan started to feel dizzy and all she could see was the barrier up ahead. She thought she would be able to stop, but she couldn't remember which pedal her foot needed to be on for the car to brake, so she continued going until there was a loud crash and the next thing she knew she was hearing the sound of sirens blaring and feeling an IV needle being shoved into her arm.

"Thank God she made it," Evan heard the doctor saying to the nurse as Evan opened her eyes one at a time. The nurse walked over and took her pulse. "How are you feeling?" she asked.

Evan nodded.

"Okay, well, you need your rest," the doctor said, and then he and the nurse left.

Evan lay dressed in all white beneath the white hospital sheets, counting the hours, the minutes, and the seconds before Kendu would come rushing through the door on his white horse, realizing that he'd literally driven her to this point.

"Evan." She heard Kendu call her name before she saw his face. Immediately her eyes looked at the clock. It had taken three hours, fifteen minutes, and ten seconds for him to come through the door.

"I'm here." Her voice was raspy. "I was waiting for you."

Kendu walked over to her, the faint scent of Chanel No. 5 continuing to linger on him. "I had to wait for the nurse to give me the okay to come in. How do you feel?"

"Happy."

He looked at her hair and touched the cut and uneven pieces. "What happened to your hair?"

"Nothing, it's perfect."

Kendu paused. "I'm worried about you."

"Excuse me," the doctor said, walking into the room. "Mr. Malik?"

Kendu turned to him. "Yes," he said.

"Your wife gave everyone a little scare."

"I'm okay though." Evan struggled to smile. "Just a little sore."

The doctor patted her hand. "Well, you get some rest. I need to speak with your husband for a few minutes."

"Knott." Evan reached for Kendu's hand, and he unintentionally took a step back. She never called him Knott, that was the name Milan called him. "Will you come back before you leave?"

Kendu paused, still caught off guard. "Yeah, sure." He walked behind the doctor toward a secluded section of the hallway.

"Mr. Malik," the doctor said, "I have serious concerns about your wife. Do you know where she was going?"

"No." Kendu hunched his shoulders. "We had an argument and she wasn't herself."

"What do you mean?"

"She was dressed up like someone else. And pretending to really be that person. I'm worried, Doctor. I'm really scared for her."

"There are some concerns. Your wife has a high level of Vicodin in her blood."

"What? What is that?"

"Prescription medication painkillers."

"Evan doesn't take any prescriptions."

"Does you wife have any history of illnesses, mental illnesses?"

"Something's going on."

"We found some cutting on her arm. It looks like she carved initials. Does she have a history of self-mutilation?"

"Self-what?"

"Mutilation. It's when people cut themselves, believing they can relieve their own pain."

"Pain from what?"

"Something traumatic. Is there anything going on between you and your wife? You said there was an argument."

"We're in the process of separating."

"Well, that may be it, or it could be something else. I would like to keep her here for a seventy-two-hour observation."

"Seventy-two-hour observation?" Kendu said, taken aback.

"I'm concerned that Mrs. Malik may have had a nervous breakdown."

Silence.

"I would like to commit her for seventy-two hours, but after that she has to be in agreement to stay, otherwise we can't keep her."

"Well, what should I do? Should I tell her?" Kendu asked.

"No, we gave her some medication that will make her sleep. It should've already taken effect. So if you'd like you can go home and come back a little later. If something changes one of the nurses will give you a call."

"No," Kendu said, "I would like to stay with her, at least for a few hours, if that's okay?"

"Okay," the doctor agreed, "for a few hours."

Kendu walked into Evan's room and she was sleeping. He sank down into the chair beside her and wondered if his rejection of her had made her crazy. It was true he wanted to leave her, but he didn't want to leave her in pieces. He could feel the fading heat from the sun going down as he looked at Evan's face, studied the slight smile she wore, and wondered what she was dreaming about.

Chaunci

"Tell the camera how you feel today, Chaunci," Carl said as he pointed the camera at her.

Before Chaunci could comment, Bridget said, "I want some emotion, some tears and drama. Curse the judge"—she flung one arm in the air—"curse Idris"—she flung the other—"and plead for us to understand that you are a good mother."

Chaunci didn't have it in her to cuss out Bridget, especially knowing it would get her nowhere. She actually hated that the cameras were following her around today and that the crew didn't see this as a true invasion of her privacy. But then again, what privacy?

She watched Idris walk up the block dressed in a camel-colored two-piece Versace suit, looking as if he were headed for a game he planned to win.

Chaunci smiled at Carl. "I feel fine. I'm sure the judge will see"—she looked Idris dead in the eyes—"that I love my daughter and that Idris has no right to come along demanding things."

Carl turned to Idris, who was passing them by. "You have anything to say?"

He nodded. "Yeah. Chaunci needs to learn to forgive." And he walked past the stone lion statue and into the courthouse. His smooth swagger lingered on the concrete steps behind him.

Chaunci walked into the courthouse and was greeted by her attorney, Sarah Washington, who walked over to her and smiled. "Good morning."

"Good morning."

"I have an offer for you that Mr. Lawson's attorney presented to me this morning."

"Is it one saying that he will go away?" Chaunci tapped her three-inch heels as she caught Idris staring at her.

"No, he's not going away," Sarah assured her. "He's put in his offer for child support—"

"I don't want his money."

"Hear me out, Chaunci."

"Sarah, I'm serious."

"Listen to me. I am your attorney, and though I will present to the court what your wishes are, it is my responsibility to give you the best advice. Mr. Lawson wants a relationship with his daughter, and the only way we could have made him go away was if the DNA test had come back negative, which it didn't. So let's consider the plea they're offering: joint custody, twenty thousand a month in child support, the first meeting at your house or a mutual place that is comfortable for the child, every other weekend during the basketball off-season, and one weekend a month during on-season. Alternate holidays."

"Absolutely not."

"Why not?"

"My daughter doesn't know him. Now I'm supposed to dump her off at his house? No, no way."

"What do you think the judge is going to give you?"

"I'll take my chances," Chaunci said, as the bailiff walked into the hall to announce that court was now in session.

"All rise," the bailiff said as the judge walked in. "Judge Randall presiding."

"You may be seated," the judge said. "We have here Lawson versus Morgan on the matter of joint custody, child support, and visitation. Have the parties come to any type of agreement?"

Idris's attorney looked toward Sarah and Chaunci. "No, Your Honor," Sarah said. "We have not."

"Are you all aware of the paternity test results?"

"Yes," Sarah said. "We've received the positive results."

"Fine," the judge said. "Now, let's hear the arguments."

"My client wishes to see his daughter," Idris's attorney said to the judge. "We were hoping to come to an agreement, but it seems that Ms. Morgan simply wishes for my client to go away so that she can go on pretending that he doesn't exist."

"And your reason for not accepting the offer?" The judge looked to Sarah.

"With all due respect, Your Honor, Mr. Lawson doesn't know his daughter. As a matter of fact, he paid Ms. Morgan three hundred dollars to have an abortion. He has never even seen this child, and I'm certain the court understands that Ms. Morgan does not feel comfortable handing her child over to Mr. Lawson, who essentially is a stranger, Your Honor."

Idris's attorney rose from his seat. "Your Honor, my client thought that Ms. Lawson had terminated the pregnancy, as this was their agreement."

"Not so, Your Honor," Sarah interrupted.

"Allow me to finish, counselor." Idris's lawyer paused. "However my client now knows that he has a six-year-old daughter and he wants a relationship with her. He is in no way seeking full custody. He simply wants to know his daughter, and I think, Your Honor, for a child not to know her father can be likened to cruel and unusual punishment."

"Not if that same father paid for this child to be medical waste when her mother was pregnant," Sarah stood up and said.

The judge cleared his throat as he looked through the file. "Well, we certainly have a situation here. The child is six years old, six years that Mr. Lawson has missed, however ironic it is. It is also six years that he never would have had, had Ms. Morgan terminated the pregnancy as he wished and apparently paid for back then. It is always unfortunate that children are caught in the middle of these situations. It is my hope that one day you two people will reach an agreement where the court does not have to be involved. However since we are not there today, the court orders as follows:

"Considering the paperwork submitted on Mr. Lawson's finances, the court orders child support in the sum of twenty-five thousand dollars a month. Joint custody to be awarded. Physical custody to remain with the mother, Ms. Morgan, and visitation awarded to Mr. Lawson, visits every other weekend and alternate holidays. Seeing that today is Wednesday, he should be properly introduced to his daughter. I can appoint a mediator if one is needed."

"I don't want a mediator," Chaunci whispered to Sarah. "What he just ordered is bad enough."

"Your Honor, we will not require a mediator, providing Mr. Lawson is in agreement. My client is willing to cooperate."

"Wonderful. Therefore the court orders that the first weekend visit take place this week on Friday. Is there a need for the court to schedule the holidays, counselors? Or can your clients come to that agreement?"

"They will come to an agreement," the counselors said.

The judge banged his gavel. "Court dismissed."

For the first time since Chaunci made up her mind that she could handle being a single mother, she felt truly helpless.

Kobi may have resembled Idris, but Kobi Sarai Morgan was Chaunci's baby and had been since the day she was born and Chaunci placed her on her breasts and promised her the world. Idris had walked away a long time ago, and now suddenly this motherfucker who didn't even know Kobi's middle name, her favorite color, or her favorite food, hadn't attended one parent-teacher conference and probably thought "PTA" was a fancy term for a three-point play—now had the audacity to demand a space in Kobi's life. And to add insult to injury, the law was on his side.

Chaunci cleared her throat and rose to her feet. She steadied herself by placing her hand on the corner of the cherrywood table. She fought back the tears and made up her mind that if she was going to cry it would be in the still of the night when no one was there but God. "Sarah," she said to her lawyer and nodded her head good-bye. She walked over to Idris, but before she could speak he said, "I don't want to hurt you, Chaunci, but I need to know my baby."

Chaunci started to level his ass, but then again she refused to give him the satisfaction, so instead she walked past him and out of the building.

Carl, waiting outside, had not been allowed into the courtroom. Pointing the camera at Chaunci he said, "Tell us what happened."

The lump in Chaunci's throat weighed heavily on her tongue. She relaxed her shoulders and smiled; too much of her business had already unfolded on camera. "I've never been opposed to Kobi having a father. And as long as Mr. Lawson holds to his side of the agreement I won't have to kill him." Chaunci batted her eyes and smiled. She knew she'd just spewed a terrorist threat, but fuck it.

She glanced at Idris, who was walking down the stairs, and then she sauntered toward her black town car, where her driver was standing with the door open.

"No more changing outfits, Kobi," Chaunci said as she sat on the soft pink chaise in Kobi's walk-in closet. "You look fine."

Kobi had taken the news about Idris a lot better than Chaunci had imagined. Chaunci had always thought that there would be a long discussion followed by a series of questions and perhaps some tears, but it didn't happen that way. When Chaunci told Kobi who Idris was and that he would be coming over in a few hours, all Kobi said was, "Okay. What should I wear?"

Kobi twirled around in her chocolate and mint green dress with chocolate leggings underneath and matching ballerina shoes. "I just want my daddy to say, 'You look beautiful!' And then I want him to say, 'I love you this much!' " She held her hands out as wide as they could go.

Chaunci arched her eyebrows. Her friends who were single mothers had always told her that no matter how much they struggled and sacrificed, all their children's father had to do was spin around, and voilà, in their children's eyes he would appear to be Daddy of the Year. And looking at Kobi, Chaunci saw the scenario unfolding before her eyes.

Chaunci peeped at the clock. Idris was already an hour late. Careful not to let Kobi sense her worry, Chaunci said, "Your daddy already told me that he thought you were the prettiest girl in the world!" Chaunci rose from the chaise. "I'm going in the other room for a moment, okay?"

Twenty minutes later and against her mother's advice, Kobi had changed her clothes again. Then she went into the kitchen, where Chaunci was sitting at the dining room table.

"Okay, Mommy, time to make my daddy a meal."

"A meal?" Chaunci looked surprised. "It's kind of late to cook something now. Your father should be here any minute."

"No, it's not, Mommy. Rice Krispies Treats and hot cocoa only takes a few minutes."

Considering that the time was steadily ticking by, Chaunci gave in, hoping that Kobi would be too distracted to notice how late it was getting.

An hour after the Rice Krispies Treats and hot cocoa were done, Chaunci was clearly upset. She hated to look at Kobi's glassy eyes because she knew it was only a matter of minutes before she, herself, broke down and cried. "I'm sorry," Chaunci said to Kobi, not knowing what else to say. Her single-mother friends had also told her such a moment would come.

"It's okay, Mommy. He might still come."

"You know it's late," Chaunci said, her heart dying in her chest. If Idris had been standing next to her she would surely slap the shit out of him. "I think you should change into your pajamas."

"No, Mommy." Kobi shook her head. "I want him to see how pretty I look."

"You wanna go out for some pizza?"

"Pizza? When we made all of these Rice Krispies Treats?"

"Okay" was all Chaunci could say. It was one thing for her to hurt, but it was a whole other thing for her baby to feel the pain.

Kobi went into her bedroom, and Chaunci picked up the phone. She was determined to find this motherfucker tonight. As Idris's cell phone started to ring, she heard a knock on the door, and someone calling her name. She hung up the phone and walked toward the door. She knew it was Idris as he pounded again.

"The bell and the phone both work," she said, opening the door.

"Listen, I'm sorry. I did some shopping in Jersey"—he held up a few shopping bags—"telling myself I was doing a good thing. I didn't know if I should bring something or what. And then on the way back there was tons of traffic and a really bad accident. I forgot my cell phone at home and I had no way of reaching you. So I know I'm late, but I'm here. I'm sorry, I am."

Chaunci looked up at him, and she hated that Kobi looked so much like him. "My baby cried for you."

"I'm sorry."

"Look," she said, closing the door behind him, "I don't care if this is court ordered. If you are going to be in and out of her life, making promises you can't fulfill, or, worse, just one day disappearing, which we both know you're capable of, then leave now, please."

"Hear me." He grabbed her hands. "Once again, I'm here now and I'm not going anywhere. Where is my daughter?"

"In her room." Chaunci led Idris to Kobi's room, where the little girl was sitting up on her bed but had fallen asleep.

"Kobi," Idris called her name softly, and she opened her eyes.

"My daddy," she said, looking at her mother for confirmation. Chaunci nodded her head and Kobi started screaming, "Oh my God!" She looked at her mother. "Do you see my daddy?"

"Yes." Chaunci smiled as Idris picked Kobi up and hugged her tightly.

"Daddy's sorry," Idris said. "I ran late. You forgive me?"

"Yes, Daddy!" She hugged him around his neck.

"Well," Chaunci said, "I'ma go in the other room and read over some articles."

A few hours passed and it was nearing midnight. Kobi and Idris read books, watched movies, and she filled him in on everything in hers and her mother's life, including answering his questions about why nobody liked Edmon. Eventually she ended up falling asleep in his arms, and he picked her up and placed her in the bed.

"Chaunci." He tapped her leg as she lay asleep on the couch, with papers in her hand. "Wake up."

"I'm up." She stretched. "You guys have a nice time?"

"Yeah." He smiled. "That's Daddy's girl."

Silence.

"How did we end up here?" Idris asked.

"End up where?"

"Here. I never dreamed of this, but it feels so good that I don't know how I didn't."

"Okay, that's interesting," Chaunci said curtly.

"You're pissed as hell with me, aren't you?"

"Idris, don't ask me the obvious. Friday is your next visit. Now good-bye."

Chaunci turned away and Idris grabbed her by the hand and turned her around. He kissed her on the cheek. "Good-night."

Jaise

Jaise sat at her formal dining room table dressed in a low-cut flowing cranberry red Dior dress. Her bare feet were crossed at the ankles beneath the table, and she watched Bilal and Jabril eat the dinner of cube steak, gravy, and baked potato she'd prepared for them.

She could see the camera's reflection in Bilal's eyes, and she wondered when would be the right time to ask him about making love or if she needed to ease into the conversation. "So what do you think of Sarah Palin giving interviews all over the news circuit?" she said to make small talk.

"What?" Bilal gave her half a grin. "You wanna tell jokes this evening? Sarah Palin is wasted space, politically anyway."

"You think?" Jaise said, not really giving a damn. What she really wanted to ask him was "When will you be fucking me?"

"Do I think? Listen, I can't entertain nonsense from someone who campaigns in front of a turkey being slaughtered. I'd much rather talk about the chances Governor Patterson has to be re-elected."

"Umm-hmmm, yeah," Jaise said in the most insincere voice, "me too."

"If he loses I think Elton John should run," he said, testing to see if she was listening. "What about you?"

"Perfect."

"You didn't hear a word I said."

"Well, hmph, I nominate Lil Wayne." Jabril laughed. "Then everybody can smoke weed."

"You lost your damn mind?!" Jaise snapped at Jabril.

"It was a joke."

"You're not a comedian."

"Jabril," Bilal said, getting his attention, as Jaise raked her fork across her plate. "Wassup with school? How are your subjects coming?"

"Huh?" Jabril said, obviously caught off guard. "School?"

"Yeah, that place you go when you leave here in the morning."

"Oh, you funny," Jabril laughed, "yeah that." He looked at the clock. "As a matter of fact, I'm on my way to go help a friend of mine out with some homework."

"And what friend is that?" Jaise asked.

"Big tittie—I mean, um, Christina."

"Why are you always running over there to help some little girl? I have told you about these li'l girls." She pointed her finger toward his face. "Don't bring no damn babies or any diseases back in here because you out there doing a two-step with your li'l-bitty dick."

"Ma!" He pointed to the cameras. "You don't know what I wanna be in life. Don't be saying that on TV!"

"I'm just keepin' it real."

"Could you keep it real subtle?" Bilal gave her half a smile. "We don't wanna embarrass him."

"Listen to the man with the gun, Ma," Jabril said. "Calm down."

"Don't test me, Jabril," Jaise warned him.

"Ai'ight." He stood up. "I'm 'bout to bounce."

"Good-bye," she said as he slid his coat on.

"Good-bye?" Bilal said low enough for only Jaise to hear. "Are you going to tell him what time to come back? It's a school night."

"Be back here in a few hours," Jaise snapped at Jabril. "And I mean it."

"Yo, my man," Jabril said to Bilal, "whatever you did to this chick, please make up so she can act right by the time I get back, 'cause she buggin'."

"You are buggin'," Bilal told Jaise as he watched Jabril leave. "I don't mean to get into your business with your son," he said as Jabril closed the door.

"Then don't."

"Slow down." He gave her a warning eye. "I do think you need to keep a tighter rein on him."

"Jabril is a good kid. He is just like every other teenager out there. For the most part you can't do nothin' with 'em. But I have seen worse, believe me."

"I didn't mean for you to make excuses for him. I understand that he's your son. But on the outside looking in, you're a little loose with him."

"So what do you want me to do? Put a gun to his head, slap some handcuffs on him, Detective?"

Bilal pushed his plate from in front of him and looked at Jaise. "What's the problem?"

"I don't have a problem."

"Liar." Bilal nodded his head. "When you start this?"

"Look, I just find it strange that it's been a month." She hesitated.

"A month and what?"

"And you haven't made love to me. Are you gay?"

"Am I gay?" Bilal looked at Jaise as if she were crazy. "You lost your mind asking me something like that? It's been a month, not a year. Your problem is you've been dealing with these lowlifes in the banks and the boardrooms and you don't know how to act when a real man is sitting in front of you. Be loved for once, appreciated, and treated like a lady. You want me to be your man? Or we just hittin' it and quittin' it?"

"I want you forever."

"Then let me treat you like a lady and not a ho. Believe me," he said, looking her dead in the eyes, "when the time comes I am more than willing, able, and endowed to handle the situation the way it needs to be handled. But I'm thirty-eight years old and at this stage of the game there's more to a woman for me than pussy."

Jaise felt like a fool, especially since he'd just put her in her place like no one else ever had. She wanted a man, and now that she had one she didn't know how to act. "I guess you're going to leave now?" she said.

"Are you putting me out?"

"No, I want you to stay. I just thought that since, you know, we just had it out that you would use that as an excuse to end this."

"We didn't have it out, we had a discussion, and even if we did have it out, where am I going? I've been here every day for a month, and I see myself wanting to be with you for years to come. But you have to let me be your man without thinking I have something to hide. Now, come here."

Jaise walked over to him, her dress clinging to her every curve. Once she reached him, Bilal placed his hands on her hips. "Let what has happened to you before go. That's the only way you're going to make room for me to love you."

Bilal's hands felt like sweet heat on her hips and Jaise felt a series of electric chills shoot up her spine. "You're right, we should love each other first," she admitted. "And, hell, who would believe you could really be in love after a month? Talk about truth being stranger than fiction." She gave a nervous laugh.

"Why don't you ask me what I believe?" He pulled her onto his lap and started kissing her softly on the lips.

Because I'm scared of what you might say . . . or might not say, Jaise thought as they began to kiss passionately. As she started unbuttoning Bilal's shirt and kissing down his chest, Carl cleared his throat loudly.

Immediately Jaise and Bilal looked up, realizing they'd forgotten about the camera being there. Before Jaise could say anything Bridget squinted her eyes and looked at Carl. "You keep it up, Carl, and you will be out on your ass. I'm so tired of you interrupting the drama when it's getting started!"

As the camera crew and Bridget packed up to leave, Bilal looked at his watch and decided it was time for him to go as well. Jaise hated that he had to leave; he hadn't even walked out the door and already she missed him. It was true that they'd been going strong for a minute now, but the fear in her heart kept telling her that certainly the time would come when he wouldn't come by in the morning to bring her a cup of light and sweet coffee, or bring her lunch. She was certain she'd talked him to death about estate sales, salvage yards, and auctions, and she could only imagine that he really wanted to go straight home after work instead of stopping by here to eat the nightly dinner she'd been preparing for him. Jaise was sure she could cook, but certainly Bilal hadn't grown accustomed to her southern way of cooking.

"Jaise," Bridget said to her before they walked out the door, "see you in the morning."

"I know you will," Jaise grumbled as she waved and watched Bilal walk out behind Bridget. "I'll call you," he said. He hugged her and kissed her lightly on the neck.

After everyone had gone Jaise sat down on the couch, every nerve in her stomach told her that she'd messed up tonight with some of the comments she'd made, but the truth of the matter was that for the first time in her life she wanted to make love to Bilal for the sake of making love.

She knew her feelings were foolish. She had to be crazy. Love took months, hell, sometimes years, and here she was trippin' after four weeks.

She looked at the clock; it was a quarter to ten. As she decided to go to bed her doorbell rang. "Jabril, you better stop losing your keys," she said, opening the door only to find Bilal standing there. "Bilal . . ." she said. She couldn't stand that she could never fight off blushing around him.

"Why didn't you ask me if I loved you?" Bilal asked Jaise.

Jaise paused and then admitted, "I was scared of what you would say, or wouldn't say."

"Ask me."

Jaise had the question playing in her mind but for whatever reason it wouldn't come out of her mouth. This was what she was scared of—loving him and him loving her back, or him loving her now and changing his mind later. This was why she had never told him that being in his arms was a beautiful feeling.

Bilal studied Jaise's face, and when she didn't say anything he arched his eyebrows and once again said, "Good-night."

He turned to walk down the stairs and she grabbed his hand. "Do you love me?"

Bilal's smile lit up the night. "Yes."

"All right," Jaise said nervously, feeling like a teenage girl who'd just revealed her first crush. Jaise took him by the hand and led him to her bedroom, where she turned the radio on and the music made love to the air as they slowly danced back and forth, kissing softly and soothingly with each lyric, each bar, and each bridge of the song. Bilal slid the spaghetti straps of Jaise's dress off her shoulders, causing the gown to snake to the Persian rug.

"Jaise . . ." He took a step back and looked at her beautiful full-figured body. His eyes caressed her every curve. "I knew you were beautiful," he said, "but I didn't know you were this perfect." He stepped back into her space and kissed her from her neck to her full cleavage, where he enjoyed tasting her chocolate nipples with the tip of his tongue, down to her wetness, where he opened her sweetness, admired the diamond glaze, and bathed his tongue with it. Sucking, kissing, biting, and licking, over and over again.

It was evident that he wanted it, even more than she wanted to give it to him. He kissed in between her thighs, and once she came he kissed a trail up her body again. Jaise lifted his shirt, revealing his beautiful, carved, and exceedingly exquisite body. He was the epitome of magnificence, the crème de la crème, the very reason why black men, no matter what part of the world they were from, were so beautiful.

His thighs were well toned and the muscle creases alone were driving her wild. By the time her eyes dropped down to his manhood, her mouth inadvertently fell open and he lifted her lip by kissing it. He pulled her to the floor and they lay before the fireplace, as he kissed her body back and forth and back again, whispering in her ear how much he wanted her and how beautiful she was.

The Isley Brothers' "Don't Say Goodnight" serenaded them as Jaise opened and accepted Bilal into her wet and creamy world. Jaise winced and moaned as Bilal's twelve inches entered her. But the way he was stroking her and twirling her nipples with his tongue, and telling her that he wanted to be with her forever made it okay.

Just as Jaise had gotten settled in missionary position, throwing her thighs on his shoulders, her sugar walls adjusting to his size, Bilal flipped her over and started stroking her from the back. She loved it, the pounding, the force, and the way that he held her wrists behind her back.

Jaise loved the feeling of her skin against his, her back against his chest, and his manliness against her ass. And just when she thought they'd almost reached perfection, he turned her over again and placed her on top of him, causing their milkyways to melt into each other.

After catching her breath she laid her head on his shoulder and ran her hands over his chest. "I know it hasn't been years . . . but I feel like this is perfect."

"Stop counting time. This is me and you. Time no longer exists." He looked her in the eyes. "I'm here and I'm not going anywhere. Accept that this is real, I'm real, and trust that I have a helluva lot more to give you." He kissed her on the lips and they began to make love all over again.

(The next morning)

"Bilal," Jaise said, as he stood in her kitchen at the stove, cooking breakfast for her, "Jabril isn't in his room. And his bed looks as if it hasn't been slept in." Jaise sighed. This couldn't have happened at a worse time. It seemed as if every time Bridget was here and it was her taping day, bullshit reigned supreme. Jaise had yet to showcase her antiquing talent or her etiquette.

"What?" Bilal looked confused. "I thought you said he usually gets up and off to school on his own?"

"He does, but he never makes his bed, ever. It's always me making it up after he leaves, and it's made up perfectly."

"Don't panic just yet." Bilal stirred the grits and dropped the catfish he was cooking into the hot and popping grease. "Call his father and see if he's heard from him."

Reluctantly Jaise dialed Lawrence's number and amazingly he picked up on the first ring. "Hello?"

"Lawrence, this is Jaise."

"I sent your welfare check out yesterday, so why are you on my phone?"

Jaise sighed. She wanted desperately to cut this motherfucker. "All I want to know is have you heard from Jabril?"

"What the hell would he be calling me for? The last time he called here he cussed me, Robyn, and the baby out. Oh no, I don't deal in that type of disrespect."

"Look, he didn't come home last night."

"That's your kid, you find him," Lawrence snapped. "You know I stopped doing him a long time ago. I told you to send him to live with me and you wouldn't, so, hey, whatever happens is on you."

"What the hell is your problem?! Jabril is your son!"

"Calm down, Jaise," Bilal said, turning over the fish he was cooking, "you don't have to argue with him."

"Who is that," Lawrence snapped, "your new boyfriend?"

"That's none of your business."

"You've always been a whore any-fuckin'-way strip-a-rella!"

"Fuck you. You must have me confused with your mother, stupid motherfucker. You think you gon' always talk shit to me because I left you. I don't—"

"Listen, is he able to tell you where Jabril is?" Bilal asked Jaise, setting her plate in front of her.

"No."

"Then hang up. What are you arguing with him for? Stop that and the issue of him acting like an ass is solved."

Jaise smiled. Was it really that simple? This was exactly why she loved him. "You're right." She hung up on Lawrence and turned to Bilal. "I hope nothing happened to my baby." Her voice trembled.

"Call his friends," Bilal said, sitting down beside her to eat. "Let's see if he went over to their place."

"I don't have their numbers."

"What do you mean you don't have their numbers?" He raised one eyebrow.

"I just don't."

"Call his cell phone."

"I did and he's not answering."

Bilal shook his head. He picked up his cell phone and called the police stations in Brooklyn and the neighboring hospitals. When he came up with nothing he looked at Jaise and she knew he was beyond pissed. "You know you not knowing his friends or having any other numbers to call is ridiculous, right?"

Jaise was offended. "Look, I know that we connected and all, but in case you haven't noticed, I don't do well with anyone telling me about my son."

"Oh, I noticed, and I noticed that's something you need to work on."

"I got this. I have been raising him by myself for many years."

"Should I kick back and listen to this or should I stop you now?"

"What?" she said, put off.

"Jaise, I'm not trying to hear that. I'm your man—"

Even in the midst of being pissed Jaise liked the sound of that.

"And if I can't tell you when I see something that you need to improve on," Bilal continued, "then who can?"

"And what if I see something you need to improve on?" she snapped.

"Then tell me."

She leaned up close to his face. "You're too much in my business with my son."

"This isn't about your business. This is about me caring. If I didn't I wouldn't open my mouth. Now, listen, Jabril is doing his own thing because he knows your bark is bigger than your bite, so he takes advantage."

"So what are you saying?"

"I'm saying that you are so busy trying to compensate for Lawrence being fucked up that you're fucking up. You are raising a man and you have the ability to do that."

"I'm not a man!"

"That's an excuse and it's a foolish one. You're his mother. Make him get a job after school, have him pay a bill, a small one, to teach him some responsibility. Make him save his money, and accept nothing less than the truth. Now, we don't know where he's at, and neither one of us is going to be able to do anything today until we know where Jabril is."

Jaise sat and stared at Bilal for a few minutes. "You really care, don't you?"

"Why wouldn't I?"

"I . . . don't know . . . I mean, I just never had a man who was really into my kid . . . at least enough to care about him."

"Listen, my mother married my stepfather when I was a kid, and not for one day did I ever feel like somebody else's child. When he was serious with my mother, he was serious about both of us. I was his son. He never used the word 'stepson.' He loved me like his own, and even to this day my brothers say that I'm his favorite."

Jaise laughed.

"So he taught me when you meet a woman and she has a child or children, if you can't accept the package then leave. More harm is done if you stay. You understand where I'm coming from?"

"I do." Jaise shook her head. "Now more than ever."

After double-checking Jabril's school and being told he wasn't there, Jaise looked at Bilal. "I really hope nothing extreme happened, but if the goddamn Brooklyn Bridge didn't fall down, taking the train down with it and this li'l mofo isn't floating on the lone piece of concrete in the Hudson River . . . and I know you hate it when I cuss . . . but I'ma kick his motherfuckin' ass." She rose from her chair. "Excuse me, but I have a headache." She headed to the bathroom, and as she stood looking through the medicine cabinet she heard a soft female voice say, "Bril, wake up."

Jaise stood stunned. She knew she'd heard wrong, at least until the girl spoke again: "Brilly Bril, wake up. We've overslept."

"You got that the hell right!" Jaise screamed, tossing the door to the guest room open.

"Are you okay?" Bilal rushed in behind Jaise. "Whoo!" He shielded his eyes and turned his back. "Is she naked? Are they naked?"

Jaise's knees wavered as she almost fainted on the floor. She gasped as Jabril hopped out of bed naked. "Oh shit, Ma." He shielded his middle while the girl he was with looked frightened and frantically started grabbing her clothes.

"That's your mama?" the girl said, "Bril, you told me this was your place."

Jaise was doing her best to talk herself out of gut punching Jabril and slapping this girl for being stupid. "I said this'll be my place in a few years," Jabril said.

Jaise slapped Jabril across his head so hard that he tilted to the side and fell down. "Ma!" She smacked him again. "Bilal! Tell her to stop," Jabril yelled as the girl attempted to run out of the room, but Jaise stopped slapping Jabril long enough to block her path.

"You came in through that window?" Jaise pointed to the open window on the other side of the room.

"Yes, ma'am," she said as she dressed frantically.

"Then leave yo' fresh ass right out that same damn window. You ought to be ashamed of yourself laying up in some boy's house when you need to be in school."

"Ma, don't make her leave out the—" Jaise shot Jabril such a look that he turned to the girl and said, "Yo, watch them bushes when you jump. Remember the last time you hurt your foot."

"The last time?" Jaise popped Jabril for a few seconds more before she started screaming again. "You lied to me! You having a damn orgy in my house! Oh my God." She started in on him again.

"Alright, Jaise, that's enough." Bilal pulled her off him, but not before she had slapped Jabril one last time for GP sake. Bilal turned to the young lady. "I think you should leave." The girl started crying as she turned toward the window. "Jaise," Bilal said, "let her walk out the door."

"Hell no." Jaise pointed. "Out the window!"

The girl cried as she placed her foot on the ledge and hopped out the window.

"Jabril!" Jaise screamed, "I'ma beat your ass. Every time you see me, know that it's on. Matter fact, you going to live with your father!"

"Ma."

"Jabril," Bilal said, "go put some clothes on."

"But—"

"Go! Trust me."

Jaise paced the floor. "I can't do this," she said to Bilal.

"You don't have a choice. He's your son."

"But he doesn't listen."

"You have to hold him accountable."

"I'ma punch him in the face!"

"And what good is that going to do? I told you before to tell him what you expect, and you didn't. Now you need to do something or else he's going to get into something he can't get out of."

"What am I supposed to do?"

"I don't know, but you have to talk to him."

"Are you going to come with me?"

"Absolutely not. That's not my place, not yet. When I marry you then we'll go in there together. But until then you and your son need to have this discussion."

"So you're just going to leave?"

"No, I'ma go in the media room and watch the news." He left her standing there.

This was the quietest that Bridget had ever been while recording. Jaise figured it was because she was getting her dramatic jollies off. She followed Jaise upstairs to Jabril's room. Jaise knocked softly and pushed the door open. As soon as Jabril saw his mother standing there he took cover.

"I'm not going to hit you," Jaise said. "I'm done, though. And I'm disappointed as hell."

"Ma, let me explain," Jabril said, seeing a look of utter disgust and disappointment on Jaise's face that he'd never seen before. "Ma, I know I was wrong."

"Oh, you know this? Good, so you'll understand that I'm done playing with you. You think that I'ma joke—"

"No, I don't."

"Yes, you do, otherwise you wouldn't have disrespected my house by laying up in here with some li'l streetwalker."

"She's not a streetwalker."

"You challenging me?"

"No, Ma, you're right," he said, intimidated. "A streetwalker."

"I'm done with you, Jabril. Yo' ass and all your li'l special privileges are cut off."

"Ma—"

"Say 'Ma' again and see if I don't backhand the shit outta you!" She paused. "I thought you'd gotten better, and here I was planning something with MTV for your birthday, but that's blown. And since you want to act crazy, then here's the deal. Get your ass a job, 'cause I'm not buying you shit. You will pay your cell phone bill or the motherfucker will be cut off. And you have to be in the house by nine on school nights and eleven on the weekends."

"Ma—"

She popped him in his forehead. "Didn't I tell you not to say 'ma' again? If you don't like my rules, then tough, because you have no choice but to get it together. I'm disgusted with you!" She stormed out of his room and immediately returned. "And hurry up and get yourself ready for school. You getting the hell outta here today!"

"Ma!" he yelled behind her.

Jaise spun on her heels. "Oh, and next year Christmas is cancelled, too. Yo' ass'll be down at the Goodwill serving in the soup kitchen."

Bridget shot Jaise a high five. "Couldn't have done it better if I'da written the script."

Chaunci

Chaunci looked up and down the street, wondering how she'd gotten here, to this place and this space, where she just wanted to escape. She had fought not to be a statistic, and here Idris had thrust her into a whole new baby mama category: unyielding, unforgiving, and labeled as interfering with her baby and the baby daddy's relationship. But that wasn't her. And, yeah, she may have been pissed, but she wasn't angry. Being angry would mean she wanted revenge, wanted to destroy her child's father, but she wanted to do none of that. She simply wanted to be left alone, and anything else she needed to deal with, when the time came, she would handle it. But the court had decided that the time for her to deal with Idris was now.

"Can we get out of the car now, Mommy?" Kobi interrupted her thoughts as they sat in front of Idris's Brooklyn brownstone.

"Yes, of course." Chaunci eyed Kobi in the rearview mirror. "Let's go." They got out of the car and grabbed their bags. Kobi skipped up the stairs and Chaunci walked behind her. A few seconds after they rang the bell, Idris opened the door. "Daddy!" Kobi yelled as he picked her up and swept her into his arms.

"How's Daddy's girl?" He kissed her on the cheek.

Chaunci hated that question; the sound of it was like nails raking across a chalkboard, and Kobi's answer was like those same nails screeching again: "I love you, Daddy."

Chaunci stood there, no longer able to fake a smile; instead she was grimacing and doing her damnedest to ignore the fact that Idris was standing at the door wearing a pair of baggy gray sweats and a tight and fitted-right wife beater that caressed his sixpack. And his shadow beard, which was usually perfectly trimmed, was now slightly rough and seemed only to enhance his sexiness. The Cool Water cologne he wore smelled like heaven as Chaunci pushed her way through the door and into Idris's living room.

Chaunci held her weekend bag in her hand and turned to Idris. "Where should I put this?"

"Oh, I have a room all set up for Kobi. You really don't even have to bother with packing her a weekend bag. You can actually take that back home with you. It's fine."

Chaunci pointed to a hot pink Chanel duffel bag. "Kobi's bag is over there. This one is mine."

"Yours? Was that in the court order?" he asked sarcastically.

"Well, you may as well call the police, especially if you think I'm leaving my baby here with you. I don't know you like that and I don't care what that judge says, I'm not leaving." She sat down on the couch and crossed her legs. "Where my baby goes, her mother does also."

Idris smiled. "Why would I call the police? I have my own handcuffs."

"Shhhh." Kobi held her finger up. "Does anyone hear that?" She paused. "Is that a dog barking?" She started running down the hall.

Idris and Chaunci walked swiftly behind her, and the closer they came to Kobi's new bedroom the louder the dog's barking was. Kobi ran into her new room, which was painted pink and white, with a chandelier hanging from the ceiling, a full-size bed with a headboard shaped like a dollhouse, every toy imaginable, and in the center of the floor was a hot pink dog bed with a brown and black Maltese puppy in it.

Chaunci was instantly pissed as she watched Kobi run to pick up the dog and kiss it. "I don't believe you brought her a dog," Chaunci said to Idris, tight-lipped. "You didn't think to ask me if she could have one?"

"Ask you?" He turned to her. "You won't even talk to me. I had to get a court order just to meet *our* daughter. Stop being so tight and we can discuss some things."

"Whatever." She waved her hand.

"Chaunci," Idris said, steadily growing tired of giving in, "listen, the dog can stay here, okay?"

"Oh, now you want to make me look like the witch in all of this?"

"I'm not doing this with you." Idris stepped away from Chaunci and over to Kobi. "Kobi, what are you going to name him? Spot?"

"Oh no, Daddy"—she shook her head feverishly—"his name is Bird."

"A dog named Bird?" Idris looked confused.

"Well," Chaunci said, "obviously the name Idris wasn't available."

The vein on Idris's neck started jumping. "Kobi, let me speak to Mommy for a minute. I'll be right back." He walked over to Chaunci, grabbed her by her forearm, and practically forced her to walk out of the room. "Check this," he said to her once they were out of Kobi's earshot. "I'm done apologizing to you. I'm done trying to make this up to you and feeling bad about the shit. Now I understand where you are coming from, but you will not disrespect me or insinuate that I'm nothing in front of my kid. If you really don't like me and you don't want to be around me, then leave. And if you don't want to leave, then get your attitude in order, 'cause I'm not havin' it." They locked eyes. "You understand?"

"Idris—"

"Do you understand?"

Reluctantly Chaunci agreed. "Umm-hmm."

"Thank you." He held her hand and the heat from his palm made Chaunci feel like she was ready to melt. "Come on, let's go back in the room," he said.

Idris walked back over to Kobi, who was patting the dog. "Hey, Kobi," he said, "I have a whole day planned for us."

"Yeah!" She jumped up and down. "Mommy, we're going to have so much fun! Where are we going, Daddy?"

"Well, first we're going down to Ruckas Park to shoot some hoops."

"Hoops?" Kobi frowned. "That doesn't sound ladylike. Didn't Mommy tell you I was a princess?"

"Lisa Leslie is a lady," Idris insisted.

Kobi looked confused. "Who is Lisa Leslie? Does she have her own cartoon?"

Idris turned to Chaunci. "She doesn't play basketball?"

Chaunci, who was holding her hand over her mouth and doing her best not to let laughter ease from her lips, said, "She doesn't like it."

"She doesn't like it?" He looked at Kobi and asked her, "You don't like basketball?"

"No."

"You ever heard of the New York Knicks?"

"The New York *Kicks,* Daddy? Do they play volleyball? I like volleyball, Daddy."

"Volleyball? You want to play volleyball?"

She shook her head. "No, I don't have on the right shoes for that. Plus, I'm not in the mood."

"Okay, so—what would you like to do?"

"Wait a minute now," Idris said as they walked into a trendy nail salon, "I don't want a manicure."

"Daddy, you need your nails done. You need your cuticles ra'tended—"

"Attended," Chaunci corrected her.

"Attended to."

"My cuticles are fine." He turned to Chaunci. "You wanna help me out here?"

"You're doing okay by yourself. You don't need my help."

"And Daddy," Kobi carried on, "I didn't want to say anything, but when we were in your house I noticed your feet need to be done too."

"I don't believe this." Idris shook his head. "Okay, baby, whatever you want."

Chaunci pulled out her digital camera, and as soon as the manicurist started doing Idris's nails she started snapping pictures.

"This better not end up on the Internet." Idris squinted. "Wait a minute, is that a TMZ reporter? Oh, God damn!"

"Color?" the manicurist asked Idris, interrupting his tirade.

"Color? You tryna be funny?"

The Asian manicurist smiled at Idris. "You like color?"

"I'ma grown-ass man, you see how big I am, and you asking me if I want some color on my nails?"

"Sir," an Asian man said from behind the counter and pointed to the manicurist who was smiling at Idris. "She doesn't speak English."

Chaunci couldn't hold it in any longer. She started cracking up laughing.

Idris turned around and gave her the evil eye. "Shut up," he said.

Kobi tapped him on the shoulder. "Daddy, I picked out a color for you."

"Y'all planned this," Idris said to Chaunci, pissed off, as he held his hands out, "but it's all good. You really got this off. But Daddy's a good sport."

"We know, Daddy," Chaunci said, standing behind Idris and massaging his shoulders while looking down at his nails. "Relax, pink is your color."

"Don't touch me," Idris snapped at Chaunci. "Don't touch me."

"Are you feeling some kind of way, Daddy?" Chaunci laughed.

"You better stop fucking with me," he said, tight-lipped.

"Remember that." Chaunci laughed as she retook her seat. She knew she was being a little too friendly and free, but she couldn't help it; this was hilarious.

When Idris and Kobi were done with their nails and feet, Chaunci said, "Should we have lunch now?"

"Yes!" Kobi shouted. "American Girl Café."

"Kobi," Idris said, doing his best not to remove his hands from his pockets, "Daddy doesn't want to rent a doll for himself. I don't like Addie."

"Why not, Daddy?" Kobi asked, as the waitress waited patiently to lead them to their table. "What did Addie do to you?"

"Look at the dress, Kobi, and what's this bonnet on her head?"

"It's her costume. Mommy has a doll."

"I sure do." Chaunci batted her lashes.

"Give me the doll," Idris snapped, as he tucked Addie beneath his arm and walked to the table.

Once they had sat down and ordered their food Kobi said, "Mommy, I have to go to the bathroom."

"Okay." Chaunci rose from her seat. "I'm coming."

Kobi started skipping toward the restroom and Chaunci found herself staring at Idris. She was sure he could read her thoughts as her mind told her to simply give in, to fold, and to just be okay with this situation, but she couldn't allow that to happen. She quickly averted her eyes and followed her daughter.

When Kobi and Chaunci returned, their food was on the table. "Daddy," Kobi said, taking her seat, "did you talk to Addie?"

Chaunci looked at Idris and mouthed, "Just say yes."

"Yes, baby."

"Well, did she ask why your napkin is thrown over her face?"

"I'm sorry, Addie." Idris removed the napkin.

"Daddy," Kobi laughed, "you're so silly. You don't apologize to a doll. She's not real. Just take the napkin off."

"I don't quite know doll etiquette," Idris said. "But I do know how to steal a fry." He took a few curly fries from her plate and shoved them in his mouth.

"Daddy!" Kobi smiled. "You can't steal my curly fries." She took one of his onion rings.

"You're stealing my onion rings? Then I'll just take Mommy's chicken fingers."

"No, you don't, buddy." Chaunci playfully popped Idris's hand. "Not without giving me a bite of your cheeseburger."

"You want me to feed you?"

Chaunci paused and before she could dissect, analyze, and compose the most politically correct answer, she said, "Boy, if you don't give me a piece of that burger."

For the next hour they laughed, joked, and enjoyed one another's company. Idris placed two hundred dollars on the table for the bill and tip, and afterward they shopped, bought new dolls, accessories, and matching clothes for Kobi and her new dolls.

Idris looked at his watch as they exited the American Girl building. "I guess we should get back home."

"Home?" Kobi frowned. "Daddy, we have one more stop to make."

"Where is that?"

"The makeup lounge."

"Oh hell no," Idris grumbled, "lipstick is where I draw the line."

Kobi poked her lip out and held her head down. "It's only for play, Daddy."

"I don't believe this." Idris sucked his teeth. "Does lipstick come in clear?"

Kobi immediately brightened up. "Daddy, you have to get your lipstick in pink. It matches your polish."

The makeup artist looked at Idris's nails and slyly started whispering to her coworker.

"What, you think I can't hear?" Idris asked her. "Huh? I can hear very well."

"Shh." Chaunci stood before him and held his hands. "Be quiet before the paparazzi jump out of the bushes and come in here. Besides, don't complain about the lipstick, complain about the mascara. Lipstick comes off easily."

Idris looked deeply into Chaunci's eyes and said, "Show me how easily lipstick comes off."

Chaunci knew she was pushing it, but she brushed her lips against his. "Like that." She took a step back.

Idris looked at the makeup artist. "Can I get my entire face done?"

By the time they were done at the makeup lounge and back at home, Kobi was sleeping and Idris felt like Dennis Rodman, minus the wedding dress. His entire face was covered with makeup, his nails were painted pink, and he'd eaten lunch with a doll.

After Kobi was put in her bed, Idris stood in front of the full-length mirror in his bedroom, staring at his face. "How the hell am I supposed to get this off?" he asked himself.

Chaunci leaned against his doorframe. "You wear your makeup rather well."

"I thought you were supposed to help me take it off?"

"I was." She eased into his room.

"Well, come on." He sat down on the edge of the bed. "I can't go another minute with this on my face."

"Give me a moment." Chaunci walked out of the room and came back with her makeup kit. She removed the facial cleaner from her bag and began to clean Idris's face. She knew being this close to him and running her hands over his lips was dangerous and would cause her to forget all of the reasons that she had sworn she would hate him for life.

Idris fingered the hem of her blouse and then asked her, "How did I do?"

She watched him place his hands around her waist. "You did well." She smiled at him, her breasts lightly touching his chin as she started to remove his eyeliner. "You're a good daddy."

They were quiet for a few moments and then Idris said, "You know I compared every woman I met after you to you."

Silence.

"All of them," Idris continued. "And I always thought about you, every day, all the time." He paused.

Chaunci bit her bottom lip and continued to remove the blush from his cheeks.

"And every time I read one of your articles I felt close to you. I loved that article you wrote on relationships. What did you call it?" He snapped his fingers. "Yeah," he said, smiling as if a lightbulb had just lit up, " 'What's Love Got to Do with It.' And I remember when you said, 'He who loves least controls the relationship.' And I remembered thinking that has to be why I never stopped thinking about you."

"Don't do this," Chaunci said quietly.

"I know I acted like an ass, but trust me, I'm grown now. I'm done with the playboy shit. I'm finished, and I'm here, and if we never get a chance to be more than what we are right now, I just want you to know that I have never stopped being in love with you."

Chaunci did her all not to cry—she was far from being the sentimental type—so she pushed the tears to the side of her mouth and said, "You are so corny. How many years did you practice that?"

"I'm corny. Ai'ight, then look at me"—Idris took one hand and cupped her chin—"and tell me you don't love me. Or better yet, I'll make it easier for you: Tell me you don't want me. Tell me and I swear that other than our daughter, I'll leave you alone. So tell me." He ran his hands over her hips and kissed her stomach through her blouse, her perfume seducing his tongue to kiss and suck her breasts through the material. Unbuttoning her blouse he said, "Tell me."

Silence. Nothing. Nada. There was nothing Chaunci could say. "You want me to stop?" He unzipped her pants.

"I'm afraid," she said, straddling his lap as they began to undress each other.

"Don't be."

"I fought for so long not to think about you, about us, about any of this. I don't know, Idris. I don't know if you'll know how to love me."

"Show me." He lay back as she began to ride him. "I wanna get it right this time."

"How was your weekend, Kobi?" Edmon's voice startled Chaunci as she walked into her apartment, where the smell of Dextra's baking currant rolls filled the air. Chaunci looked into Edmon's face and realized that she'd forgotten about him. Not once had he crossed her mind. Not when butterflies were filling her belly, not when she kissed Idris, made love to him, cooked for him, and made love to him again before she had left and returned home this afternoon. Not until this moment when she looked into Edmon's face did she remember him and his place in her life.

She knew he had to be beyond pissed if he was sitting in her living room with Bridget and the camera crew.

"I had so much fun with my daddy and my mommy!" Kobi

screamed in excitement. "We went to American Girl Café, the makeup lounge, and I have a new puppy. His name is Bird. The next dog I get I'ma just name him Dog."

"That sounds really nice," Edmon said, speaking to Kobi but never once taking his eyes off Chaunci.

"Kobi," Chaunci said, placing her bag down on the couch, "why don't you go play in your room for a while."

"Okay, Mommy." Kobi waved. "Bye, Mr. Edmon."

"Bye, sweetie."

Once Kobi was in her room and her door slammed shut Edmon stroked his chin. "Where have you been all weekend?" he said a little too calmly.

"Oh, Mr. Montehugh," Chaunci said in her best valley-girl voice, "is it possible that we can meet at the office perhaps tomorrow and discuss the article?" She attempted to play off the reason for his visit.

"Fuck that shit. Now, I asked you, where have you been? You spent the weekend with this man?"

Chaunci paused. Her whole life was spinning on its ass on TV. This was not supposed to be a soap opera about her life, but an infomercial about why people needed a *Nubian Diva* subscription. "I couldn't just drop my daughter off at his house. I didn't know him like that."

"That's her father. What are you talking about? You couldn't stay for a few hours and bring your ass back home? So what else did you do with this motherfucker? Did you fuck him?"

"Oh, my," Bridget gasped. "Well I'ma just have to clutch my pearls."

"I don't think now is the time to discuss this," Chaunci said, tight-lipped. "You are way out of line. This is not the time."

"Is that a yes, you fucked him? Let me know so we can end this shit."

Chaunci thought about how this would've been the perfect time to tell Edmon how she felt—maybe not share the details of how she was doing more than riding Idris's dick, but that she was loving him, and feeling him, and wanting him. But nothing in life could ever be that simple. Edmon was too entangled in her dreams, in her life, and in her struggle to maintain her status quo. She couldn't afford to be spewing out a bunch of carefree words about a weekend filled with carefree actions.

She swallowed. "Edmon, I am really sorry." She walked over and grabbed his hand. "I didn't mean to be inconsiderate, and I know that we have been having some trying times, but I really want us to work past this, okay?"

Edmon stood astonished. "You really think I'm crazy?"

"Damn, Edmon, I just apologized. What more do you want?"

"Let me ask you this again, while I think we have a chance to part amicably. Did you sleep with him?"

"No," Chaunci said a little too quickly.

"Do you still want to marry me?"

"Cut." Bridget stepped in between them and turned to Edmon. "I didn't know she was engaged, and that caught me a little off guard, so I wasn't able to direct you. So do you mind saying that again?"

"Not now, Bridget," Chaunci snapped as she grabbed Edmon by the arm and pulled him to the side. "Edmon, baby, I care about you."

"You never answered my question." Edmon looked at Chaunci with a disbelieving look on his face.

"I said that I care about you deeply."

"That's exactly what you said." Edmon walked toward the front door and opened it.

"Edmon, wait."

But he didn't. Instead he continued down the hall and Chaunci watched him step onto the elevator. As she thought about what had just happened, she heard Bridget behind her. "Carl," Bridget attempted to whisper, "perfect scene. There won't be any need to edit this."

Evan

Evan had her publicist release a statement to the papers, the gossip sites, and the bloggers that she was in the hospital after a car accident, and the cause was due to stress, as she'd been working long hours with her charity and had fallen asleep at the wheel. It was almost believable considering her life had returned to semi-normal.

Kendu had been home all day for the last two weeks; the scent of Chanel No. 5 no longer lingered on him; and that along with the shot of lithium the hospital gave her before she signed herself out made her feel sane.

They were in the middle of a family photo shoot for the cover of *Essence* magazine. Kendu's story of rags to riches and the money he'd raised for his charity had attracted national attention.

Evan sat on the floor, with her arm draped across Kendu's lap, and Aiyanna stood behind the leather wing chair Kendu sat in, an awkward position for a family photo, but one that Evan insisted the photographer take and she was adamant that they use it for the cover. She could feel Kendu pushing her off of his lap after the picture was taken.

"You all are really a lovely family," the photographer said. "What's your secret?"

"Love." Evan smiled. "Nothing but love."

Kendu looked intently at Evan. His life was extremely controlled by image and position and bullshit about what other people thought and their values and opinions. He'd only been home around the clock because he was scared to leave his daughter with Evan. And he hadn't called Milan, because he couldn't think of any way to explain that he needed her to hold on just a little while longer. So he took the hit on the chin and risked losing the woman he loved forever, because he knew if he called her or he went to Soho and Milan told him she was leaving him, the script would flip and he would be the one to act crazy.

Evan tried not to look in Kendu's eyes. She knew he was only doing this because of his image, and since he was this year's recipient of the Arthur Ashe Courage Award, the last thing he needed was a scandal. So she decided she would take what she could get. Besides, if she couldn't have him the way she wanted and the way she needed, then his reputation would pay dearly for it.

"Mrs. Malik," the governess called, walking into the dining room and standing near the door, "Bridget is on the phone."

Evan looked at the photographer. "Are we done?"

"Yes, we are?"

"Great"—Evan turned to Kendu—"honey, I have a lunch date with the girls: Jaise, Chaunci, and *Milan*." She rolled her eyes. "So I'm sure that's why Bridget is calling." She looked back at the governess. "Tell her that I'm on my way."

The Club

When Evan arrived at the Russian Tea Room, Jaise and Bridget were already seated and the camera was rolling. Evan was confident that in her gray and white diagonal-striped Fendi dress she looked beautiful; the long bell sleeves covered the scars of her self-inflicted wounds and the voices in her head were silent for the moment. She walked over to Bridget and Jaise and air kissed them both on the cheeks. "Darlings." She batted her eyes.

"Hi, sweetie," Jaise said. "How've you been?"

"Wonderful."

"Really?" Bridget said. "You want to tell the camera why you were in the hospital?"

"My publicist released a statement."

"I mean the real story."

"Bridget, you're pathetic," Evan dismissed her, waving her hand. "Histrionics at any and all cost."

"Pretty much the name of the game."

"You know what," Jaise said defensively, "why don't you give it a rest, Bridget. She doesn't have to keep explaining herself."

"Okay, well, why don't you explain yourself," Bridget said snidely. "Explain why a woman of your caliber would fall in love with a Brooklyn cop. Not the chief of police, not the captain, but a low-level detective. Would you like to explain that to the camera?"

Jaise twisted her lips. "What business is it of yours? Bilal is a great man. You act as if his being in my life is a secret. He's been in front of the cameras."

"My sentiments exactly, so why don't you explain."

Evan looked confused. "What happened to Trenton?"

"He was cheating on me."

"So you just up and dump him?" Evan batted her eyes. "And for a cop? Are you crazy?"

"Look," Jaise said, clearly agitated, "so what if he isn't rich."

"So what if he isn't rich? Did you forget about your little alimony situation, or are you really that desperate? Damn, Jaise, be for real. If you get remarried your forty thousand dollars a month in alimony stops. My God."

"Well, I'll be damned," Bridget said. "Mo' drama unveiled." She looked toward the camera and arched her eyebrows. "Stay tuned. So if you marry a broke man, Milan won't be the only has-been, is that what she's saying, Jaise?"

Jaise cut her eyes at Evan. Her alimony settlement was something she didn't want anyone to know about, not since her divorce decree had a gag order in it. Jaise never thought the details would slip out, let alone on national television. "Who said I was getting married?"

"I don't believe this." Evan shook her head. "You have hooked up with the local fuckin' Jamaican cab driver."

"He's not a cab driver."

"He might as well be. What's the difference? As a matter of fact, a cab driver makes more money."

"Why is everything about money? Maybe I actually love him."

"What does love have to do with it?" Evan shook her head. "You would really lose it all for a cop?"

"You losin' all for a football player." She looked Evan over. "Everyone knows what you were really in the hospital for. It's no secret that you have a mental health diagnosis. People talk, doctors get paid off. Please, that shit is all over the Internet, which is why you released a statement saying the opposite. So when you get your thoughts in order, you tell me about my man, broke or otherwise."

"Fuck you, Jaise."

Jaise crossed her legs. "No, honey, for all intents and purposes"—she pointed at Evan—"fuck you."

"Is that the new language for friends?" Bridget smiled. "Oh, and before I forget, Chaunci and Milan are on their way, and I need you two to be extrasensitive to Milan. No references to broke bitches spewed around, keep the welfare comments to yourself, and don't ask her if her EBT card works here, because clearly this place doesn't take food stamps."

"Is she doing that bad?" Evan asked.

"Unfortunately, she is." Bridget sipped her drink. "I just spoke with her last night, and she was sounding so pitiful."

"Where was she calling you from?"

"I think she was walking the street, because I could hear the wind whipping in the background."

"But they had so much money. How could they really be broke?" Jaise questioned.

"How many rich crackheads do you know?" Bridget asked.

"None."

"Exactly."

"Well," Jaise said, concerned, "should we give her money?"

"That's awfully thoughtful of you, Jaise," Bridget said, holding up her glass for the waiter to refresh her martini, "considering Milan called you a trashbox."

Jaise practically choked on her drink. "Are you serious?" She cleared her throat.

"Looks like we've gotten here right on time, Milan," Chaunci said as she and Milan walked in the door flashing mile-wide smiles. "I swear I heard someone calling your name." She looked at Jaise, Bridget, and Evan. "Seeing as how the bitches have arrived"—Chaunci snapped her fingers—"let the chatter continue." She laid her Ferragamo clutch on the table, and she and Milan took their seats.

Evan stared at Milan and she could clearly envision her riding Kendu's dick. "Milan, Kendu and I—"

Milan couldn't help how quickly her neck whipped around. "You and Kendu what?"

"Were thinking of asking you to be our new baby's godmother."

Milan started to cough. "Excuse me?"

"You're pregnant?!" Jaise exclaimed. "Is that what's wrong with you?"

"No," Evan chuckled, "not yet anyway. But we are working on a baby. Aiyanna wants a little brother or sister."

Milan looked around the room. She wondered if anyone else besides her and Chaunci heard the bomb ticking.

"Congratulations." Jaise smiled. "Now, maybe you can judge your own business and stay out of mine." She looked Evan over.

"I guess they stopped selling dogs," Milan said as she crossed her legs one way and then nervously crossed them the other way.

"Was that supposed to be a joke?" Evan snapped.

Milan sipped her drink, and said in the interests of peace, "Yeah, it was a joke."

"So how long have you been trying to have a baby?" Jaise asked Evan.

"For the last two weeks."

Milan looked around. The bomb had stopped ticking; it had exploded.

"Ladies," Evan continued on, "my husband and I are getting it on all day long." She sipped her drink. "I swear I'm turning into a freak. Every morning around nine we begin to make love all day."

"Wow, Evan, I mean, I have to admit it took me a while to have sex in broad daylight," Jaise confessed.

"Well, what is this," Milan said, "confessions of the trashbox hookers?"

Bridget smiled and winked an eye at Jaise. "Told you."

"Are you calling me a hooker, Milan?"

"Sure did. And what are you going to do? I'm so sick of this whole reality TV, cameras, and all of this other bullshit. Fuck it, I don't like you." She looked at Jaise. "And you, Evan, are pitiful. So I tell you what, shut the fuck up, keep my name outcha mouths, and don't say shit else to me."

Chaunci leaned against Milan's shoulder and whispered, "I didn't wear the right shoes to be bustin' these bitches up."

"Why the hell are you so angry?" Jaise looked taken aback.

"You know what," Milan snapped, "cut the innocent, peace-making bullshit."

Evan looked at Milan long and hard, and the more she tried to contain herself the less control she realized she had. "Jaise, ignore this broke-ass, low-budget sleaze."

"Don't tell Jaise to ignore me. You need to be telling your man that."

"I'll kick your ass!" Evan reached across the table, and Jaise pulled her back.

Evan started screaming and Bridget snapped, "I can't believe you just held her back! This isn't the Layaway Hos, this is the *Millionaire Wives Club*. We don't postpone shit!"

Jaise turned to Bridget. "You know what, I'm getting real sick of you. Most producers on these shows are quiet, and people don't even know who they are, because they know how to shut up. But you, you are in everything! I can't wait until this show is over because then I can look at each and every one of y'all and tell you to kiss my ass."

"I know that wasn't the peacemaker," Milan snapped as security rushed into the room.

Chaunci looked at security and spat, "I just had a flashback, so you know what, this may as well be the reunion show, because I'm done, and don't call me for another goddamn get-together." She looked at Milan. "Let's go."

"Let's." Milan grabbed her bag as she and Chaunci stormed out of the restaurant.

Bridget looked at Evan and Jaise, who were being shielded by security. "What are you two pissed off for? Smile, they've just guaranteed us a second season."

It'll Be a Motherfucker

Milan

The morning when it hit Milan that she'd been lying in Kendu's bed, grooving for far too long to silence and dancing with loneliness, was when she realized she didn't have any more tears left.

It's not as if she didn't know from the onset that she'd been holding on to nothing. It's just that nothing had ever felt so good as it did today . . . well, yesterday . . . back when they had enough passion between them that Milan could emotionally afford to ignore the obvious, that he was married and had a family. But not anymore. Not today, at least. Milan knew she had to leave, because if she didn't, she would be fighting for the rest of her life and the rest of her love with Kendu, to desperately get in where she fit in.

She'd applied for an apartment on Church Avenue in Brooklyn on an emotional whim, a spur-of-the-moment type of thing, when she couldn't reach Kendu no matter how much she'd called or how many messages she'd left. She did it because she needed to make believe—at least at the time—that she had the nerve and the heart enough to say, Fuck him, she didn't need him, despite how bad she hurt inside. So, she combed the paper, found an apartment, completed the application, and a few days later, surprisingly, she was approved. And yesterday, when her soul whispered to her that her willingly lying in Kendu's bed, two weeks after not hearing anything from him, was too long, was when she went straight from work and signed the lease.

Milan looked around at the beautiful space she was leaving behind and knew that she'd worn out her welcome. She'd derailed her own plans and this time she had to get back on track. To hell with the name brands, the wealthy friends, and all the other artificial things that controlled her life.

She had to leave, especially now that she had the keys to her new place in her purse and the moving men were downstairs with her boxes of clothes and some of the things she salvaged from her old place with Yusef.

Milan threw her purse onto her shoulder, grabbed her last box, tossed the keys to Kendu's apartment in the middle of the floor, and walked out the door.

She attempted to swallow the lump in her throat repeatedly, but it felt as if the ball of emotion resting on her tongue was too much to push back into her stomach. This left her with no choice but to accept that the pain of leaving here would be around for a while.

"Ready, ma'am?" the driver said to her, as he placed his keys in the truck's ignition and turned his aged baseball cap around backward.

"As ready as I'll ever be." Milan forced her lips to curl into a smile.

"Let's be out then."

Milan looked out the window as the driver pulled off. She closed her eyes for the remainder of the ride. She didn't care about the route the driver took. All she wanted was to arrive at her new place.

Twenty minutes of riding with the wind cutting across her face, and then Milan opened her eyes and the driver said, "Looks like we're here."

Milan didn't respond. She looked at the people walking swiftly up and down the mixed block of apartment buildings, row houses, and single-family dwellings. Milan was moving into a fifth-floor apartment in a tall brick building filled with mixed-income people, some working and some chilling on the block. It was a far cry from the upscale apartments of doormen, dog walkers, and living lavishly. Instead this was real life, and real shit went on here.

Strangely enough, as if she were suddenly high off contact, Milan didn't feel like she had hit rock bottom. She felt on top. Like she was able to do this—this place and this space was freedom, a detox of sorts, where all the fucked-up love could ease from her pores and let her become sound again.

As Milan placed her keys in the door and the movers brought in her things, she knew this was where she was supposed to be.

After an hour of moving boxes into the one-bedroom flat, and the moving men had gone, Milan felt as if she had mastered her situation. But then, unexpected or perhaps expected, yet unwanted, tears filled the back of her eyes and her heart started melting into an emotionally drained piece of shit. Suddenly, she felt empty. Like all that she'd been through, the glitz, the glamour, the money . . . the millions . . . and millions . . . of dollars . . . and all she had left, and all she'd been able to accomplish in all of her thirty years . . . was nothing. Absolutely nothing.

Milan crouched to her knees in the middle of her wood floor, among the sea of boxes, and cried until she couldn't cry anymore.

Evan

"You sure you can't be Daddy's date?" Kendu teased Aiyanna as he stood in her doorway dressed in his two-piece black Armani suit.

Aiyanna coughed as she sat up in bed. "Daddy, can you stay home and I can be your date in front of the TV?"

"Well, that's awfully selfish of you, Aiyanna," Evan blurted out as she walked up next to Kendu in her royal blue cocktail dress and placed her hands around his waist. "This is very important to Daddy, and that should mean more to you than him staying home."

"I just feel really sick." Aiyanna looked at Kendu with tears in her eyes.

Kendu brushed Evan's arms from around his waist. He walked over to Aiyanna's bed and kneeled beside her. "You really want Daddy here with you?"

"Yes."

He unbuttoned his jacket. "Ai'ight, then I'ma stay here." He pressed his hand against the back of her head. "She has a fever," he said, looking at Evan.

"She also has a nurse." Evan walked over and grabbed Kendu's hand. "And you don't need to stay home. Aiyanna is fine. You just have her spoiled. There is more to life then the life and times of Aiyanna Malik. You are the recipient of the Arthur Ashe Courage Award for the all the hard work you do with our charity. You deserve this."

"But she's sick."

"Aren't you always telling me she will be okay?"

Kendu nodded.

"Well, then she will be fine. This is an opportunity of a lifetime. Now, I insist that our child understand that Mommy and Daddy love her but we have to go."

Kendu stared at Aiyanna and held her hand. "You know I love you, and when I come home I'll read you a story, no matter the time."

"Daddy, please stay home with me."

"This is enough," Evan interjected.

"Back up, Evan." Kendu shot her a look that told her to take it down.

Kendu cleared his throat. "Listen, Daddy does spoil you a lot, because you're Daddy's main girl. But I think it's important that Daddy attend this function. After all, I'm getting the Arthur Ashe Courage Award. Do you know who he was?"

"No." Aiyanna shook her head as Kendu wiped her tears away.

"He was a great man," Kendu said, his voice animated. "And he loved his community, and he did a lot of things to help other people."

"Like you do, Daddy?"

"Exactly, and you know why I do that?"

"Why?"

"Because when Daddy was a little boy I didn't have a mommy or a daddy. I lived in a lot of foster homes, and when I turned ten your granny adopted me. So it's my way of giving back to my community."

"So you're a great man too, Daddy?"

"Of course he is." Evan smiled.

"You're like Superman, Daddy?" Aiyanna laughed.

"Yeah"—Kendu chuckled—"I think I like being on the same level as Superman." He placed his right hand like a visor over his eyes. "It's a bird . . . it's a plane . . ."

Aiyanna stood up on her bed. "No, it's my daddy!"

"Aren't we well all of a sudden?" Evan said. "No standing on the bed, and we will see you later."

"Bye." Aiyanna sat back down and poked her lips out.

Evan waved and walked out in front of Kendu, who turned around and whispered to Aiyanna, "You can stand on the bed. Daddy paid for it."

"Sweetie," Evan said to Kendu as they walked the red carpet, "would you be still so we can pose for a few pictures?"

"Aiyanna is calling me." He pulled his BlackBerry from his pocket.

Evan snatched it from his hand and before he could protest she turned it off and tossed it in her purse. "It's your show tonight. If it's an emergency the nurse has my cell phone number."

"Kendu! Kendu!" a few reporters yelled, as he and Evan posed for pictures. "How does it feel receiving such a great reward?"

Kendu smiled and said, "Like Superman." And he headed inside to the ceremony. He mingled with a few of his teammates and athlete friends, while Evan felt like a superstar in her own right as many of the athletes' and entertainers' wives were dying to know how she managed to be taping for such a hit series.

When the awards ceremony began, Evan was boiled over in excitement when Michael Jordan was there in person to present the award to Kendu. "On behalf," Michael said, "of every great athlete that is here, that ever lived, and ever will be, we present to you, Kendu Malik, the great Arthur Ashe Courage Award!"

Everyone stood up and the crowd erupted in cheers.

Evan kissed Kendu on the cheek. He stood up and walked toward the stage.

"Man," he said into the mic once he reached the podium. "Wow." He looked around. "God is good. When I started doing this, I never thought of recognition or admiration. All I thought about were the kids and making a difference . . ." As Kendu continued on, one of the escorts for the awards ceremony walked up to him and whispered that he needed to speed things along, because he had an emergency at home. "Thanks to all of you." His mood quickly changed. "God bless." He hurried backstage, where one of the backstage assistants told him he needed to call home.

"Kendu," Evan said as she rushed backstage, "what happened? Why'd you cut your speech short?"

"It's an emergency at home." He dialed Aiyanna's nurse. "What's the problem?" he said when she answered.

"Aiyanna," the nurse's voice trembled, "started having convulsions, and before I knew anything she'd fallen off the bed and hit her head. She won't stop bleeding! The ambulance is on its way. We will meet you at the hospital."

"What's wrong?" Evan panicked.

"Aiyanna," Kendu said as he started walking swiftly toward the car. "She started having seizures and she hit her head. The nurse said something about a lot of bleeding. I knew I should've stayed home!" he said as he jumped into the car and sped up the highway.

Milan sat on the edge of the nurse's desk wondering how she would tell Kendu that she'd moved, both mentally and physically. That there was no way she could continue to love and to live like this, especially since she was losing herself in the process.

"Eight-year-old girl, convulsing," she was startled to hear as EMT workers burst through the doors with doctors running beside them. When she looked up, Kendu was staring her in the face and the doctors were spitting orders at her about what they needed to do. Milan broke her gaze from Kendu and swiftly began to follow the doctors' orders.

As they transferred Aiyanna to the hospital bed, Milan started cutting Aiyanna's clothes off of her and asking Kendu and Evan questions. "What happened?"

"She was sick earlier," said Aiyanna's nurse, who was also there.

"What was she sick from?"

"I'm not sure," the nurse said. "I thought she was feeling better because she started playing. I left the room for five minutes and when I came back she was unconscious, having seizures, and had hit her head."

"Does she have a history of seizures?" Milan did her best not to look at Kendu for longer than she had to.

"No," the nurse said.

"Any family history?"

"No." Evan shook her head. "Stop asking us questions and help my child!" she cried.

"I'm trying," Milan said as she looked at the doctor. "This is a lot of bleeding. Her blood should've started to clot by now."

The doctor squeezed the IV. "This is not good."

"What's not good?" Kendu asked in a panic.

"You need to leave," the doctor said to Kendu. "Please, we need you and your wife to leave the room."

"I'm not leaving my daughter."

"Mr. Malik, I'm trying to explain to you—"

"You can't hear? I'm not going any-fuckin'-where."

Milan looked at Kendu and then to Evan. "Please. I know you are upset, but this is standard procedure, and we can't get to the bottom of this if you're in here. Please." She looked Kendu in the eyes. "Leave. We will keep you informed every step of the way."

"I need to know what's wrong with my daughter."

Milan grabbed Kendu's hand. "Let us find out."

Kendu stood there.

"Please."

Kendu stepped reluctantly out of the room with Evan following behind him.

The team of doctors examined Aiyanna and sent samples of her blood to the lab. "She needs a blood transfusion," the doctor said. "Her blood's not clotting, and she's losing a lot of it."

"What's wrong?" Milan asked, suppressing her panic.

"I don't know, but I know we have to do this in order to save her life."

"I'll go and tell the parents," Milan said.

"Yes," the doctor said, "and go quickly. We need to find out in a hurry who's the match or if they both are. That would be even better."

Milan walked swiftly down the corridor and was met midway by Evan and Kendu, who were visibly upset. "What's going on?" Kendu spat.

"Listen," Milan said, "Aiyanna's blood won't clot."

"What do mean it won't clot?!" Kendu snapped.

Milan could tell by the vein jumping in Kendu's neck that he was two seconds from kicking somebody's ass. "Knott," she said, knowing that calling him by that name always calmed him, "Aiyanna is really sick." She looked over at Evan. "And in order for us to help her we need to give her a blood transfusion. And we need your consent."

"And if we don't give it?" Evan asked, hating the scent of Milan's perfume.

"She will die," Milan said.

"Milan, you can't let my daughter die," Kendu said. "Not my baby."

Evan turned to Kendu and began crying on his shoulder.

Mixed emotions raced through Milan's head, but this was not the time to analyze how she needed to detox from this relationship. There was no way she could continuously deal with all of this. "I need you to help me help you," Milan said.

"Look," Evan said in a panic, "I keep trying to make the doctors understand that I believe Aiyanna has Addison's disease, and I keep trying to have her tested, and nobody is listening to me." She looked Milan in the eyes. "I need someone to see that I need help."

Milan felt nauseated. This was too much weight to carry. "Do you know how rare Addison's disease is? And how painful those tests are? Do you have a family history of that?" Milan looked at Evan strangely.

"Don't fuckin' tell me about my baby!" Evan started to scream. "I know what is wrong with my baby!"

"Wait a minute." Milan attempted to get things under control. "This isn't about you, this is about Aiyanna! She needs help, and we are trying here. Now, you need to get it together. Your daughter will die if she doesn't get a blood transfusion, and then what will you have to argue over? Now, I need you two"—she pointed to Evan and Kendu—"to get it together and be strong for your daughter. We are trying to assist you, not battle with you. Now, you need to be tested so we can see what your blood type is and make sure you're not carrying any diseases. Or would you rather stand out here and argue than give your daughter blood?" She paused. "Now let's go," Milan said as she gave a heavy sigh and led them to an examination room, where the phlebotomist took their blood and sent the samples to the lab. "As soon as the results come in, I will be back," Milan said as she walked Evan and Kendu back to the patients' lounge.

A half hour later the lab technician delivered the results. "Thank God," Milan said as she opened the chart and compared it to Aiyanna's. Milan stared blankly at the pages. She knew for sure she'd seen wrong or maybe she didn't understand. Hell, it had been a while since she had practiced nursing, so maybe she had this whole deal wrong.

"What are the results?" One of the doctors walked over. "We need this immediately."

Milan didn't answer.

"Nurse Starks, do you hear me talking to you?" the doctor asked.

"Oh yes . . . yes, doctor."

"So what are they?"

"They don't match." Milan swallowed.

"What do you mean they don't match?" the doctor asked.

"They don't. The father has type B blood."

"And the mother?"

"A."

"The child has O positive. That's not possible." The doctor took the chart. "Well, it's here in black-and-white. Are they the natural parents or is she adopted?"

"She's not adopted, I can assure you of that," Milan said. "Besides, she's the spitting image of her mother."

"It's clear, then," the doctor continued, "he's not the father." The doctor handed the chart back to Milan. "And quite frankly I don't give a damn who is. I have a little girl in there who will die if we don't get this transfusion going. Now, if I need to I will have the social worker call the judge and we will have an emergency hearing allowing us to give her blood from the hospital's bank."

"Can I just talk to them before you do that?" Milan said.

"Yes," the doctor said, "and hurry."

Milan walked over to Kendu and Evan and they both stood up. "Listen"—she cleared her throat—"we ran the test."

"Get to the point," Kendu said in a panic.

"I am, and we have the results, but Aiyanna . . . can't receive blood from either of you."

"What?" Evan said, put off.

"What the hell does that mean?" Kendu spat. "Of course my baby can have my blood."

"No, she can't."

"Why not?"

"Because it doesn't match." She looked Kendu dead in his eyes, but seeing that her words hadn't registered she continued on. "Aiyanna has O positive blood, and unless you have another donor we will need to pull from the hospital's supply. We screen the blood carefully, so it will be okay."

"Wait a minute," Kendu said as if he were still pondering what Milan was saying. "What are you saying to me about our blood not matching our baby? Is that normal?"

Milan attempted to brush him off. "It happens, Kendu, but that's not important."

Kendu stared at Milan and she averted her eyes. "I asked you a question," he said, "and you're bullshittin' me?"

"Listen, I will explain it to you later, but right now this is what you need to deal with: Your daughter needs you to sign this consent. I'm begging you to please do it, because she can't wait much longer." Milan shoved the papers in front of them and they scribbled their signatures on them. Afterward she quickly left the room and headed to the operating room, where they were prepping Aiyanna and awaiting the consent.

An hour later Milan sat at the nurse's station, distressed. Maybe she was mistaken; maybe Aiyanna was Kendu's child. She looked down at Aiyanna's chart . . . *Blood types don't lie,* she thought.

A voice interrupted Milan's thoughts. "Can I speak to you for a minute?"

She looked up and it was Evan. "What is it?" Milan asked.

"Can we speak someplace private?"

Milan led Evan to an empty room and closed the door. "I'm listening."

"Thank you for what you did earlier, with Kendu. I didn't know the blood wouldn't be a match."

"You didn't know," Milan snapped. "How didn't you know?"

"I didn't." She paused. "I just thought that Kendu was the—"

"Was the what?" Milan squinted her eyes. "The right choice, the right man, or he had the right money? You aren't shit, you know that?!" Milan spat. "Nothing. I had fuckin' regarded you as higher than a mole, but I see you're lower than that."

"I didn't come here to argue with you."

"No, you came to feel me out and see if I would be willing to keep some bogus-ass secret of yours, but make no mistake, I'm not. So you can keep your goddamn thank you."

"You know how much he loves his daughter?"

"She's not his daughter." Milan pointed into Evan's face.

"You hate me that much?" Evan batted her extended lashes.

"If you don't tell him I will."

"Are you threatening me?"

"You got twenty-four fuckin' hours to figure out if it's a threat or not."

"Milan!"

"Get the fuck out my face," she said, tight-lipped.

The doctor walked into the room. "Ladies, is everything okay? We can hear you down the hall. Why are you back here?"

"Doctor," Milan said, "everything is fine. Mrs. Malik was upset and confused, and I just wanted to explain some things to her."

"Okay, well"—he tapped Evan on the shoulder—"come and let me speak to you and your husband."

"My baby is out of surgery?" Evan wiped tears from her eyes.

"Yes, she is," the doctor said as they walked to the family waiting area where Kendu was.

"Everything looks great," the doctor said. "We need to run some more tests, but at least we were able to stop the bleeding."

"Can she come home?" Kendu asked.

"Not tonight, but I hope in a couple of days."

"Thank you." Evan smiled. "Can we see her now?"

"Of course, but she needs to get some rest."

"We'll only stay for a few minutes and then we'll leave."

"I'm not leaving," Kendu said. "I'll be spending the night."

"That's not necessary," Evan said. "You need your rest."

"Don't," he said to her and then looked at the doctor. "What room is she is in?"

Milan stood back and watched them walk down the hall toward Aiyanna's room. She knew she needed to tell Kendu, but then again, maybe she didn't. Hell, she didn't need to get involved, and the whole thing was too damn confusing and complicated anyway. And what exactly would she say, "Aiyanna isn't your baby?" And then what?

She looked at the clock and saw that her shift had ended. She grabbed her coat and started down the corridor toward the elevator.

"You need a ride?" one of her coworkers yelled.

"No," she said, "I need a good train ride to help me clear my head."

"All right, good-night."

"Good-night." She stepped on the elevator and the doors closed behind her.

Jaise

Jaise tried to act as if the cameras weren't following her around as she thought about how Jabril had been creeping through the house all week, stuttering, starting sentences and not finishing them, half eating his dinner, and when he didn't have to work at the afterschool job he had started at McDonald's, such as tonight, he was going to bed around eight.

"Jabril is into something he has no business being in," Jaise said to Bilal, who had just come in from work. He looked at the food Jaise had prepared for him and smiled, as he shifted his gun holster to unload his service revolver. Bilal was around all the time now. "What makes you say that?" he asked, placing his gun in the closet's safe.

"Because I know this little boy. Acting depressed. I swear if he has an STD I'm getting his jimmy cut off. Period."

"Oh, that's real motherly of you. Why don't you just ask him what the problem is?"

"I did. The other night I said, 'Jabril, don't let no li'l tramp cause you and me to have problems.' "

"Jaise, you have to chill with spazzin' like that," Bilal said kissing her on the lips. "He's not going to tell you anything if you're making comments like that."

Jaise didn't respond. She simply rolled her eyes.

"Where is he now?" Bilal asked.

"In the bed."

"It's eight o'clock," Bilal said as the bell rang.

"Exactly." Jaise rose from the couch.

"After I eat I'll go and talk to him." He watched Jaise walk to the door. "Damn, girl," he said flirtatiously, "look at that ass. Who is your man?"

"Don't you worry about him. All I need to know is your name." She laughed while opening the door.

"Well, I'm glad motherfuckers is laughin' over here!" A mahogany brown woman with streaked honey blond hair, wearing a cropped denim jacket, a tight wife beater that showcased her cleavage tattoo of ME AND RAFIQUE, a pair of silver jeans with rhinestones going down the side of each leg, and a pair of Thin Mints high-top Pastry sneakers on pushed her way through Jaise's front door.

The woman shoved a crying girl ahead of her into the living room, the same girl Jaise had caught in Jabril's room over a month ago and made leave through the window. "Is this where the li'l negro live?" the woman spat at the girl.

"Who are you?" Jaise said, confused. She looked at the girl. "And why are you in my house?"

"Tell her." The woman pushed the young girl on her shoulder again. "Tell her who you are and then call his ass in here." When the girl didn't respond quick enough the woman said, "I said tell her who you are!"

"Chris . . ." the girl cried, "Chris . . . tina."

"You ain't no goddamn Christina," the angry woman spat. "You ass is baby mama. Tell her your name is M.C. Brilly Bril's baby mama."

"Brilly Bril?" Bilal said, confused.

"What?!" Jaise screamed in disbelief. "Come again? Baby mama?!"

"Oh, you ain't know?" the woman screeched. "Well, seems your li'l thug don't know how to keep his thing in his pants."

"My li'l thug," Jaise snapped. "Who the fuck are you? Am I being punk'd?" Jaise asked.

"Not at all, dear," Bridget said. "This is all your life."

"And this right here," the angry woman said, pointing to her daughter's stomach, "is all him!"

"Are you trying to say that my son got your daughter pregnant?"

"Ah hell, nawl," Christina's mama spat. "Did you follow this li'l fool home to see if his family was slow? Why is she asking me the obvious? I sure hope this li'l boy ain't retarded."

"He ain't retarded," Christina cried.

"He is retarded," her mother snapped. "His mama's crazy. Look at her. She don't know shit. Is she high? You better not be pregnant by no damn crackhead's baby!"

"Bilal," Jaise turned to him, "if you don't lock these motherfuckers up now—"

"My name ain't motherfucker, it's Al-Taniesha." She swerved her neck.

"What kinda shit is this?" Jaise said in stunned disbelief.

"Jabril!" Bilal yelled up the stairs. "Come here."

"Yeah," Jaise screamed, "get your ass down here! Right now!"

"What, Ma?" He opened the door of his room and peeked out. When he saw Christina and her mother he looked as if he'd seen a ghost.

"Oh yeah," Jaise said. "Bring yo' ass down these stairs right now."

"That's him?" Al-Taniesha snapped at her daughter. "Look at this skinny motherfucker here, lookin' like T. I."

"Listen," Jaise said to Al-Taniesha, "you need to calm down all of what you're saying about my son!"

"And what you gon' do?"

"Ma," Jabril interrupted, "chill. That's my girl. I got her as the screen saver on my iPhone. She's my number one friend on My-Space."

Christina whined, "I knew you was the truth, Bril."

Jaise smacked Jabril so hard that he fell onto the couch. "What I tell you about these li'l hoochies, huh? And of all the tramps on Easy Street you go knock up Keyshia Cole's goddamn sister. "

"I swear," Bridget said, "Junior should've been the reality star. He's a natural."

"My daughter is not a hoochie, tramp. And I ain't Frankie. You the one over here raising Young Jeezy. All I know," Al-Taniesha said, looking around the living room, "is that you got cameras up in here makin' videos, y'all livin' in the Grand Arbor section while we over there in Lafayette Garden, and you don't even have plastic on yo' shit. So it seems to me that Jabril gon' do the right thing because he has more than enough to share."

"Share?!" Jaise completely lost it. "Share what? He just turned seventeen years old. He ain't got shit. You wanna know what Jabril has? A pair of fuckin' jeans he paid for and some sneakers he bought last week. These are my things. I live in Grand Arbor. Jabril just has a room here. This, all of this is my shit." She turned to Jabril. "Just when I think you are improving you pull a stunt like this. Well, I tell you what, if this child is having your baby—"

"If?" Al-Taniesha spat.

"Yes, if. I'm not claiming some random girl's baby. Are you crazy? We do a DNA test like Maury Povich around here."

"Ma," Jabril said, "Christina's straight. Ain't nobody else ran up in that. Tell 'em, Christina."

"You got that, Bril. Ain't nobody else been here but you."

"Yeah, 'cause I got that ass sewed up." He gave her half a grin. "I'ma be a good father, too."

Jaise smacked Jabril in the back of his head. "Spell 'father,' Jabril? It's spelled day care, child support, life insurance, medical insurance, lonely nights at home when you can't get no girl, 'cause this mama ain't babysitting."

"You got that right, girl. 'Cause I'm doin' me," Al-Taniesha spat. "Grandma is gettin' her swerve on. I have raised my kids. Time for me to get my hair and nails done when I feel like it. I ain't gon' be tied down to no crib. Hmph and I got me a li'l young 'un too, Rafique, at home waitin' on me right now."

"Ma, this is my baby," Jabril insisted.

"Shut up! You don't know anything. You just stopped playing with G.I. Joe last year. You don't know nothin'. Be quiet. You are not claiming some random baby, because this fresh-ass little girl was over here riding your dick, instead of doing her school work! I have plans for you. You're going to college, not to child support court or to welfare to give your social security number. Hell no, I'm not having it."

"So what are you saying?" Al-Taniesha spat. "That you want me to kick yo' ass now or after the baby's born?"

"Then I guess it'll be on an' crackin'!" Jaise snapped, slipping her shoes off.

"Ain't nothin' but a word." Al-Taniesha spat, taking off her earrings. She reached into her purse, pulled her Vaseline out, and rubbed it on her face.

Bilal and Jabril stepped in between the two women. "What are you two doing? Stop it! Now listen." Bilal looked at Al-Taniesha. "You need to leave."

"And don't come back!" Jaise pointed over Bilal's shoulder. "Until you and the li'l ghetto bird you had have a blood test in hand."

"Ma," Jabril said seriously, as he walked over to Christina and grabbed her hand. "I love her and if things go as planned I wanna marry her."

"Awwl, Bril." Christina wiped her eyes. "That's the realest shit I ever heard."

"Yeah, that was sweet," Al-Taniesha said. "I wish Rafique would say some shit like that to me."

"Oh . . . my . . . God. I need a moment. Jabril, just tell Christina good-night and you'll talk to her later, because we have some things we need to discuss."

"That's wassup," Al-Taniesha said as they walked toward the door. "We gon' get at y'all soon, so you go on and handle that. 'Cause we got a crib that need to be bought. Milk higher than a ma'fucker now, shit. And WIC ain't what it used to be. So get at me when you got it figured out how we gon' do this."

"Ai'ight, Christina, boo," Jabril said before he closed the door. "I'ma come through and see about you probably tomorrow."

"Don't make me and the baby wait too long."

Jabril closed the door and turned to Jaise, who screamed in his face, "Have you lost yo' fuckin' mind?! What the hell are you gon' do with a damn baby? You can barely take care of yourself!"

"I been doin' a damn good job of it this long!"

"What is that supposed to mean? And don't cuss in my face!"

"Hmph, we both know my ole dude ain't nowhere around, and don't get me wrong, Bilal, I like you, but before you she was too busy stressin' over a dude who wasn't even beat for me. And now all of a sudden she wants to be my mother?"

"I don't appreciate that, Jabril. I know I haven't been the best mother, but I have been there. I have done my best with what I had. And, no, you shouldn't have had to see me in some of the positions that I've been in, but give me some credit. Do you know the life you're setting up for yourself?"

"Anything gotta be better than the life you set up for me."

Jaise stood with tears in her eyes. Jabril's comment rocked her to the core. Bilal looked at Jaise and then to Jabril. "Let me speak to you for a minute," he said.

"Yo Ma," Jabril said, noticing his mother in tears, "I'm sorry. I didn't mean that. I know you've been trying."

"It's okay, just go on and talk to Bilal."

"See," Jabril said as Jaise left the room, "everything I do is wrong."

"Jabril," Bilal said, "listen, I'm not here to judge you or anything like that. Now, I get it, your father wasn't there and your mother didn't always make the best decisions, but you have to get through that, because the moment you decided you wanted to be a father was the moment you decided you wanted to be a man, so are you having this baby or what?"

"Hell yeah, I'ma have my baby. I ain't gon' be like my father." Tears trembled his voice. "I'ma be there for my baby, and I'ma love my girl. I'm not gon' put my hands on her and none of that whack-ass shit he did. I'ma love her the way you love my moms. I'ma be like you." Tears rolled down his cheeks.

Bilal walked up to Jabril and gave him a hug. "You already a man."

Jaise walked back into the room and noticed Jabril crying. "Is everything okay?"

Jabril wiped his eyes and walked over to his mother. "I'm sorry, Ma, for speaking to you the way I did."

"It's okay. Some things need to be said." She held Jabril in her arms and at least for that moment he felt like her baby again.

Chaunci

"Okay, bitch," Chaunci said, handing Milan a straw and a personal-size bottle of champagne, keeping another bottle for herself. "I brought you out here to listen."

"You didn't need to bring me to Jones Beach to listen. It may be spring, but it's cold as hell out here. We could've stayed at your house, or you could've come to my apartment," Milan complained while lying back on the small plastic chaise in the sand, as the evening wind whipped bits of sand toward the sky and blew her hair away from her face. She and Chaunci were two of the few people out here and among them were lovers and a few souls sitting on the edge of the water letting the cold waves run over their feet.

Chaunci sat next to Milan, and they both began champagne sipping through a straw. Chaunci looked at the gray sky and then back to Milan. "I just really need a sistah girl talk right now. And I need you to listen," Chaunci said.

Milan sipped. "As long as we don't get arrested for having this liquor out here in the open, I don't have any problems with listening. Otherwise," she said, pausing to take a sip, "a sistah might need some help with bail money. I'm a bit strapped."

Chaunci turned to her. "You're getting on my nerves."

"Okay, okay." Milan waved her hands in defeat. "Proceed."

"And allow me to give you the cue for when I'm soliciting your opinion."

"You are the opinionated one, not me."

Chaunci sighed. "Anywho, I told you about Idris taking me to court—"

"How did that turn out?"

"He has every other weekend and alternate holidays."

"How did you feel about that?"

"Defeated, and now I'm confused as hell."

"What makes you confused?"

"Hold it." Chaunci sat up. "Didn't I ask you to listen? Not give me a therapy session?"

"Then stop going around the point. Get to the shit."

"When I took Kobi to Idris's the first weekend, I stayed."

"What, for a few hours? That's understandable."

"Longer than that."

"Until she fell asleep?"

"No." Chaunci paused. "All weekend."

"Oh, okay, so what, are you pregnant now? 'Cause I know you fucked him."

"One of my pet peeves is when people think they know me," Chaunci griped. "Let me tell you the story."

"I'm listening."

"It was an accident."

"What?"

"Me sixty-nining him, letting him hit it from the back, and when I started riding him I knew at that point I had completely lost control."

Both women cracked up laughing. "This is really not funny." Chaunci chuckled. "This is really ridiculous. Like, I don't behave like this."

"Like what?"

"As if I've been waiting around for the last six—seven—years pining over his ass. And all it took was for him to whisper sweet nothings and voilà I was back to being with him."

Milan sucked air into her cheek and released it slowly from the side of her mouth. "Sometimes you need those sweet nothings to feel appreciated."

"No," Chaunci said, "I can appreciate me." She pointed to her chest. "I don't need him to do it."

"Maybe you had to learn that."

"I knew that already. I did. You don't understand. I was okay with me and my life, and I wasn't looking for self-discovery, so how could I not stand my ground and be pissed with him? What the hell was wrong with me that I slept with him? I mean, Edmon handled his business, so it wasn't the dick."

"So what about Edmon? Are still marrying him?"

Chaunci silently searched her thoughts. "I had this vision that Edmon and I would be a power couple. Making moves and conquering the world. Here I had one of the most prestigious, and wealthy, and financially supportive men in the world who wanted me, Miss Brooklyn-around-the-Way-Girl, to be his wife."

"So you feel like you owe him? Like he's responsible for your success?"

"I am indebted to him for believing in me and my dream, but I don't owe him anything, if that makes any sense."

"Why don't you just say that you were on this egocentric wave for a minute? You felt entitled to have a man of his caliber, and you were comfortable with that, until loneliness started kicking in."

"But why was I lonely?"

"Because a relationship without love is a disaster. Just like a relationship with love and no boundaries is destruction. Plain and simple. That's why we're friends: We're on the same boat just on opposite ends. You—no love, but commitment, well," Milan said, slurring slightly, "until you cheated. And me—I had nothing but love."

"I couldn't have said it better myself." Chaunci nodded her head.

"So what are you going to do about your situation?"

"I have to find a healthy medium. The problem is I don't know what that means."

"Well," Milan chuckled, "it could always mean movie night at my house and you don't even have to call me before you come. I won't hold it against you."

Chaunci fell out laughing. "I have to come check out your new place. How is it?"

"It's different. It's quiet and it feels normal. I don't feel like I'm faking the funk or looking to maintain this damn lifestyle that I can't afford, and I damn sure don't lie in bed at night wondering why the day has passed and Kendu hasn't come."

"How did he take your moving?"

"I didn't tell him."

"He doesn't know?"

"Nope."

"I guess he'll be stalking your ass. Do you still love him?"

"I love him until my chest literally hurts. Do you know, before I left I didn't see him for two weeks? Two whole weeks. He didn't call, come by, nothing, and then I had to listen to his wife brag about them making a baby."

"Maybe they were. Maybe they are."

"Well, he better make sure the motherfucker is his, because the first one isn't."

Chaunci spit out the champagne she had in her mouth. "Come again?"

Milan shook her head. "Aiyanna is not his."

"How do you know that?"

Milan recapped the story of how Aiyanna had been rushed to the hospital. "The blood didn't match."

"I don't understand," Chaunci said. "I heard you, but I feel like I heard wrong."

"A child's blood has to match the blood of one of the parents. You cannot have Evan with A blood, Kendu with B blood, and Aiyanna with O blood. It's like math: One plus one is two every time. It can never be three."

"I can't believe Evan, but then again, I can."

"So, can you imagine how I feel, loving this man too damn much, really, and knowing he's loving a child who's not his. And staying with a woman who's lying to him."

"Maybe he knows."

"He doesn't know."

"If I were you I wouldn't tell him."

"I'm not. That's his family. They deserve each other."

"Is Aiyanna okay, though?"

"She's out of the hospital now. But the doctor doesn't know what's wrong with her. She has to go see an infectious disease specialist. But I tell you one thing, I wouldn't put shit past that crazy-ass Evan, and I wouldn't be surprised if Aiyanna being sick has more to do with her mother and less to do with some rare disease."

Chaunci slurped the last of her champagne. "Milan, I'm glad I'm drunk, because there are some things you just can't process if you're sober."

They clinked their bottles. "Ain't that the truth," Milan said as they watched the waving sea. "Nothing but the truth."

Jaise

For three solid weeks Jaise acted as if nothing had gone on with Jabril that needed her attention, or required her to sit down and map out a new plan. One that involved a teenage son who was about to be a parent. She had no idea where to start or what to tell him. All she knew was that she had to say something to him, because according to Al-Taniesha, who'd been calling her house twice a day, "This li'l niggah has six months to get his shit in order."

But Jaise's denial was not about Jabril; her denial was about her being thirty-five and a single mother who had tried and retried, and tried again to maintain a balance of being this child's mother, his friend, his critic, and his support system. Yet a monkey wrench had been thrown into the deal—a baby that, like it or not, was on its way.

This was not what she had dreamed of for Jabril. A lifetime of baby mama, child support, and barely-making-it drama. She envisioned him as one day outgrowing his silliness and suddenly becoming Ivy League with the ability to make it happen for himself.

Not this, not having to figure out how to take care of a baby and take care of himself at the same time.

Jabril walked into the kitchen where Jaise was cooking dinner for the three of them. "Ma, can I hollah at you for a moment?"

"Yeah." She paused. "What's going on?"

"I noticed that you've been quiet ever since you found out about Christina."

"I'm disappointed, Jabril. I mean, we've been through some things together, but damn, I never expected this."

"Me either, Ma. But I have to deal with it."

"Well, Jabril, I don't know how to deal with it."

"Yes you do, Ma. You deal with it like you taught me to deal with things: head-on. We don't look back. We keep it movin'."

Jaise blinked. "Who did you say taught you that?"

"You did. You never gave up, Ma. You were always right there, fighting whatever came your way," he said, hunching his shoulders, "and I guess you know I gotta be the man you raised me to be."

Jaise couldn't believe what she was hearing. Had her son grown up in front of her eyes and she had missed it? Had he really just become a man without Jaise having a self-help book to help her do it? Well, damn, maybe she wasn't that bad of a mother after all.

"Okay, Jabril, I guess we're in this together."

"So does that mean I can invite Christina over?"

Jaise did her best not to twist her lips. "Yeah, and I guess you need to invite her ghetto-ass mama, too."

"She ain't ghetto, Ma. She got a lot of class."

"I just told Christina," Al-Taniesha said, popping her chewing gum, "I thought y'all motherfuckers was tryna pull the okeydoke. I'm glad y'all called 'cause word up I was bought to bust a crip walk out this motherfucker."

"Come in." Jaise swallowed, promising herself that she would do her best to accept Christina and her family, but the mere fact that she'd just opened the door for them and already wanted them to leave wasn't a good sign.

"Dis my man Rafique." Al-Taniesha pointed to the man dressed all in lavender with a pink boa around his neck walking behind her into Jaise's living room.

"But er'body calls me Lollipop," Rafique said, flinging his wrist, and for a minute there Jaise could've sworn he was switching his ass.

"Umm," Jaise stuttered, "Al-Taniesha and ummm . . ." She pointed to Rafique.

"Lollipop," he answered.

"Yes, Lollipop, this is Bilal."

"Hol' up." Rafique snapped his fingers. "Al-Taniesha," he attempted to whisper, "we gon' need to roll. You know I got them two warrants for indecent exposure and that niggah there is five-oh."

"How you know?" she attempted to whisper back.

" 'Cause he arrested me before."

"Is everything okay?" Jaise asked.

"We scraight," Rafique insisted. "Lollipop is da hell scraight."

"Where's Christina?" Jaise asked.

"She's comin'," Al-Taniesha answered. "Li'l T.I. helping her out the car."

"His name is Jabril."

"Yeah, him."

" 'Niesha," Rafique said with a high-pitched twang, "this fish is pa'yaid. Ho' shit." He picked up a piece of Jaise's china. Lowering his voice while covering his lips, he said, "You know how much I could make on the street for this?" He flung his wrist.

"Rafique," Al-Taniesha attempted to whisper back, "be quiet. I told you we couldn't lick them off. Christina started crying as soon as I mentioned it."

"Ai'ight, ai'ight, baby. We gon' let 'em live, we gon' let 'em live."

"We would appreciate that," Bilal said. "We certainly don't want any problems."

"Told you he was five-oh," Rafique said. "This niggah all in my mouth."

"Hi, Ms. Williams, how are you?" Christina said as she walked in with Jabril holding her hand.

"I'm fine, honey." Jaise smiled, noticing that Christina was a very pretty girl who resembled Ki-Ki Palmer. "I hope you guys are hungry," Jaise said, showing them to her dining room.

Jabril and Bilal respectively held Christina and Jaise's dining chairs out, while Rafique sat down and left Al-Taniesha standing there. "Don't catch no beat down," Al-Taniesha spat. "You better have some class."

"Oh, 'cuse me," Rafique said, throwing his hips to one side. "Lollipop's fault." He stood up and pulled Al-Taniesha's chair out.

Jaise attempted to hold it together for Jabril's sake, and from what Jabril had told her about Christina, she was a sweet girl, so Jaise promised herself that she would hold her tongue and not lose her damn mind over the fact that she would be tied to these people for life.

"So," Jaise said, smiling while attempting to hold a conversation that didn't involve the word "niggah" or "motherfucker," "Chris, what are your plans after the baby is born?"

"Moving in here," her mother interjected. "We done already worked it out."

Jaise batted her eyes. "What?"

"She gon' come live here. You got all this room, this your grandbaby, and we gon' have to share this responsibility. Why should my man be the only one losing sleep behind a crying baby?" She looked at Bilal.

"And Lollipop needs his sleep." Rafique snapped his fingers.

"Aren't you a lively li'l thing," Bridget said. Everyone had forgotten she was there with the camera crew.

Jaise looked at Al-Taniesha. "If I were you I wouldn't get my hopes up."

"And why not?"

"Ma, chill," Jabril said.

"You know what, Jabril, no. These people are not coming in here and turning my life into stone-ass crazy."

"But, Ma, it's not Christina's fault."

"Jabril, I'm only thirty-five years old. This being a grandmother shit is not my steel-o."

"Well, how you think I feel?" Al-Taniesha spat. "You lucky, your ass is old, but I'm only twenty-nine—"

"Thirty-nine, baby." Rafique tapped Al-Taniesha on the hip. "Thirty-nine."

"Would you shut the fuck up!" Al-Taniesha snapped.

"Oh, wait a minute, I know you ain't telling Lollipop no shut the fuck up, ya stank ass."

"My ass don't stank. Yo' ass be the one stankin', drippin', and all kinda shit. Now don't show off in front of company."

"You love me, don't you, girl," Lollipop growled. "Wit' yo' feisty ass."

Al-Taniesha blushed and turned back to Jaise, whose mouth had dropped open. "Don't be acting like y'all don't argue," Al-Taniesha said. "Just 'cause you on this show the shit don't make you better than nobody else." She looked at Bridget. "What's the requirements? I've been on *Wife Swap* and I got three kids . . . three kids and four daddies. What? A bitch like me is what y'all need. 'Cause I will turn it out."

"Three kids . . ." Bridget grabbed a napkin to write on. "Four daddies."

"My baby is the truth. They don't know you, baby," Rafique screamed as Al-Taniesha hopped out of her seat.

"They'll be like hold up, wait a minute, is that"—she shielded her eyes—"Al-Taniesha Rayquana Jankins? They don't know, baby." She snapped her fingers. "They don't know."

"They ain't ready for you, 'Niesha. They . . . is . . . not . . . ready for you."

Al-Taniesha sat down. "Now, where were we? Oh yeah, li'l Fifty-Five Cent done knocked up my Christina. So what we gon' do about this?"

"Listen," Jaise said, "Christina cannot live here."

"Ma, can we please talk about this later?" Jabril said.

"No," she said, tight-lipped.

"Jaise." Bilal waved his hand under his chin.

"So my advice to you all," Jaise continued, "is to figure out some other alternate plan for this child's living arrangement."

"Ma, I'ma move," Jabril blurted. "I'll find us a place."

"Shut up, Jabril. You can't even scrape five dollars together."

"Christina," Al-Taniesha said, "you ain't tell me li'l T-Pain was broke. This is some bullshit. Listen," Al-Taniesha said, turning to Jaise, "what do you say you keep your son with you and I keep my daughter at home. I don't know how y'all roll, but we goes to college around my house."

"Don't sleep," Rafique added. "We believe in Ed'jacation."

"So," Al-Taniesha carried on, "Christina has already been accepted to NYU, so I guess since we family now we gon' have to take care of our grandbaby."

Jaise blinked repeatedly. This shit was crazy, but somehow in the big scheme of things it made sense. "You know, Al-Taniesha and Rafique, I guess you're right."

"It's Lollipop," Rafique said as they started to eat. "If we gon' be family, y'all gon' have to call me Lollipop."

Chaunci

"Idris," Chaunci said, her eyes combing him as she stood at his front door, "thank you for letting me bring Kobi over this weekend. I know you didn't have to."

"She's my daughter. She can come over whenever she wants to."

Chaunci leaned from one foot to the next. She knew Idris was wondering if she would change her mind and cross his threshold. "You know, I'm . . . going out to dinner with Edmon."

"I know."

"Idris," Chaunci said as if she were exhausted, "it's not that I don't—"

Idris walked down the three steps that led from his front stoop and stood before Chaunci. "Whatever you decide, I am okay with that. I'm grown, you're grown, and we're parents. We don't have time to figure out what went wrong and how to fix it. We just have to be, just find a way to coexist peacefully. You will always be my first love, my love, my daughter's mother. But I am okay if the closest we ever get to rekindling a relationship is the weekend we shared."

"I just can't jump into this."

"I know, and I love you for that. Just be as honest with yourself as you're being with me." He kissed her on the forehead. "Enjoy your night and I'll bring Kobi home on Sunday."

The eerie part about Chaunci meeting Edmon at the restaurant on top of the Empire State Building was that that was where he'd proposed to her. He'd rented the entire restaurant, hired the chef, had a candle-lit table, and the rest was today's history.

Chaunci wanted desperately to love Edmon. She wished at the moment that she had allowed herself to form a love thang or some type of emotional connection with him, because then maybe this day wouldn't be happening and this evening wouldn't be the last they would share. The problem was Edmon was not the type to understand that she needed space, because her mind was filled with dreams that had nothing to do with him.

She just hoped that he was adult enough to swing with at least being tolerable; after all they had the magazine.

"Chaunci," Edmon said as he walked over to the small table in the center of the rooftop. "I see we had a memory worth rekindling." He smirked, taking his seat.

She kissed him on both cheeks. "Edmon, don't start."

"I'm not a kid, and this is not a race."

Chaunci shook her head. Already this was going at a disastrous pace. She wanted to look him in the eyes and tell him, Fuck it and fuck him. They were done. But she didn't; she owed him enough to at least deliver his heartbreak with respect.

"Edmon," Chaunci said, moving the wineglasses out of the way and taking his hand, "I have really appreciated having you in my life, and I know I haven't been the easiest person to understand all the time."

"Don't insult my intelligence. I'm forty years old and I have no time for long speeches."

"So then maybe you can tell me, what do you do when your mind says, 'Don't look back,' but your heart tells you that you have to?"

"Idris. This is about Idris," he insisted.

"It's more than that."

"No, it isn't."

"I have something to give you." Chaunci slid her engagement ring into his palm. "I'm sorry."

"You're right, you are," he snapped. "You are sorry, and I can't believe that I fell for you."

Chaunci faked a smile as the waitress came over and took their order. "I'm trying to be an adult about the situation," she said as the waitress walked away.

"Being an adult," Edmon said, "would've meant telling me from the beginning that you didn't love me and that you have been pining all of these years over some fake-ass ballplayer."

"Edmon—"

"Don't Edmon me, I'm pissed-the-fuck off. What did you think I was going to do, sit here and act like I was above being upset and that it was okay for you to walk all over me? You know I own part of your magazine. I could sell the shit."

"Listen, if you want to sell it, sell it. What the hell do you want me to do? I can't help it if my heart won't do what my mind tells it to."

"You can't help it," he said more to himself than to Chaunci. "Well, you know what, Chaunci," he said, rising from his seat, "I can't help it either." And he walked out.

Chaunci sat there for a moment, her mind racing with a thousand thoughts of how this could've ended differently. She looked from one side of the restaurant to the next, greeting the other customer's glances with a smile. She held up her glass of white wine and said, "Well, Chaunci, here's to you."

———————

After driving around for hours, stopping by her apartment, and then coming back out and riding around even more, Chaunci found herself right back where she had started, sitting in her car, in front of Idris's house. She thought at least a million times how she should ring Idris's bell and fall into his arms.

But she didn't know if she would be happy living in such a fairy tale. It was true that she loved Idris, but the Idris she loved was the Idris she had known more than six years ago, before the pregnancy, before life set in, before she knew that being every woman was more than a song. She loved him, yes, but could she run and jump in his arms . . . she didn't know. And because she was so uncertain and so unsure, she decided she needed more me time, to know who Chaunci was and what Chaunci wanted. Suppose Edmon sold part of her magazine? She needed to be focused enough to deal with that, not fucking, not lying up in Idris's arms as if all that mattered in the world was having a man. She needed to get things back in order for Chaunci and find a balance between being in control and submitting to love.

Tears sat at the base of Chaunci's eyes as she started her engine again, made a U-turn, and headed back to her apartment.

Jaise

"Jabril!" Jaise walked out of her bedroom and screamed, "Come get these bags for me please."

"I'm not the bellhop," he said, walking past her.

"No, but you will be hearing bells if you keep talking smack."

Jaise walked behind Jabril as he carried her bags. "I'm trusting you, Jabril, to behave while I'm gone. Please don't let me come back and find you've made another baby."

"Ma, would you cool out? You're coming back tomorrow night."

"It only takes five minutes, Jabril."

"Ma, I start my new job at the mall and I'm not going to mess that up. And I definitely am not going to mess up your trust in me."

"You have all the numbers, right?"

"You could always come with us, Jabril," Bilal said. "There's more than enough room. We could bike ride—"

Jabril laughed. "Bike ride? Yo, I'm not bike riding in the spring with a grown man."

Bilal cracked up. "Yeah, that does sound a li'l suspect."

"You feel me?"

"Yeah, I got you."

"You two done speaking in uneducated code?" Jaise asked.

"Ma, it's cool, stop worrying," Jabril said.

"Okay. And you keep Al-Taniesha and Lollipop's ass out of here."

"Alright, let's go," Bilal said, taking Jaise's suitcases from Jabril. "Damn, baby, what do you have in these things?"

"Not too much, I hope," Bridget said, "because the Super 8 doesn't have that much space."

They ignored Bridget and continued out the door. "Jabril, here," Jaise said, and handed him some money and a credit card, "only for emergencies."

"Okay, Ma."

"Call me."

"Okay, Ma."

"And if you eat over at Christina's, smell the food first, I don't trust them."

"I got you. You can go now."

"And if that trick, Al-Taniesha—"

"Alright, Jaise," Bilal said.

"If that bitch," Jaise whispered, "tries some shit or talks crazy to you, call me, 'cause I will leave and come kick her fuckin' ass."

"Ma, I got you." He pointed to Bilal, who was holding the door to his Deuce and a Quarter open. "You can leave now."

"Thank you." Bilal laughed as he and Jabril exchanged dap.

Jaise looked at Bilal's car and said a silent prayer, and then she figured sometimes prayer needed a little human intervention. "Sweetie, we can always drive my car. Please, I really am scared we may break down in this."

"You think I would put you in jeopardy like that, Jaise?"

Jaise didn't respond; instead she got in the car and they took off. Jaise watched Jabril in the side mirror until he became a small figure in her sight.

"I worry about that boy," she said to Bilal.

"He'll be okay. He's making a lot of good changes."

"Yeah, he is."

Bilal smiled as they got on the highway. "You know," he said, "the other night we had a man-to-man talk."

"Really?" Jaise couldn't believe it.

"Yeah, he came up to the station."

"Jabril?"

"Yes, your son."

"What did he say?"

"He told me that he liked me and he thought I was cool, but that you were his mother and he loved you. That he'd seen you cry enough and that the next tear you shed he was gon' kick ass behind it."

"Say that again." Jaise whipped her head around.

"You heard me. He told me if I wasn't going to treat you right then not to come back again."

"And how long ago was this?"

"Last week."

"And why didn't you tell me that? I would've gotten in his ass about being disrespectful."

"Nah," Bilal said, "we have an understanding."

"And what else did you two talk about?" Jaise asked as a smile lit up her face.

"That's between me and Jabril. Nothing bad, I would tell you that. But just some man-to-man things."

Jaise and Bilal laughed and talked about everything under the sun as they drove four hours to a docking station for the Martha's Vineyard ferry. Jaise, Bilal, and the camera crew got out of their vehicles and looked at how beautiful everything was. From the crisp breeze to the blossoming branches on the trees.

"They must be running a special on this," Bridget said to Jaise, as Bilal walked over to one of the employees at the docking station, "otherwise this has to be his whole damn salary."

"You don't know that," Jaise said defensively.

"I tell you what, it's not much, but we have a little room in the van if you need to leave with us."

Before Jaise could respond Bilal walked over to her with a be-wildered look on his face.

"What's wrong?"

He started patting his back jeans pockets. "I can't find . . . ," he said, continuing to frisk his pockets, "my wallet."

"Oh hell no!" Bridget said. "Your broke ass'll never set up me and my crew!" She snapped her fingers as Bilal ignored her and walked back to his car. "Carl, let's go," she said. "He pulled the old missing wallet trick." She looked at Jaise. "You rollin'?" she said in a hurry, " 'cause we're outta here."

"I'm not leaving him here like that."

"Pathetic," Bridget said as they screeched in reverse out of the parking lot, made a U-turn, and hauled ass back onto the highway.

"Something is wrong with her," Bilal said, walking back over to Jaise.

"Did you find your wallet?"

"Yeah."

"Where was it?"

"It had fallen under the seat. Are you ready to get on the ferry?"

Jaise hoped she was hiding her hesitancy well. "I'm as ready as I'll ever be." She smiled nervously.

After a half-hour ride on the ferry to Edgartown, Jaise and Bilal were back in his car riding through the country roads until they ar-rived at what appeared to be a Norman Rockwell painting come to life. Set back three hundred feet from the entrance of the cob-blestone driveway lined with weeping willow trees was a beautiful and well-restored hundred-year-old, red farmhouse with white wooden shutters, double screen doors, a winding wraparound porch with round pillars on each corner, two rocking chairs, a porch swing, and ceiling fans. The closer they got to the property the better Jaise could see the hanging gas lantern flickering above the doors.

"This is beautiful," she said as she noticed how oak and ever-green trees were growing everywhere. She could hear the ocean roaring behind the house and she could see a slight view of it from the side. She'd traveled all over the world and had seen some of the finer things in life, but she had never imagined that something so simple, yet so grand, could outshine all of them.

"Bilal," she said as they parked, "you didn't have to rent this property."

"Okay," he said, allowing her comment to dangle in the air. He walked to the back of the car and started taking the luggage out.

"You could've . . . you know . . . ," she said, hopping out of the car and walking over to him, "just taken me to the movies."

Instantly he stopped what he was doing. "Think about what you just said. Did you really want me to just take you to the movies?"

"Well . . ."

"Whenever you say 'well,' that means no."

"How do you know that?"

"I know you."

"It's just that this looks really expensive, and, I mean, come on, you're not rich. And . . . because I am . . . I don't want you to feel obligated—"

Bilal placed Jaise's suitcases on the ground and walked over to her. He placed his hands on each side of her and on the roof of the car. Looking down at her he said, "If I couldn't afford this, if I couldn't afford you, if I couldn't afford anything that I wanted, then I wouldn't have it. So get the thought that I'm a broke-ass cop out of your mind and enjoy me. I'm here, we're here, and we damn sure ain't here to do a buncha talkin' because we can do that at home."

Jaise was so turned on by his forwardness all she could say was "Damn."

He kissed her and his tongue caused her nipples to harden. "Let's go."

As they stepped onto the porch the double doors opened and a smiling and short-statured black woman in a maid's uniform was standing there. "Sir, I didn't expect you so soon." She waved her hand, ushering them in. "Come on in here."

"Ma'dear," Bilal said, "how've you been?"

"I've been okay, but you and the mistress are early."

"Yeah, but it's fine." He pointed to Jaise. "This is my lady friend, Jaise. Jaise, this is Ma'dear. She oversees the property."

"Pleasure to meet you." Ma'dear smiled. "Pretty girl," she said, looking toward Bilal. "Well, sir, I'm going to leave now. I have the refrigerator stocked with all the groceries you like and the fireplace is started."

"Thank you," he said as Ma'dear waved and walked out the door.

"Sweet lady," Jaise said. "Does she own this place?"

"You startin' again, Jaise?"

"No," she said, smiling because she knew that she was. "Not at all."

For the next hour Jaise and Bilal toured the house, and Jaise's jaw dropped at all the spectacular views, especially when she stepped onto the balcony off the master bedroom and realized the back of the house sat atop a cliff and the ocean was below.

"Jaise." Bilal called her onto the terrace, where he had music playing softly and two glasses of champagne. "I need to ask you something."

"Yes?" She sat down at the table and wondered why there was a pear-shaped engagement ring floating in her glass. "Bilal . . ." It clicked. She looked at the ring and immediately tears filled her eyes. Jaise hated to cry, and truthfully she didn't know if she was crying because of how crazy she was about this man or because she didn't have the heart to tell him she didn't wear fake diamonds—and a ring this size, coming from a man who drove a broke-down thirty-year-old car, would have to be fake.

Bilal got down on one knee, and Jaise knew right away she would say yes. She didn't know quite yet how she would adjust to everyday living, but if push came to shove, she could always get therapy for that.

"You know I love you," Bilal said, "and I want to share my world with you."

All twenty-five dollars of it, Jaise thought. "I know, honey," she said.

"So," he said, taking her left hand, "will you marry me?"

Jaise didn't hesitate. She'd never been in love like this, and, besides, it wasn't as if she hadn't stashed any cash. This wasn't about money; this was love. For the first time in her life something was about true love. "Yes, I will marry you!"

"I know you'll be giving up a lot," Bilal said.

Jaise couldn't think about how much money she was about to give up, because then she would run the risk of telling Bilal no. "I'm gaining everything."

"Pretty much, especially since I'm worth ten times more than Lawrence."

"I mean, I can always work full-time, and Jabril is working. Wait a minute, what?"

"I'm wealthy. Very wealthy."

"Excuse me?" Jaise took a step back. She was sure she had heard wrong.

"I made a lot of money in the stock market before it went belly-up."

"But you're a cop."

"I know, but I'm a cop because I want to be, not because I have to be."

"I don't believe this shit," Jaise said, pissed.

"Wait a minute, are you upset?"

"What the hell do you think?! This isn't *Comin' to America*. You acted like a broke ass for what?"

"It's just my style. I don't let anyone know I have money. That's why I brought you here to my house. I wanted to ask you to be my wife and show you all that I want to share with you."

"You took me on that raggedy-ass date, with that shit getting in my hair, grease spots on my dress? Do you know how much I paid for that dress? And then you scared me half to death driving up here, and all along you're wealthy! Oh hell no."

"Does that mean you're not going to marry me?"

"I'm going to marry you because I love you, but I'm pissed as hell. Wait until Bridget finds out about this shit," she said. "And you might as well find another car, because I will not ride one more minute in that broke-down jalopy."

"Don't talk that way about Leroy, baby."

"Leroy needs to be donated to the junkyard for scrap metal."

Milan

After the hospital gave clearance, Milan agreed to let Bridget and the camera crew follow her around at work and then ride home with her on the train. This view of her life was a far cry from the million-dollar apartment with the killer view that she had had when this whole thing started. This was sure to be one hell of a season finale.

"Milan," Bridget said to her as they exited the subway, "I want you to cry and scream when you walk through your apartment. Talk about the crackheads and the pimps that are your landscape. Geezus, I smell an A-list award."

"There are no pimps and crackheads who are my landscape," Milan said. She took a deep breath. This was her last taping, and then she would be done with reality TV. Period.

"This is reality TV," Bridget snapped, "so get to pretending!" She walked behind Milan into the building and up to her apartment. The mixture of physical exhaustion from work and mental exhaustion from being on the show was wearing her thin. She could've sworn as she opened her apartment door that she smelled cigar smoke.

As she closed the door behind her she heard a soft click and then she saw a pastel yellow stream of light on the wood floor. Instantly her heart jumped as she turned around and spotted Kendu sitting on the couch, taking a strong pull off his cigar and releasing the smoke into the air. From the look of things he'd been waiting for hours.

"How did you get in here?"

"Keys." He tossed them across the room.

Milan wasn't sure why, but she started walking backward. The one time she needed Bridget to say something and intervene she was quiet.

"How—how," Milan stuttered, "did you get keys to my place? How did you know where I lived?"

"I have enough money to get keys to the White House if I wanted to. But for now, this one-bedroom Church Avenue flat will do. So tell me, what the fuck you call yourself doing?!"

"Can we talk about this later?" Milan's heart jumped in her chest as she pointed to the cameras.

"I don't give a damn about those cameras anymore. Fuck it."

"Zoom in, goddammit!" Bridget yelled at Carl. "Get all in their faces with the camera."

"Where you been all night, Milan? Matter of fact, where you been for the last three weeks?"

"Are you stalking me?" Milan asked nervously.

"Answer my question!"

"I was working!" she screamed. "Do you see what I have on?" She pulled at her nurse's uniform. "And, furthermore, I'm tired, Knott. Did you think I was going to lie and wait in hell forever? No, I'm done."

"I can't believe you gon' move out on me, Milan. On me?"

"What difference does it make, you didn't want me! Every time I turned around it was Evan this and Evan that. Evan doesn't give a fuck about you, I do. I love you. That bitch used you. You ain't shit in her fuckin' life."

"It wasn't about Evan!" he yelled as he stood to his feet. "It was about my daughter. But you're too fuckin' selfish to understand that. I've been trying to get shit straight so that I could be with you. So that I could be the man you needed me to be."

"I laid there and waited for you for two fuckin' weeks and you never called me, not even once. How long did you think I was supposed to be nothin' in your life? I was fuckin' you every night, and every day you were home with that bitch!"

"Oh . . . my . . . God . . . ," Bridget said, stunned. She closed her eyes and clasped her hands as if in prayer. "Thank You for this Emmy." She opened her eyes and looked around the room. "I'd like to thank the Academy."

"You damn right, that's my wife and my daughter, and I don't have to apologize to you for being with my family. You should've accepted your fuckin' position instead of trying to be in competition. I swear to God, I'm glad I never married your ass."

As soon as Kendu said that, they both felt how fucked up it was. Kendu stood quietly and Milan felt her body crumbling to pieces. She stumbled out of her spot a little and then without warning she reared her hand back and with all her might she slapped him so hard that a spritz of spit flew from the center of Kendu's mouth.

Tears blinded Milan, and for a moment she started breathing as if she were asthmatic. "I don't believe you just said that to me," she said, as if finally starting to process everything they'd been through.

"Milan." Kendu reached for her hand and she snatched it back. "Wait, baby, we need to talk about this."

"Talk about this?" She laughed in clear disbelief. "Talk about what?" She wiped her eyes.

"Us."

"There's no us. We're done. Go home to your family."

"Milan—" He reached for her again.

"I swear to God, if you touch me again, I'ma smack the shit out of you."

"Don't be like this." He walked closer to her.

"Fuck you, Kendu. Really." Milan pushed him in his chest. "You think I love you enough to accept anything? You really think that Evan and Aiyanna are your family? You just don't know. Let's talk about this. So you really wanna talk? You really wanna talk to me? Okay, let's talk about how your daughter ain't yours. Let's talk about how you're standing here and you look like the dumbest motherfucker in the world to me right now."

"What you say about my daughter?"

"That's not your fuckin' kid. You couldn't even give her blood, and you know why? Because you're not her damn daddy. Evan played the shit out your ass, and from where I'm standing you asked for the shit!"

"Don't say that," he said quietly. "Why would you say some shit like that?"

"Because it's true!" she screamed at the top of her lungs. "Evan doesn't give a damn about you. She doesn't know who that damn child's daddy is, but I can tell you one thing, I betchu she knows who the fuck ain't her damn daddy."

"Milan," Kendu said, backing her into a corner. She could see the pain in his eyes. And before she could wonder what it would be like to witness Kendu's strength folding to kryptonite, tears were rolling down his cheeks. He spoke quietly again, "So you knew and you didn't say anything to me?"

"It wasn't my place."

"It wasn't your place," he said more to himself than to her. "It wasn't your place. Everybody knew but me. What, y'all were laughing at me? Look at this fool. You hate me that much, Milan?"

"Hate you?" She blinked. "Me loving you is what has me standing here."

"Yeah . . . I'm sure."

"Knott." She reached for him.

He took a step back. "Nah, it's cool . . . I got this. Just give me a minute." And he stormed out the door.

Milan knew she'd messed up, and she knew he was too calm not to be ready to kill Evan. "Knott!"

Milan ran after him and Bridget yelled, "Wait!" "The van is parked outside. You can ride with us!"

"Evan!" Kendu yelled, bolting into the house, swinging the front door so wildly that he rattled the frame. "Evan!" He looked in the living room and she wasn't there. "Evan!" He screamed as he ran down the corridor and into the kitchen, where he unwittingly bumped into her, causing her to spill the bottle of bleach and the cup of hot oatmeal in her hands.

"What the fuck is that?" Kendu screamed. "What the hell are you doing?!"

"Nothing," Evan said nervously, "I was just—just—nothing."

Kendu paused and then snapped, "Were you going to feed her this? Have you been making her sick?"

"Are you crazy?" Evan yelled. "Why would you accuse me of some shit like that!" She pushed him in his chest and he smacked her across the face.

"I've had enough of you!" Kendu grabbed Evan by her collar. "You always fuckin' tryin' me. I should choke the shit out of you!"

"Do it!" Evan held the side of her face. "Do it."

"I will." Kendu sneered. "Right after you tell me this." He grabbed Evan roughly by her chin and lifted her off the floor by her neck, the bleach that had splashed against his chest steadily turning his black hoodie white. "And don't fuckin' lie to me. Is Aiyanna mine?"

Evan struggled to move her head, but there was no way she could speak with Kendu gripping her by the neck.

"Kendu!" Milan ran into the kitchen and over to him. "Please stop."

"Catch that angle, Carl," Bridget said. "This is one helluva season finale."

"Bridget," Carl said, "this is a little rough. I think maybe we need to call the police."

"Just do your job!"

Kendu was oblivious to the conversation going on around him. He pressed his fingers deeply into Evan's cheeks. "I asked you a question!"

"Let her go!" Milan pushed him. "You gon' kill her!"

"Answer my fuckin' question," Kendu spat.

"Daddy!" Aiyanna came running out of her room. "Why are you screaming like that?"

"Go in your room!" he yelled at Aiyanna, never taking his eyes from the child's mother. He could see in Evan's eyes that her age-old lie had exploded in her face. Now he was certain he had to kill her, and as if death were in the palm of his hand, Kendu reared back and smacked Evan so hard that she slid across the room and hit her head on the front door.

"Daddy!" Aiyanna screamed. "Don't hurt my mommy!" She threw her small body on Evan.

Kendu picked Aiyanna up, and as he was moving her out of the way Evan was able to crawl outside. She struggled to stand up, and everyone followed her out onto the front lawn. She watched Milan beg and plead with Kendu to stop. Milan grabbed his hands and looked into his face. "Stop it, please," she spoke quietly, calmly, and with a voice that radiated I love you a thousand times. Evan couldn't believe what was unfolding before her eyes. She charged toward Milan, but when Kendu blocked her path, it was as if she'd hit a brick wall.

"You better not touch her," he said.

"Oh . . . my . . . God!" Evan screamed. "Oh . . . my . . . God!" She looked at Kendu and squinted her eyes. "You want this bitch? After everything I did to keep you loving me, you've been using me?"

"Is Aiyanna my child?"

"Hell no," Evan spat with venomous rage, "she ain't yours, motherfucker!"

"Don't say that, Mommy!" Aiyanna ran over to her and screamed. "Don't say that about my daddy!"

"He ain't your fuckin' daddy. You ain't related to this motherless bitch! This bastard's a stranger!" She took a step back, and all the sanity she'd felt leaving was finally gone. All she could see was kicking Kendu's ass and running over him and this bitch Milan.

Evan hopped in her fingerprint-activated Mercedes, revved the engine, and whipped her car in the direction of Kendu.

"Mommy!" Aiyanna screamed, running in front of her father. Evan's brakes screeched as she tried to stop, but it was too late. Aiyanna was thrown into the air and landed on the hood of the car.

"Aiyanna!" Kendu yelled as he ran over to her, and everyone on the estate started to panic.

"I told you we needed to call the police!" Carl screamed. "This isn't right. It's gone too far."

Evan crouched to her knees. She could hear Kendu yelling and screaming, "No . . . not my baby," and she could hear people buzzing around her, but she couldn't make out what exactly they were saying.

She wasn't sure why the police were there, when they needed an ambulance for Aiyanna. The problem was relating that to somebody . . . because she couldn't speak . . . but then again . . . someone must've read her mind, because the ambulance arrived and Aiyanna was carefully placed on the stretcher. Then the police lifted Evan from the ground and placed her in handcuffs.

Evan

The moon's reflection bathed Evan's exposed back as she stood in the center of the bamboo floor, dressed in a violet evening gown. Jaise had bailed her out of jail, and she'd been home for two days contemplating what she needed to do and where her life should go from here.

Her bare feet crackled as she walked through the bits of broken and crushed glass from the window she'd pushed her arm through in an effort to chase away the dark-haired phantom who called her name all night.

She kept her right shoulder hunched forward as she felt the sea's breeze blowing against her skin and raising the hair on the back of her neck.

Everything haunted her, from the seagulls flying above to the echoing of her own voice. And everything haunted her because it was all finished. Everything: the show, her marriage, her ability to be God to Aiyanna and to control Kendu's emotions, the limelight, the money . . . her life . . . everything. Everything that she needed to use to hide from who she really was—it was over. All she had left were the whispers in her head, calling her out to sea.

And she had to go—no two ways about it; she had to answer Poseidon's call. But first she had to let these motherfuckers know. Evan ran her hands through her wild and untamed hair, brushing it from her shoulders so that it fell down her back. She splashed on some Chanel No. 5 and applied lipstick from her chin to her upper lip. She brushed both sides of her face with blush, and with dark eyeliner she painted half of her eyelids. She looked at herself in the mirror and saw majesty. She couldn't be more beautiful, and everyone watching her would know. She flicked the video camera on, stood back, and began to speak. "I am a survivor, and my life isn't finished until I say it is. Fuck the fat lady, I have to sing. I have loved every one of you to death. My daughter, my man, my life . . . and what have I gotten in return? Silence. Gloom. Hell. I have always wanted a reason to genuinely smile, to feel good about life, and yet every day and every step of the way it was a tussle. So I pray you all understand why I have to make my own way. I don't know where I'm going, all I know . . . is where I've come from."

Evan quietly stepped away from the camera. She gathered the beaded hem of her long and flowing gown, swept it over her forearm, and walked out to the back of the estate. The surface of the earth beneath her feet changed from grass to sand, to bits of rock . . . to water. A smile lit up her face as a thought entered her mind: She would touch the moon.

As she started on her journey the water rose around her, and Evan began to slowly disappear into the night. She closed her eyes and somewhere in the midst of darkness the chariots came, the limelight faded, and the curtain fell.

*Live from the Four Seasons Ballroom,
It's the Reunion Show!*

The Club—Reunion

*M*illionaire Wives Club brought the station its highest ratings ever. The show was an instant hit, the women were all reality stars, and it seemed as if everyone in America had an opinion about their lives, making this one of the most anticipated reunion shows ever.

Jaise took a seat on one side of the host and crossed her legs. She sat alone on a blue chenille sofa across from Milan and Chaunci, who sat together on the adjacent sofa.

"Welcome," the blond host with the too-bright highlights said to the camera and the live audience. "My name is Don McBride, and we have quite a show planned for you today," he said, holding a stack of blue index cards in his hand. "We are here with our Millionaire Wives to catch up on their lives." Don sat down. "So ladies"—he nodded his head at them respectively—"Jaise, Chaunci, Milan, I think we should start by saying that we are dedicating this show to Evan. As some of you may know," he said, looking toward the camera, "Evan passed away a few weeks before the first episode aired."

Jaise wiped her eyes, while Milan swallowed the guilt in her throat, and Chaunci shook her head in sorrow. "She was a great part of the cast," Don said, "and she is definitely missed."

The studio went dim for a moment as a large photo of Evan appeared in the background. After a few minutes of silence, Don tried to get the show back on track. "So," Don said, clapping his hands together, "on a brighter note, we have our first question." He looked at Jaise. "Taylor, from Union, New Jersey, wants to know what's going on with you, Jaise. She said that she related to your life and wants an update."

Jaise shot a Barbie-doll smile at the camera. "Thank you for your question, Taylor. It's good to get the niceness out of the way first," Jaise said as she flicked her hand, showing off her pear-shaped diamond engagement ring and matching wedding band, "because then we can get to what the hell I've been wanting to say for the last few weeks. Now about me." She pointed to her chest. "I'm married, my husband is stankin' rich, thank you very much. We were married last month on a small island he owns in the Bahamas. Jabril has a son, Jabril Jr., or my little J.J., as I call him. Jabril is also a straight-A student and he wants to attend More-house in the fall. Now"—she looked at Milan—"on to lowering the boom on your ass."

"We weren't friends," Milan sneered, "so you shouldn't have shit to lower to me."

"Well, I do." Jaise pointed her finger." 'Cause seriously, I wanna kick your fuckin' ass."

Milan crossed her legs and rolled her eyes to the ceiling. "Air and opportunity," she said, and looked Jaise directly in the face, "is all that lies between us."

"And about three more months!" Bridget yelled, as she walked onto the stage. "Save that for next season. Do you know how high the ratings will turn out to be, please put that ass-kickin' on pause, until the new contracts are signed."

Jaise rolled her eyes at Bridget and continued on, "Milan, you are the reason that Evan killed herself. Yo' ass!" She pointed.

"Evan killed herself because of her own demons," Chaunci said, getting into the argument.

"Milan fucked her husband!" Jaise shouted.

"No." Milan sneered again. "The day she decided to put another man's baby on him, is the day she fucked him better than I ever could."

"How dare you?!" Jaise shouted.

"Let me tell you something," Milan said, "I'm not saying that I was right, but I am not responsible for Evan losing her mind. For once in my life I didn't give a damn what anybody else thought or what anybody else wanted. I allowed myself to love and to be in love with my best friend. And no, I didn't give a damn that he had a wife, and yes, I made love to him . . . good love to him; several times. But I will not apologize for it."

"Wait a minute, Milan," Chaunci said. "Now, you're my girl, but right is right but wrong is what you are."

"I loved him!"

"He was married," Chaunci said.

"Thank you," Jaise interjected.

"You act as if we are still together."

"Well," Don said, "that brings us to our next question." He turned to Milan. "Janice, from Murfreesboro, North Carolina, wants to know 'Are you and Kendu still an item?'"

Milan swallowed. "Kendu and I are friends and that's all either of us can handle right now. He's in the process of adopting Aiyanna; that's his focus and I am my own focus."

"This is such bullshit," Jaise snapped. "All of a sudden you are the poster child for getting your shit together? Please, you are a home-wrecking tramp. You tore this family up, and now you act as if you are proud of the shit?" Jaise started clapping. "As a matter of fact, why don't you give yourself a hand. Evan is dead and you've won."

"Wait a minute." Chaunci jumped in. "Don't be trying to come at her as if she's responsible for Evan getting out of jail on bail, overdosing on pills, and getting the bright idea to swim out to sea. Did you forget she was poisoning her daughter?"

"Thank you," Milan said, and clapped. "Does Münchausen syndrome by proxy ring bells for you? Aiyanna wasn't sick. Evan was feeding her damn Pine-Sol and bleach and all sorts of shit. Are you kidding me? And you want to blame me for that?" Milan pointed to her chest.

"Yes, she was wrong," Jaise said, "but she needed a friend, she needed help, not for her husband to have a mistress."

"Speaking of Aiyanna," Don said, "where is she?"

"At home," Milan answered, "with her father, Kendu."

"Speaking of fathers," Don said, "how's Idris, Chaunci?"

"He's fine." She blushed.

"Are you two an item?"

"No, but we haven't closed the door on being an item, Don." She chuckled.

"And Edmon?" Don pried. "What ever happened with your magazine?"

"He sold me his interest. We ended up parting like adults."

"Do you think you'll ever get back together?"

"No, but maybe one day we can be friends again."

"You two are really fuckin' selfish," Jaise snapped. "Like your love life is so important."

"Well, everyone can't be perfect," Milan said.

"When you invest in your own man then you'll find out how perfect life can be."

"Boorring!" Bridget said. "Listen, on to something people want to hear about. I would like to introduce you to Yusef 'Da Truef' Sparks."

Yusef walked out onstage wearing a white unitard and knee-high wrestling boots. He sat next to Bridget. "I told you I was coming back, Milan," he said, "but you didn't believe me."

"Yusef will be starring in his own reality show, *Da Truef: A Wrestler's Story.*"

"This is too much for me." Jaise sighed. "Nobody cares that Evan isn't here?"

"Yes, Jaise," Milan said, "believe it or not, I care."

"We all care," Chaunci said, "but we're all different, and I guess that's what makes—"

"The show a success," Bridget cut in. "We don't have time for sappy shit. Forgive each other when the commercial comes on." Bridget stood up. "Be sure to join us next season when we bring our new housewife on: lottery winner Al-Taniesha!"

Al-Taniesha stepped onto the stage and paraded back and forth like a pageant winner in a full-length red rabbit coat. "Y'all ain't seen shit. I ain't nothin' like these bougie bitches." She snapped her fingers. "So be sure to look out for me and my baby, Rafique."

Rafique joined her onstage wearing a hot pink three-piece suit. "It's Lollipop!"

Bridget stood up and said to the camera, "Be sure to join us next time for a new season of *Millionaire Wives Club!*"

"Milan," Bridget could be heard saying as the cameras faded to black, "get your shit. We just canceled your broke ass for next season."

Acknowledgments

To My Father, who is the God of Abraham, the God of Daniel, and the God of the three Hebrew boys, I say thank You for continuing to love me despite myself, and thank You for Your grace and Your mercy, for it is sufficient.

To all of my ancestral African American authors who wrote when it was illegal, who wrote because they had something to say, and who wrote because the voice in their hearts and in their heads said to do so, I say thank you, because without you who knows where my stories or I would be.

To my mother and father, who love me unconditionally, thank you for all that you do . . . oh, and my children thank you, too.

To my husband, who is grilling the barbeque chicken I want right now, although it's nine o'clock at night, thank you, my love, for you are truly the best.

To my children, Taylor, Sydney, and Zion, whom I love and spoil soooooo much, you are my life!

To my family, my grandma, my aunties, my uncles, and my cousins, I love you dearly! To my in-laws in Siparia, Trinidad, W.I., thanks for your support!

To my "little" cousin Malik (the best artist in the world), although it is almost twenty years later, I promise to never tell your mother your secret. You know, the one where you had me call your school and tell them you had an emergency, and needed to leave right away. That will forever be between us.

To my church family at Philemon Missionary Baptist Church, thank you for all of your support. I love you and many blessings!

To my Ballantine/One World family, thank you all for everything seen and unseen that you do. Melody, thank you for your patience and your faith in my ability. You guys are amazing!

To my agent, Sara Camilli, thank you so much for everything!

To my friends, you are all so special to me, I don't know what I would do without you. Thanks for being there.

To my best friend in the world, Kenya Williams, thanks for all the laughs, the times we cut up, even the times we've cried. Thank you my sistah, for you are truly a best friend!

To my friend Dywane Birch, stay exactly as you are, my brother.

To K'wan and Keisha, one day we will get all the money we're supposed to.

To my homegirls: Nakea, Tiffany, Danielle, Keisha, and Adrianne, who all love reality TV like me, I wrote this one for you!

To my crew at work: Cynthia, Diane, Terry, Tanya, Angel, Shannon, Maurice, Natasha, Marcia, Tamika (although you have a new crew—LOL), and to the one who walks past my office every day and calls me "Spring," Shafequah and to all of my co-workers who I talk, laugh, and work hard with, thanks for your conversations, for making me laugh, and most of all thanks for your support! You'll never know how much it means.

Saving the best for last: the fans, readers, bookstores, websites, and message boards, thank you so much for your support in all of my literary ventures. I have some very dedicated readers who have been riding with me from the beginning, you know who you are, thank you, thank you, thank you.

Be sure to email me at tushonda111@aol.com and let me know your thoughts. Oh, and check out me and my girls on Three Chicks On Lit every Wednesday at seven on www.blogtalkradio.com/chicksonlit.

And now without further ado I say to you, "Turn the page and let's do the damn thing!"

Love ya!
Tu-Shonda

ABOUT THE AUTHOR

TU-SHONDA L. WHITAKER is the *Essence* bestselling author of *The Ex Factor, Flip Side of the Game,* and *Game Over.* She received the Ella Baker and W. E. B. Dubois International Award for fiction writing. She lives in New Jersey with her husband, two daughters, and son. Visit her on Facebook, MySpace, and Twitter.